THE DUKE'S HAMMER

The Duke's Guard Series,
Book Five

C.H. Admirand

ARE YOU SIGNED UP FOR DRAGONBLADE'S BLOG?

You'll get the latest news and information on exclusive giveaways, exclusive excerpts, coming releases, sales, free books, cover reveals and more.

Check out our complete list of authors, too!

No spam, no junk. That's a promise!

Sign Up Here

www.dragonbladepublishing.com

Dearest Reader;

Thank you for your support of a small press. At Dragonblade Publishing, we strive to bring you the highest quality Historical Romance from some of the best authors in the business. Without your support, there is no 'us', so we sincerely hope you adore these stories and find some new favorite authors along the way.

Happy Reading!

CEO, Dragonblade Publishing

Additional Dragonblade books by Author C.H. Admirand

The Duke's Guard Series
The Duke's Sword
The Duke's Protector
The Duke's Shield
The Duke's Dragoon
The Duke's Hammer

The Lords of Vice Series
Mending the Duke's Pride
Avoiding the Earl's Lust
Tempering the Viscount's Envy
Redirecting the Baron's Greed
His Vow to Keep (Novella)

The Lyon's Den Series
Rescued by the Lyon
Captivated by the Lyon

Dedication

For DJ, the keeper of my heart, and love of my life. I miss you.

For Arran McNicol, my editor, who gets me back on track when my brain is moving at a different speed than my fingers on the keyboard.

For my loyal readers, thank you for reading my books and letting me know how much you love my stories.

Author's Note

Dear Reader:

Hardheaded Heroes and Feisty Heroines…what's not to love?

This book is for all of you who continue to read the books that live in my mind and my heart, with characters that continue to whisper to me long after I've written their story and shared it with the world. Thank you, from the bottom of my heart.

Settle into your comfy reading spot with a cup of tea (or tasty adult beverage) while I tell you a story…

PROLOGUE

JAMES GARAHAN SAT at a table in back of one of the filthiest taverns in the underbelly of London…waiting for his quarry.

Attuned, and observant, to his surroundings, he watched the serving lass approach. Something was off. His instincts on high alert, he noticed her limp was more pronounced. As she set the tankard of ale on his table, her sleeve shifted slightly, revealing a ring of dark purple circling her wrist.

Until that moment, he had not realized how strong the need to protect her had become. He would get to the bottom of why she was being abused, and by whom and when—but had to tread carefully. He could not compromise his assignment. "Thank ye, lass."

She nodded and quickly looked away. He reached for her arm, and she flinched. Even a blind man could see the signs. He had not been to the tavern in a few weeks, and in that time her situation had changed—it worsened.

That changed everything. He would need to push harder this time. "Have ye thought about me offer?"

She lifted the corner of her apron to wipe a splash of ale from the table. With a quick glance over her shoulder at the tavern keep, she answered, "Aye."

"On me honor, I want to help—not harm—ye, lass. I know of a position offering a fair wage for an honest day's work."

"Melinda!" the owner yelled.

The fear in her eyes scraped Garahan's gut raw. "Did ye pack yer bag like I asked ye to?"

"I can't leave."

The owner called her name a second time, and she stumbled, but righted herself, in her bid to answer the summons.

Garahan had taken the man's measure the first time he entered the tavern—an overweight man with soulless dark eyes that only brightened if a coin was waved beneath his nose. He did not trust the owner.

Concern for the lass filled him. He would make a point to return in two days' time instead of five. He drained his tankard and left a coin on the table for the lass. He needed to speak to her, but it would draw unwanted attention to her—and to him. If he were to continue to utilize this establishment to gain the information he needed, he would have to be patient.

Mayhap the lass would change her mind.

As he made his way through the darkened alleyways toward Grosvenor Square, the lass lingered on his mind. The alleyways had brightened, and the cobblestones were no longer littered with refuse, by the time he realized he wanted more than to make a difference in her life—he wanted her to trust him so that she would be a part of *his* life.

Convincing her to trust him, and take that chance, would be difficult enough. To open her eyes to the possibility of letting him into her heart would take a miracle.

Garahan rubbed at the scar around his throat. The good Lord owed him a miracle.

CHAPTER ONE

THREE DAYS LATER, Garahan returned to the tavern. He was not here for information—he had come for the lass. He spied her on the other side of the room. From the slant of her shoulders, he knew something was wrong.

He made his way through the inebriated crowd to sit at his usual table in the back corner and waited for her to notice him. He watched as she wended her way through the customers, fending off hands that grabbed hold of her. When a man pulled her onto his lap, Garahan tensed, poised to interfere if the bugger's hands strayed further. It would be a pleasure, breaking the man's fingers—one at a time.

The man abruptly let her go, and Garahan buried the need to teach the bastard to keep his hands off *his* woman. He felt the bottom drop out of his stomach—she was not his...yet.

He compartmentalized his thoughts and vowed to deal with them later. He smiled at the lass when she approached, holding a tankard filled to the brim with ale. The large red handprint on the side of her face and split and swelling lip had him asking, "Who struck ye?"

She set his ale on the table. The first time he'd been to the tavern, his ale was in a dirty tankard. After befriending the lass, his drink was served in a clean one. She gripped her apron and stole a glance at the overweight owner. Meeting Garahan's gaze, she lifted one shoulder in answer.

Either she was afraid to say, or she wanted him to believe it did not matter.

He leaned across the table. Pitching his voice low, he rasped, "Ye matter, lass. Let me help ye."

He was unprepared for the tears welling in her soft brown eyes. They magnified the expression lingering there—worry wrapped in fear, and for a heartbeat...hope. The urge to take her in his arms battled with his steely control. He wanted to promise to protect and defend her. But the need to give her all of the things in life he knew she lacked from observing her these last weeks was even stronger.

How could he have these feelings after such a short time? He'd only noticed her that first night because as she struggled to rush, she limped between the tables and men lingering between them. She pretended not to hear the comments about her face, her form, and her unattractive—to some—limp.

In Garahan's opinion, a limp was the same as a scar—earned from an event that would define one's life from that moment onward. He was determined to find out what happened to the lass, in order to complete the picture he carried of her during those times when they were apart.

Unease filled his gut, but he kept his expression neutral for her sake. "'Tis been a long day, and I've a powerful thirst." He lifted the tankard to his lips and took a healthy sip. Setting his drink down, he reached into his waistcoat pocket, withdrew a coin, and placed it on the table. "Thank ye, lass."

She lowered her gaze to his hand, and instead of shying away from him as she had in the past, she raised it again to look into his eyes. *Progress.* But she had yet to answer the question still hanging between them.

"Ye don't have to speak." He lifted the ale to his lips again. "All ye need to do is trust me. There's a position waiting for ye—with a clean place to lay yer head, plenty of water, and enough food to fill yer belly."

"Melinda!"

She spun around, stepped wrong on her weak leg, and would have fallen if not for Garahan's quick reflexes. "Have a care, lass."

The tavern owner glared at Garahan. "Unless you plan to share the coin you'll earn in that one's bed, you'll refill the rest of the empty tankards."

Her face lost every ounce of color. Garahan was an excellent judge of character. 'Twas shock and betrayal, not guilt, on the poor lass's face.

Garahan rose to his feet, at the same time as one of the miscreants. The other man reached for her—whether to get her attention to refill his ale or to act upon what the tavern owner hinted at, Garahan did not know, nor care.

The man looked up at Garahan, changed his mind, and returned to his seat.

Before Garahan could repeat his offer of a more suitable job, she moved through the crowded room to serve the ale. He glanced down at the table and noticed the coin he'd placed there remained.

If he guessed correctly, the lass would earn another slap or bruise if she did not take payment for his drink. He picked it up and walked over to the bar, while keeping an eye on the crowd as the fair lass served drinks on the other side of the room. He tossed the coin at the man behind the bar, who caught it.

"I'd challenge ye for impugning the lass's reputation, but I doubt ye've ever been on the field of honor."

The man's eyes widened at the suggestion before he snorted with laughter. "I'm more at home in back alleyways."

Garahan shot his hand forward and grabbed hold of the man's shirt front. "If ye ever suggest such a thing about the lass again, I'll know, and will return for the pure pleasure of breaking every bone in yer body."

The man's Adam's apple bobbed up and down before he nodded.

"Now then, I'll be returning to me table to enjoy the rest of me ale. Ye'll apologize to the lass, and explain ye were mistaken. The lass's favors are *not* for sale. Do I make meself clear?"

When he remained silent, Garahan twisted his hand so the man's stained shirt was choking him. Satisfied he'd gotten his point across, he released it enough for the man to speak. "I'll tell them," he said.

Garahan shoved the man backward. "See that ye do." He returned to his seat and lifted his tankard to take a sip, glaring at the tavern owner over the rim of his mug.

The man cleared his throat and told everyone to be quiet. "I...uh...may have made a mistake just now. Melinda does not take coin for her favors—" He looked right at Garahan, narrowed his gaze and boasted, "She gives them for free!"

Garahan slammed his tankard on the table and shoved to his feet. He clamped down on his fury and pushed tables and men out of his way. He reached across the bar, grabbed the man by the throat, and lifted him off his feet. The owner who would pay for defaming the lass.

He heard the shouts and knew wagers and coin exchanged hands. He wasn't after brawling, but he had a point to make, and bugger it, he would make it! "I should cut out yer tongue for speaking such evil in the face of innocence!"

When the tavern keep's face drained of color, Garahan slammed his fist into the man's face. His hand was poised to strike again when the door to the tavern burst open and slammed against the wall—twice.

A deep voice called out, "Problem, Garahan?"

He looked over his shoulder at Gryffyn Tremayne, one of Captain Coventry's men, who stood ready to do battle. "I have things under control."

Tremayne shrugged, walked over to the bar, and stared at the man bleeding from his mouth and nose. "Any chance of getting a drink in this place?"

Garahan ignored the bleeding man and grumbled, "Ye're late."

"I know."

"Ye aren't offering an excuse?"

"Why?" Tremayne asked. "We both know I'm late."

Garahan surveyed the room and noticed he and Tremayne were the center of attention. The hair on the back of his neck stood on end. Where was the lass?

Ignoring the owner, who held a blood-soaked, dirty rag to his nose, he asked Tremayne, "Did ye see a slip of a lass with dark brown hair and an angel's face?"

"Nay, I was—"

A terrified scream had them running to the back of the tavern. Garahan tried the door, but it was locked. He put his shoulder to the door and broke it down in time to witness the miscreant from earlier grabbing hold of the front of Melinda's gown.

Garahan roared. The man jolted and looked over his shoulder.

When he saw Garahan, he shoved Melinda away from him. Her gown tore as she was thrown to the floor. Garahan started to go to her, but the rush of adrenaline pulsing through his veins could not be ignored, and he turned toward the man who would pay for harming the lass.

"See to her," Tremayne ordered him. "I'll take care of this rubbish and hold him for the Watch." He lifted the man off his feet and tossed him through the window into the alleyway, then leapt through it after him.

Garahan bent down on one knee and brushed a hand to her cheek. "Ye're safe now, lass."

Her eyes were closed. Had she fainted from shock, or hit her head on the floor?

"Lass, open yer eyes. 'Tis James."

She slowly opened her eyes and met his steady gaze. "I'm sorry."

"Ye have nothing to be sorry for." He slipped out of his frockcoat, helped her to sit up, and wrapped it around her. It would hide the fact that her gown had been torn, but not the fact that the poor lass couldn't possibly weigh seven stone!

"Do you think ye injured your ribs when ye landed on the floor?" he asked. Her eyes lost the glazed look, and a fraction of his concern eased. "I'll pick ye up, but don't want to hurt ye."

He swept her into his arms and stood. Her sharp intake of breath was telling—she had been injured. He felt the hitch in her breathing, a distinct pause. She was in pain. "Where does it hurt, lass?"

"I injured my ribs last night."

He didn't ask how. He buried the need to exact revenge deep and promised, "Ye'll never have to suffer such again, lass. Trust me."

She laid her head against his chest. Her hot tears soaking his frockcoat were answer enough for him. Concern for her injuries, and her reputation, shot through him. "I cannot hire a hack, as I rode here on me horse. We'll have to ride double. Do ye mind?"

She mumbled a reply, but it was muffled against his shoulder. When she settled in his arms, he knew the horse would not be a problem.

He stepped over the pile of splintered wood that had been the door and carried her through the main room of the tavern. Garahan swept his gaze around the room, one man at a time. No one challenged him. When they reached the door, he turned around. Leveling a look at the owner, he said, "I'll be back—and God help ye then!"

Tremayne waited outside with the attacker, who was slumped against the side of the building with his hands bound behind his back. When Melinda trembled in his arms, Garahan reassured her, "Lieutenant Tremayne is with me, Melinda. He served in the King's Dragoons, until he was injured."

"A pleasure, miss." Tremayne turned to Garahan, saying, "I'll deliver this one to the Watch and meet you later."

Garahan nodded. It was understood neither of them would divulge the address—or whom they worked for.

Tremayne glanced at the woman in Garahan's arms. "Are you going to hail a hackney?"

"I rode here on me horse. We'll ride double. He's a strong lad and can easily carry the two of us," Garahan answered.

Tremayne studied the horse for a moment before warning, "Watch your back."

"Aye, ye do the same."

The small hand that settled over his heart nearly had him stumbling as he approached the hitching post. "Ye have nothing to fear, lass," he assured her. "I mean ye no harm." He lifted her onto the back of his horse and mounted behind her. "We've a passenger, lad," he said to his horse. "Mind yer step, now."

The horse whinnied in reply as Garahan pulled her onto his lap. Bloody hell! He'd hauled bags of grain that weighed more! He set his worry aside, knowing Mrs. O'Toole and Mrs. Wigglesworth would soon discover the extent of the lass's injuries, tend to her...and feed her.

The need to be the one to take care of her wasn't as much of a shock as the desire to hold her in his arms and never let go. She was not his intended...yet—but she could be. He didn't question the thought, or the attraction as his mother's words echoed in his ear: "Once ye see her, ye'll know her, and faith, ye'll love her."

He always thought his ma was full of blarney when she said such things to them. But as he rode through the night with the lass's slight weight leaning against his heart, he wasn't so sure.

"Rest now," he urged. "We've a maze of streets before we reach our destination. I'll wake ye when we arrive."

"If my employer paid me a wage instead of room and board, I could repay you."

"I'm thinking the blackguard did not feed ye half enough, lass, in exchange for working for him. Worry not—I'll be settling up with him in a day or two."

"I broke a pitcher last night—he'll expect payment from me!"

"If he doesn't pay ye a wage, how does he expect ye to come up with the coin?"

"He always finds extra tasks for me to do in repayment."

Judging from the state of the tavern—and the lass—she'd faced even more hardship than he'd realized. "What else could he expect ye to do?"

"Be waiting for the man who collects the waste from the chamber pots, and the woman who delivers milk." Garahan was muttering about getting up at dawn when she added, "Then there's the wood that needs to be split to fit in the hearth—he doesn't like to waste it."

He didn't bother to tell her what he thought of that arrangement. "Leave it to me. He'll be more than happy with what I give him."

"But I still won't have the coin to repay you!"

He clamped his jaw shut, to keep from letting go of the string of curses behind his teeth. Instead, he concentrated on avoiding the carriages and others on horseback.

She stiffened in his arms. "It isn't true," she rasped.

"What isn't?"

"I never sold myself."

"Ah, lass, I never thought ye had. Ye've a pure heart, and a soul to match."

"How could you possibly know?"

Garahan couldn't remember having a conversation like this with a woman—or wanting to. He'd best watch his step in order to avoid distractions and keep his vow to the duke. When he felt her shift in his arms, he answered, "'Tis in the depths of yer eyes. Anyone can see it."

"Then how can I repay you?"

God save him from stubborn lasses! She was like a dog after a bone, and the edge of panic was back in her voice. He did not want her worry to escalate. "Will ye leave off asking if I tell ye?"

"Aye."

"After Mrs. O'Toole and Mrs. Wigglesworth check yer injuries—and they are properly tended to—we can discuss it. There's work enough, cleaning and cooking. I promise ye will be able to earn the coin to pay me back, if ye agree to me terms."

"I agree."

"Then will ye close yer eyes?"

She laid her head against his heart once more. Could she hear the way it pounded? Before he embarrassed himself by asking, her breathing slowed, and she relaxed fully this time.

He savored the feel of her. Beneath the lingering odor of ale, he caught a hint of rosemary. He leaned closer to her head—it was stronger. He inhaled, soothed by the herbaceous scent and feel of her. Though she was slight, her curves were womanly.

Cursing himself for even thinking such things, he did what he always did on an assignment—separated what he was feeling from what he was thinking. He had a job to do, but first, he had to deliver the lass to the duke's town house, and His Grace's caring staff. Then he and Tremayne had a member of the *ton* to ferret out and the lord's lies to expose.

No one slandered the duke or his family on his watch! They would either make reparations publicly, or the men of the duke's guard would be forced to take action.

As his arms were full and his hands on the reins, he mentally cracked his knuckles in anticipation.

He looked forward to a satisfying bout, sparring—trading punches—with one of his cousins, or Tremayne, as he would be handy. The thought of it gave him something to look forward to instead of discovering if the lass's lips tasted of tart cherries or sweet blackberries.

The temptation was strong...but his will was stronger. He could wait a day or two more before sampling her full lips.

Bollocks! Ma was right!

CHAPTER TWO

THE LOSS OF heat woke her briefly, until a soft warmth covered her. Melinda drifted between dozing and wakefulness. In the quiet, she ruminated over everything that occurred after leaving her cousin's tavern. The last thing she remembered was giving her promise to let James Garahan—her scowling knight in shining armor—help her. He knew of a position where she could earn a decent wage.

Relief filled her. She would have a way to repay her cousin for the broken pitcher and whatever other trumped-up expenses he would come up with.

"Is Melinda still sleeping, James?" a soft voice asked.

She slowly opened her eyes to find her savior staring down at her. Her heart began to beat faster at the concern, and an emotion she hadn't seen in a long time—affection—in the depths of his dark brown eyes.

"She started to wake when I placed her on the cot," he answered, never looking away from her. "But drifted off again once I covered her with the quilt. Lass, I'd like ye to introduce ye to Mrs. O'Toole. Mrs. O'Toole, meet Miss Melinda Waring."

"Thank you for letting me stay here until I can start my new position," Melinda said.

The gray-haired woman turned to James again. "She reminds me of Mignonette and Mary Kate."

He ignored the statement.

Curiosity piqued, Melinda asked, "Who are Mignonette and Mary Kate?"

Mrs. O'Toole replied, "Mignonette was injured when intruders ransacked Madame Beaudoine's shop."

Having only recently arrived from the country, Melinda had no idea what shop that would be. "Madame Beaudoine?"

"One of the most sought-after modistes in London. Mignonette was one of her seamstresses."

The word *was* could mean one of two things: either the young woman's injuries had proven fatal, or she was no longer employed by the modiste. "You said *was*—" Melinda began before Garahan interrupted her.

"Me cousin, Sean O'Malley, was on hand to rescue the lass and bring her here."

Did Mrs. O'Toole open up her home to those in need? The woman's gown was a soft dove gray—and of excellent quality—as was the pristine white apron she wore over it. Mayhap this was her uniform when working with abused young women.

It pained Melinda to ask, but they had not told her what she wanted to know. "Then she did not recover?"

"Do ye always jump to conclusions, lass?"

She frowned at him and answered his question with a question. "Did she succumb to her injuries?"

Mrs. O'Toole answered, "Not at all. She fully recovered, and saved Sean's life."

Melinda turned to look at James. "Your cousin?"

He nodded. "There was a point where we did not know if he would survive."

"It all worked out in the end," Mrs. O'Toole said. "They are happily married and living at Chattsworth Manor. The viscount is one of

His Grace's cousins."

What did a viscount and a duke have to do with James's cousin and Mignonette? Melinda was about to ask just that, but then she remembered: "Who is Mary Kate?"

James looked at Mrs. O'Toole, who smiled and answered, "A young woman who was sorely abused by her employer. James happened to be on hand when the poor thing was let go—in a most grievous way."

Did James and his cousin make a habit of rescuing young women? "We have something in common. Would you mind if I speak to her?"

The older woman shook her head. "She was only here for a brief time. Long enough to heal before Their Graces took her with them to their country home in the Lake District."

Unease slithered up Melinda's spine at another mention of the duke. "Their Graces?"

"Aye, lass," James said. "I've brought ye to the Duke of Wyndmere's town house, and will be leaving ye in the excellent care of his cook, Mrs. O'Toole, and his housekeeper, Mrs. Wigglesworth—who should be along shortly."

Fear tangled inside of her. She sat up, looked around, and asked, "Where is here?"

"We've tucked ye into the room near the pantry," Garahan answered. "Mrs. O'Toole stores her herbs, bandages, and the like in here."

"I don't belong here." Melinda shoved the quilt off her legs and tried to stand, but her weak leg buckled beneath her.

Garahan moved like lightning and scooped her up before she could hit the floor. "Whatever maggot ye've got in yer brain, ye'll ignore it and listen to reason."

"How could you even think of bringing me from where you found me to the duke's home?" She didn't wait for an answer. "Is he here? Will he demand to know who I am and why I am here?"

Garahan started to place her on the cot, but changed his mind. He obviously didn't want her to try to bolt again. He sat in the chair with her on his lap.

"You have to let go of me," she said.

"Ah, lass, ye ask too much of a man."

Mrs. O'Toole tut-tutted as she bustled about the small room, setting out herbs, small jars, and linens. "The water should be hot now. I will be right back. Explain things to her, James."

Melinda watched the woman leave before pushing against James's hold on her. He didn't budge an inch. "Please let me off your lap."

"What do ye intend to do if I set ye on yer feet?"

"I should leave," she answered.

He mumbled something she could not quite hear.

"What did you say?"

"Not a thing, lass."

Mrs. O'Toole returned with a tray, containing a steaming pitcher and a few small bowls. She placed the tray on the table beneath the cabinets. "You cannot leave until I tend to your injuries."

Melinda wanted to argue with the woman, but James tightened his hold on her for a moment, as if to remind her she could not leave—yet. Her rescuer was turning out to be more stubborn than she'd anticipated.

Well, she was too. Did he think because she was in an untenable position at the moment that she did not know how to speak up for herself? He did not know her! Before she left to begin the promised job, she would tell him a bit about herself in order for him to understand she had not been working for her cousin by choice, but by necessity.

"It is only my ribs that pain me, Mrs. O'Toole. I'd be grateful for your help and promise to repay—"

"Enough of yer obsession with repayment, lass!" James abruptly stood and walked over to the cot. With a gentleness she had not expected, given his angry tone, he placed her on it. "I have an appointment and need to leave ye in the care of Mrs. O'Toole. Ye will do as she bids. Understand?"

She lifted her chin high and met his frustrated glare. "I am not a child and will not be spoken to as if I were."

"I cannot take care of Melinda properly until you leave, James," Mrs. O'Toole added.

He inclined his head and said, "If ye need me cousin for anything, Mrs. O'Toole, Emmett is guarding the perimeter."

Melinda was confused. "I thought your cousin's name was Sean?"

"I have more than one, lass."

"Does he also rescue abused women?"

James chuckled. "Not as yet, though it's early days."

"Do you work for the duke?"

"Aye."

Getting information out of James Garahan was proving to be difficult. "Is part of His Grace's good works caring for abused women?"

"Well now, lass. The duke has assumed responsibility for more than one woman since I've worked for him."

She narrowed her eyes. "I hesitate to ask..."

"I'll answer to the best of me knowledge. What do you want to know?"

"Just how many women is the duke responsible for?"

James paused, leaving her to wonder—was it his job to search the bowels of London for abused women?

"His Grace takes his responsibility to his title—and his family—seriously. Twenty-two, I'm thinking, but that does not include the whole of his staff at his estates—he has four at the moment, and two he has a vested interest in, as they belong to his cousins."

"Good heavens! His Grace is to be commended for his support of women whose lives changed upon the death of their parents or relatives."

Garahan walked toward her. When he reached her side, he asked, "What happened to yer parents, Melinda?"

Her belly clenched and her heart ached as she recalled how swiftly her mother and stepfather had succumbed to an ailment of the lungs. Losing them within months of one another was a shock—but not as much as the realization she could no longer live at the vicarage.

She licked her lips to moisten them—her mouth was so dry. "They're gone."

"Gone?" he asked.

"My mother passed suddenly from a lung ailment that went undetected. My stepfather soon after."

"How did ye come to be working for that—"

"Cousin," she interrupted. "On my stepfather's side. My only living relative, and a distant connection at best."

"What of your stepfather's home? Was it entailed?"

"He was a vicar. The new vicar and his family were moving in to our home. I had no choice but to accept my cousin's offer."

His frown was fierce. "He lied to ye."

Melinda shrugged. "It wasn't apparent until I arrived in London."

"Ye had nowhere to turn."

She sighed. "Not until you offered me a position that would pay a fair wage for an honest day's work."

"And ye shall have it. Won't she, Mrs. O'Toole?"

The older woman's eyes were suspiciously moist. She blinked and answered, "Of course she will, though Miss Waring will have to choose which location she'd prefer to work at."

"How many locations are there?" Melinda asked.

"Were ye not listening?" James asked. "The Duke of Wyndmere has four estates, and two more that he helps oversee."

The reality of the situation was not lost on Melinda. She opened her mouth to speak but couldn't force the words out.

She shook her head, and James placed a hand to her shoulder. "Ye have plenty of time to make yer decision, lass. Let Mrs. O'Toole see to yer ribs. We'll talk again when I return."

Before she could find her voice, he bent, brushed his lips to her forehead, and was gone.

"Well now," Mrs. O'Toole said, trying unsuccessfully to hide her smile. "Did you know James's nickname is the Duke's Hammer? Not many people would dare to argue with a man of his reputation."

Melinda digested that bit of information about her rescuer. "I see."

"Try not to rile the man unduly, Miss Waring. Now, let me take a look at your ribs and your ankle—or is it your hip? I noticed you limping."

Melinda blew out the breath she'd drawn in when his lips were pressed to her forehead. "The limp is from childhood—I fell out of the tree I was climbing and landed on my leg. It did not heal properly."

"Does it pain you?"

"Not all the time."

"Well, just your ribs, then."

Melinda cleared her throat. "Er...if you would not mind, I think my back is not healing either."

Mrs. O'Toole frowned. "What happened to your back?"

Melinda met the woman's direct look. "My cousin."

CHAPTER THREE

G ARAHAN HAD TAKEN the time to change into his normal attire, his uniform of the tailored waistcoat, frockcoat, trousers, and fine linen shirt—and the blasted cravat—before leaving the duke's townhouse. His black garb was familiar to most now, in and around London, denoting him as one of the Duke of Wyndmere's private guard. The symbols of his homeland embroidered over his heart were the only nod to his heritage—and that of his brothers and cousins, who were also members of the duke's guard.

He arrived at Captain Coventry's home at the same time as Tremayne. They met on the sidewalk, but did not speak. The corner of Hart and Lumley was a busy one. As with the building Coventry lived in, the walls had ears.

They bypassed the captain's apartments on the lower level and ascended the stairs to his office. Tremayne knocked, and they were ushered inside.

"From the look on your face, Garahan, you have more to report than I was expecting," Coventry said.

"Aye. There was trouble at the tavern—"

Coventry interrupted, "Which one?"

"One of the more rundown places I gather information for ye... 'Tis likely ye wouldn't know of it."

"Do not be so sure of that," Coventry said. "Before the duke hired you, I used to frequent establishments in parts of London I will not permit my wife or stepson to go."

"How is the lad?"

Coventry smiled. "He's taller and looks more like his father every day. Michael would be so proud of him."

"From what ye've told us," Garahan said, "the lad's father would be proud of the way ye helped raise the lad in his stead."

Coventry frowned. "I do not think my friend intended for me to marry his widow."

"What else do you think Lieutenant Thompson had in mind," Tremayne asked, "if not that?"

Garahan stared at the captain—at first glance, one might think the retired naval hero would be an easy target, given the eyepatch and sling. But he knew from experience that most who underestimated the good captain did so at their peril. Garahan had fought alongside Coventry and had been impressed with his strength, agility, and ingenuity. "Ye honored yer word to him before the Battle of Trafalgar. Afterward, ye took care of his widow and two-year-old son for a decade."

Coventry held Garahan's gaze but did not speak. Garahan continued, "Ye made certain they had food on the table, and a roof over their heads in this very building—where Miranda was able to earn a living wage as housekeeper. I'm thinking ye more than kept yer word to yer friend."

"I never intended to fall in love with her—I sincerely doubt Michael anticipated that happening."

Tremayne chuckled. "Having met your lovely wife, I am quite sure that was his intention all along. He loved his wife and knew, given the time you would be spending watching over them, that you would come to have feelings for the two of them. The lieutenant wanted her to live a full life—and for his son to have a father. I'd say your marrying Miranda was his intention all along."

Coventry held Tremayne's gaze for long moments without speaking. Finally, he nodded. "I had not looked at the situation from that perspective. Michael trusted me with his heart—Miranda and young Michael. A wise woman informed me that one's heart has the capacity to hold more love than one could possibly imagine. It seems she was right."

Garahan chuckled. "Me ma has taught me brothers and meself the same. I've watched me O'Malley cousins try to resist the women they were meant to fall in love with—'twas a battle well fought. The moment they stopped fighting was the moment they realized a man could keep more than one vow in his lifetime. The one pledged to the duke, to protect his life and that of his family, and the other the day they promised to love one woman for the rest of their lives."

"Enough talk of vows and promises," Coventry said. "What have you learned?"

Tremayne spoke first. "Lord Corkendale was overheard slandering Viscountess Chattsworth at White's, and Countess Lippincott at Tattersalls."

Garahan was incensed on behalf of the viscount, the earl, and their wives. Coventry's reaction—his green eye darkening to nearly black—was his only outward sign of anger.

Garahan would do all in his power to expose the source of the rumor and end it. Though in the back of his mind was the need to return to Grosvenor Square to see how the lass he'd rescued fared. Although he'd left her in the capable hands of Mrs. O'Toole and Mrs. Wigglesworth, he had thrust her into a situation not of her own making. He only hoped the lass would accept the help the two women would offer.

"Neither lady has been to London in an age," Coventry said. "We need to confirm if the rumors and slander are from more than one source. If not credible, we can encourage the person repeating such claims to cease—or go directly to the supposed source to put an end to the lies."

"I'm always in favor of encouraging—" Garahan began.

Tremayne interrupted him, "Like the tavern keep's broken nose—very persuasive." Turning to Coventry, he said, "I'll check with one of our contacts at White's."

Coventry seemed to be digesting what Tremayne had said. He stared at Garahan. "See if you can speak with one of the grooms at Tattersalls. Report back to me—downstairs. It's my turn to be up with little Emma—she's teething and kept Miranda up most of last night."

"Ma told us to use *Poitín*, or a bit of the Irish, on a babe's gums. She also said we always quieted faster if Da rubbed our gums." Garahan grinned. "He had bigger fingers."

"Isn't that homemade brew illegal in Ireland?" Tremayne asked.

Garahan shrugged. "There's a lot that's *illegal* back home. We can discuss it over a pint another time."

"After you check in with—"

"I take it from what you are not saying that you rescued another young woman earlier, Garahan," Coventry said.

"Aye. Tremayne was there to aid in her rescue. Either one of us can fill ye in on the details after we come back with the names of the blackguards spreading the latest round of vicious slander against the duke's family."

"Excellent," Coventry agreed. "Now, if you'll excuse me, I need to check on my ladies. I anticipate being up most of the night, so do not worry about the hour. Oh—don't knock, use one of your signals instead."

Garahan grinned at Tremayne. "Mourning dove or owl?

Coventry chuckled. "Mourning dove—it should sound soothing to little Emma."

"Dove it is," Garahan said.

THE WHITE-HAIRED GROOM at Tattersalls greeted Garahan with a nod. "I've been expecting you since yesterday."

"Have ye now?" Garahan asked. "Then ye must've heard the latest *on dit*, Burton."

"Aye, though I didn't believe a word of it. I met Viscountess Chattsworth more than a year ago. There were a few *on dits* circulating at that time, too, if I remember correctly. Members of the *ton* have little to do with their time except to create salacious gossip about one another...for sport."

"Aye, ye have the right of it. Coin to be gained from wagers placed that could ruin a person's reputation in a heartbeat. What did ye hear?"

The groom motioned for Garahan to follow. "Walk with me. I have a gelding that was still a bit restive after a trio of *Pinks* spooked him earlier this afternoon."

"Never understood why a man would need more than one waistcoat," Garahan mumbled.

The groom chuckled. "Or the need to use an excessive amount of starch in their cravats." The two shared a look of understanding, then the groom said, "After I see if the gelding has settled down, you can accompany me while I continue on my rounds. Don't worry, the horses won't repeat what they hear."

"Smarter than most men," Garahan said. "Lead on."

"Now then, I do not know where the rumor started, but I know one of Baron Corkendale's footmen was heard repeating the tawdry tale." Burton sighed. "I do not like repeating it, but I trust you'll get to the bottom of it—and end it."

"Ye have me word," Garahan promised. "What did ye hear?"

"Neither Lady Calliope's babe—nor Lady Aurelia's—were fathered by their husbands."

"If not Viscount Chattsworth and Earl Lippincott, then who?"

Burton held Garahan's gaze, frowned, and answered, "You."

Garahan stopped mid-stride. "Bloody *fecking* hell! When would I have had the time? I've been filling in for me cousins at the duke's four estates since last year. I just returned from Penwith Tower in Cornwall."

"I heard there was a bit of excitement."

Garahan shuddered, remembering the sequence of events. "Ye could say that. Did ye also hear a crooked excise official nearly succeeded in hanging me cousin, Finn O'Malley?" He didn't wait for the man to answer. "The bleeding bugger was holding Finn's wife captive—there on the scaffold—forcing her to watch as the lever was pulled."

Burton grabbed hold of Garahan's arm. "I thought that was an exaggeration."

"Nay. 'Twasn't."

"You got there in time?"

"Aye. It took three of us to save me cousin."

"Three?"

"Tremayne was beneath the scaffold. I was on the platform. It took the two of us to lift him up high enough for the rope to go slack."

Burton nodded. "And the third man to cut him free."

"Aye." Garahan rubbed his throat, remembering the time *he* had been the one with the noose around his neck. Finn had saved his *arse* that day. They were even now.

"And Mrs. O'Malley is well?"

"Aye," Garahan said. "Mollie and Finn are expecting a babe come summer. Now then, what can ye tell me about the footman? Anything that comes to mind will be a help."

"I heard it secondhand," Burton reminded him. "Not much to tell other than the footman seemed to be boasting. He would not have been if he knew of your reputation—or whom you worked for."

"I can use that to me advantage." Garahan held out his hand and thanked the groom. "If ye hear anything further, send word."

"I will, and Garahan?"

"Aye?"

"I've known you, and your brothers, since you first set foot on English soil. I'd trust any of you with my life—and my wife's. You are innocent, and you should know that I've already started a counter-rumor."

Garahan's brows rose. "And what might that be?"

"You plan to challenge the footman."

Garahan snorted with laughter. "It sounds fine, but not likely, as I'm not a member of the quality and prefer a knife or me fists to defend meself."

"I didn't say you plan to meet him on the field of honor."

"What rumor did ye start, then?"

"You aim to challenge the footman to a bare-knuckle bout."

Garahan narrowed his eyes, considering the idea. "Now that sounds like something I'd do—but not in Town, mind. I wouldn't ever do anything that could possibly reflect on the duke's reputation—or that of his family."

"I took that into consideration when I let it be known you plan to hold the bout on the grounds at Chattsworth Manor."

"Ye're either a genius, Burton...or a bloody *eedjit*! Faith, but I like the idea! Have ye started accepting wagers yet?" Burton shrugged, and Garahan asked, "How much of a percentage are ye taking?"

"I'm not at liberty to say," the groom answered, "but I want you to know the coin collected will be going to a good cause."

"What might that be?"

"The injured and widows of those who sacrificed their lives serving in His Majesty's forces."

Garahan clapped a hand on the older man's shoulder. "A fine cause. One that will please those who will verify me whereabouts at the time in question. Ye'll let me know when ye learn the footman's name—and anyone else behind this heinous slander? I won't be the only one determined to make the truth known."

Burton nodded. "Viscount Chattsworth and Earl Lippincott will succeed as they did when this happened before."

"Don't forget the Duke of Wyndmere," Garahan reminded him.

"If anyone can expose a member of the *ton* bent on destroying another's reputation," Burton said, "it is His Grace." He locked the door behind Garahan.

Garahan waited to hear the bolt slide into place before leaving. Fighting the urge to smash his fist into the corner of the building as he rounded it, he strode to where he'd tethered his mount. "Let's be off, then, lad." He gained the horse's back and confided to his loyal friend, "We've more problems than I'd anticipated. I need to speak to Coventry and King before we can return to Grosvenor Square this night."

Retracing the route he took to Tattersalls, he worked through the possibilities as to whom the footman had overheard. Was it Corkendale, or some other lord out to destroy the duke by attacking the reputation of the men in his private guard? Mayhap it was a matter of jealousy, as it had been the first time vicious rumors were being spread about Lady Aurelia and Lady Calliope.

He admired the strength, compassion, and caring both women displayed—whether under fire from a madman attacking the duke's estate in the Lake District...or facing down verbal slings and arrows while continuing to attend the endless round of entertainments of the Season, to show the world they were innocent.

As he approached the corner of Hart and Lumley, his thoughts turned once more to Melinda. Mrs. O'Toole would have bound her ribs by now. Between the duke's cook and housekeeper, they'd coddle the lass. Garahan had a feeling in the pit of his stomach that it had been a long time since anyone had.

He dismounted, and the overpowering need to hold the lass in his arms swept up from the soles of his boots. *If Ma's right—and the lass is meant for me—the timing could not be worse.*

CHAPTER FOUR

M RS. O'TOOLE'S HANDS shook as she bathed the red and swollen welts on Melinda's back. "Why didn't you tell James about your back?"

Melinda was glad she couldn't see the older woman's face. If her back looked as bad as it felt...it must be a mess. The warm cloths draped across her back eased some of the pain.

When she didn't answer, Mrs. O'Toole paused to lay a hand on Melinda's elbow. "I think I should summon the physician. Some of these wounds are infected, and I do not relish the idea of lancing any of them."

Melinda's stomach flipped over at the thought of anyone slicing the wounds open to relieve the pressure and cleaning out the infection. "I don't have the coin to pay for a physician."

"Don't you give it another thought. James would not want me to hold off. His cousin, Sean, nearly lost his arm to infection. If not for their cousin Emmett taking quick action, he would have."

"Emmett is a physician?"

"A gifted healer. I'll ask him to look at your back, then we'll see if we need to summon the physician.

"Would you stay with me while he examines my back?"

"Of course. It wouldn't be proper otherwise." Mrs. O'Toole fell silent. Finally, she said, "I wish James was here. He may insist on the physician and not want his cousin seeing you in such a state."

"Injured?"

"Your back exposed," the woman answered.

"Would he rather let the infection set in?"

Mrs. O'Toole sat in the chair beside the cot and frowned at Melinda. "Shame on you for thinking anything of the kind. James, Emmett, Sean—and the rest of the men in the duke's guard—are compassionate men who are very good at what they do."

Melinda sighed. "Forgive me. I did not mean to slight him." She paused, then asked the question that had been tugging at her: "What exactly do they do for His Grace?"

"Protect the duke and his family."

"By doing what?" Melinda asked.

"Whatever it takes." Mrs. O'Toole rose from the chair and said, "I'm going to send Mrs. Wigglesworth in to sit with you while I speak to Emmett."

"Thank you, Mrs. O'Toole," Melinda said. "It's not that I'm not grateful—it's just that neither my father nor stepfather ever raised a hand to me..." She let her words trail off. The shock had not waned, though it wasn't the first time her cousin had struck her in the last few months.

"What could you have possibly done to have your cousin beat you?"

"I refused to *entertain* one of my cousin's friends."

"Good Lord!" Mrs. O'Toole paused in the doorway. "I have no idea what James will do when he hears you were treated so abominably."

Melinda needed to tell her the whole of it. "He said he would only have struck me twenty times with the rod if I hadn't thrown the pitcher at his head." The tightness in her chest eased once she confided in the woman.

Mrs. O'Toole's eyes filled. "How many times did he strike you?"

When the first tear fell from the kindly woman's eyes, Melinda confessed, "I stopped counting after twenty."

"I shall be right back. Do not move!"

If she had not been in so much pain, she would have laughed. She should have said something to James when he swept her off her feet—but the pain had momentarily stolen her breath, and she hadn't been able to speak.

Whenever he tightened his hold on her, in his bid to protect her, excruciating pain had radiated across her back where the thin wooden rod had left its mark. She didn't have to ask; she knew she would carry scars from this most recent beating for the rest of her life.

At least she wouldn't have to look at it. Her childhood dream of marrying a kind, handsome man had evaporated. What man would be able to look past her current circumstances and see the heart of her? If there was such a man...he would have to be able to stomach her twisted leg and scarred back.

Accepting spinsterhood as her future, she closed her eyes and prayed for strength to endure the treatment required to battle the infection.

"Oh, you poor dear!" Mrs. Wigglesworth proclaimed, entering the room. "That cad! Do not worry—our James will take care of that bounder."

"He cannot! My cousin is bound to be angry enough when he realizes I won't be working tomorrow."

"My dear girl, how did you manage to work while in so much pain?"

Melinda shivered. "Until earlier tonight, when James and his friend burst through the door to the back room—interrupting...er...coming to my rescue—I did not have any other choice. Unless I wanted another beating."

The housekeeper reached for a lightweight quilt and laid it carefully over Melinda's back. "That should take care of the chill. Mrs.

O'Toole and Emmett are in the kitchen discussing the herbal poultice that will be best to draw out the infection."

Relief spread through Melinda. "They won't have to lance it?"

"We will not know until Emmett examines your back."

"And I won't be making any promises I cannot keep," a deep voice boomed from the doorway. A tall, broad man—dressed in black from head to toe—stood in the doorway, a tray in his hands. "I'm Emmett O'Malley, cousin to James." If James and his cousin both worked for the duke, why did James dress as if he were a laborer—in coarse-woven, earth-toned trousers, shirt, and jacket—while Emmett dressed in clothes that had obviously been tailor-made for him?

He walked over to the long, narrow table beneath the cabinets and set the tray on it. "Ye must be the lass I've heard so much about. Miss Melinda Waring, is it?"

She blinked, and the fair-haired man squatted next to the chair. She still had to lift her head to meet his intense green eyes. He appeared taller than James, but maybe it was the width of the man's shoulders. They were wider than James's.

He studied her face and said, "Yer pain must be great. Mrs. O'Toole described the wounds on yer back. I'll need to see the severity of them to judge for meself if the poultice will do the trick."

"If not?" she asked. The expression on his face changed from concerned to neutral—she had no idea what the man was thinking now. Mayhap it was best she did not.

"Well now, let's not be too quick to make a decision without all of the facts."

"I've brought the herbal you asked me to prepare for Melinda to drink." Mrs. O'Toole set the steaming mug on the table.

"Thank ye, Mrs. O'Toole." He rose to his feet. "In case ye were concerned, I'll have ye know that Mrs. O'Toole and Mrs. Wigglesworth have doctored meself, and me cousins, more times than I can count since we started working for His Grace. When things are a bit beyond their great experience, they call on meself before summoning the physician. Will ye allow me to see how far along the infection is, lass?"

What could Melinda do other than agree? "Aye. Thank you."

"Don't be thanking me till we discover what's what. If it is as I expect it to be, ye'll be able to have the herbal draught before I tend to yer back…if not, ye'll have to be patient—and brave to wait until I'm through treating ye."

She watched as he removed his frockcoat, rolled up the sleeves of his black cambric shirt, and walked over to the table. Dipping his hands in a bowl of steaming water, he used a round of soap and washed thoroughly. Drying his hands, he turned to the women and nodded.

"Are ye ready, lass?"

She saw the confidence in his gaze and relaxed. "Aye." The cover was gently removed, and a chill seemed to set into her very bones. She shivered.

"Easy now, lass. I'll do me best not to hurt ye."

"Are you applying the poultice?" Melinda asked.

"Not as yet. I need to remove the strips of linen to see—"

The silence that followed was worrisome. Was it worse than she feared? It had been painful, but she'd managed to bear an entire day with her chemise and gown rubbing against her wounds. How bad could it be?

He cursed beneath his breath—but his voice was so deep, it was easy to hear him.

"It's bad, isn't it?" she asked.

"Aye," he answered. "Ye've bits of fiber stuck to some of them. Why did no one care for yer wounds, lass?"

"There was no one I could ask."

Emmett mumbled something she could not quite make out. She decided not to ask.

"Not to worry," he assured her. "Once those fibers are removed, we'll try the poultice next. It'll feel hot to the touch—but won't burn ye. 'Tis the combination of healing herbs that make it feel hot on yer inflamed skin."

She tensed, resolving not to make a sound throughout the treatment.

"Ready, lass?"

"Aye."

Calling on the same control she used when her cousin landed the first blow, she prayed she would not embarrass herself by crying out. She felt a slight pressure, and then sharp pain when the first of the fibers was removed.

"Hang on, lass. We've a bit more to go."

Her head swam and her stomach tried to rebel—but still she clung to his words and the hope that the promised drink would be warm and filled with herbs that would ease some of her pain.

The hot, damp weight of the poultice between her shoulder blades took the sharp edge off the pain. Her head felt light when Emmett removed fibers from welts on the middle of her back. She bit down hard on her bottom lip and managed to keep from crying out. Once again, the warmth of the poultice eased some of the pain.

She cried out when he began to remove bits of fibers from the welts on the base of her spine. She drew in a sharp breath through gritted teeth.

"Ah, lass, I'm sorry to cause ye pain. 'Tis the worst of the infected welts—the closer I looked, the more I found. The pain will ease in a few moments. Let the poultice do its work."

She drew in one breath and then another, relieved to discover he was right—the worst had passed. Then it felt as if something popped. "Did the bag of herbs break?"

He cleared his throat before answering, "Nay, lass—'tis doing what it should...drawing the infection out. 'Tis a good thing."

A wave of dizziness swept through her as she imagined what Emmett saw. Odd how she could hold on while he removed strands of fibers from the wounds and then cleansed most of them. But listening to his description planted an image in her brain that had her head spinning.

"Mayhap you should not tell me what you are doing," she rasped, as the edges of her vision grayed.

"Stay with me, lass," he coaxed, lifting and then reapplying the herbal treatment.

"Can't," she whispered as the darkness pulled her under.

MRS. WIGGLESWORTH LOOKED up from where she sat beside Melinda. "She's fainted."

"'Tis probably for the best," Emmett said. "I don't know how the brave lass survived the beating, let alone the pain of cleansing her wounds. Where did me cousin say he rescued her from?"

"He didn't," Mrs. O'Toole said. "The poor thing was so pale and had a faint mark on her check where she'd been slapped."

"Her lip had been split," Mrs. Wigglesworth added.

"Any other injuries I should know about?" Emmett asked.

Mrs. O'Toole shot up from where she sat. "Her ribs! She mentioned landing hard on her side and feeling something give."

Emmett frowned, drew in a breath, and finished checking the last poultice. "We cannot allow her to lie on her back for at least another day—the pain will be unbearable."

Mrs. O'Toole nodded. "We'll rouse the poor thing, give her the herbal draught, and wrap her ribs."

"I'll leave the two of ye to it, then, shall I? Me Garahan cousins are prone to jealousy. I wouldn't want to be provoking James unnecessarily. 'Twill be bad enough when he finds out I've tended the poor lass's injuries on her back."

"James knows he can trust you," Mrs. Wigglesworth said.

"Aye, but if he's attracted to the lass—and with her angel's face and soft brown eyes, I'm thinking he might be—'tis best not to rile him."

He washed his hands and dried them, rolled down his sleeves, and donned his frockcoat. "If ye need me, I'll be patrolling the perimeter."

Mrs. Wigglesworth asked, "Shall I inform Jenkins we need the physician?"

"Let's give the lass a chance to rest and let the poultices, and the herbal drink, do their job. I'll return in an hour to check on her. If you need me before then, send word."

"Thank you, Emmett," Mrs. O'Toole and Mrs. Wigglesworth said at the same time.

He paused in the doorway, stared at the young woman Garahan had rescued, and wondered when his cousin planned to return to wherever he'd found the lass—to extract payment for what was done to her. Emmett planned to accompany James when he did.

He strode along the hallway, determined not to let his frustration show until he was alone. Emmett intended to make the man who'd beaten the lass pay, and if James was not interested in the lass, well then, so much the better. Emmett's admiration for the lass had grown from the moment he'd spoken with her, through the treatment, until she'd given in to the pain and fainted.

He paused in front of the door that led to the alley. He'd made up his mind. His cousin was in for a fight.

Miss Melinda Waring was a lass worth keeping!

CHAPTER FIVE

TREMAYNE AND GARAHAN could hear Coventry's daughter screaming through the closed door.

"We should wait," Tremayne said.

"Coventry's daughter has strong lungs," Garahan replied. "But she'll need a breath soon—wait for it, then give the signal."

A few minutes later, their opportunity came.

The door opened, and Garahan glanced down at the red-faced babe in the captain's arms. "Easy, lass," he crooned. "Yer poor da doesn't know what to make of yer tears yet." He used the tip of his finger to brush one away. "Ye're skin's softer than a rose petal."

Miraculously, Emma stopped crying to listen to him. "There's a lass," he said with pride. "Never met one I couldn't charm just speaking to them."

"Is that a fact?" Tremayne asked.

Garahan grinned. "Aye, 'tis a well-known fact women are partial to the lyrical sound of an Irishman's brogue."

"I'll remember that when the boys come sniffing around my daughter."

Garahan smiled as he freed a curl clinging to the babe's lashes.

"The rum isn't working tonight," Coventry said as he took a step away from Garahan. Emma's little face scrunched up. Before she could cry, he moved back to stand beside Garahan.

"Rum? Did ye not listen to me when I told ye what me sainted ma said about babes and teething?"

Coventry glared at him. "I do not keep a ready supply of Irish whiskey on hand."

"Faith, ye're in luck." Garahan whipped his flask out of the inside pocket of his frockcoat, handing it to Tremayne. "Hold on, lass, while I wash me hands."

Garahan washed and dried his hands, returning with a shot glass.

Tremayne uncorked the flask and poured while Garahan said, "'Tis a magical elixir, and 'tis said the *Fae* bless every batch of mountain dew brewed in me homeland." He dipped his finger in the whiskey and handed the glass off to Tremayne. Garahan whispered, "Open yer wee mouth, darling girl."

To Coventry's surprise—and Tremayne's—Emma opened her mouth and clamped down hard on Garahan's forefinger. "She's got strong jaws. I'm thinking she might let me hold her for a bit. With yer permission, captain."

Coventry locked gazes with Garahan. "I never figured you for a family man...though I never thought I'd be one either."

"Ma still reminds me in her letters that the Lord works in mysterious ways. She made sure I helped with me younger brothers and then our cousins—we've more than the few that are working for the duke. May I?" Garahan asked.

Coventry pressed a kiss to his daughter's forehead and handed her to Garahan.

He whispered nonsense words, and when the babe was settled in his arms, he gently pulled his finger free, dipped it in the tiny bit of whiskey left in the small glass, and waved it in front of her face.

Emma smiled, babbling until his finger was close enough to grab. She pulled it toward her open mouth. Without looking away from the precious babe in his arms, Garahan said, "Why don't ye have a seat, captain? I have news. 'Tisn't good."

"I have information as well," Tremayne said.

"Emma usually stays quiet when I walk around the room," Coventry said.

"Ma taught me to rock side to side," Garahan said. "I'll do that first, then walk if she fusses." With a glance at the bottle of rum, he grinned. "A wee bit of rum ought to set ye to rights, captain."

Coventry stared at Garahan, who sensed the captain was trying to add this to what he knew of him. Until this moment, only his family had witnessed his way with babes and children.

The duke may refer to Garahan as "the hammer" because of his ability to encourage detractors to talk—sometimes with words, sometimes with force. But Garahan's *true* gift, according to his ma, was his ability to calm babes and children. It used to confound him when he was young. Eventually he accepted it as his lot when, time after time, he'd enter a room where a babe or one of his brothers or cousins were crying. As soon as he started talking, the little ones would stop crying and pay rapt attention to him.

His brothers ribbed him about it the older they got, but in a brotherly way. They were raised to believe, and understand, that everyone had a gift in life that they were meant to use for good. Hadn't his ma told him that when he complained about his O'Malley cousins having better gifts? Michael had the gift of sight, and Emmett the gift of healing.

"You never cease to amaze me, Garahan," Coventry said. "You meant what you said when you met me. You never saw me as half a man, did you?"

"Why would I, when ye're not?"

"I could not see past what had been before the Battle of Trafalgar...and what was left of me after," Coventry said. "I never thanked you for that, did I?"

Garahan looked at him. "I'm thinking ye have a time or two." Then he smiled at the babe in his arms.

"You saw a need to be filled and brought it to my attention. Bayfield, Masterson, Hennessey, and Tremayne," the captain said with a nod at Tremayne, "all served His Majesty until their injuries ended their military careers—like mine had." After pouring two shot glasses, he handed one to Tremayne, and lifted the other.

Coventry raised his, as did Tremayne. "To Garahan, the man behind the idea to form a group of injured military men who are not as they appear. Men who were still strong in spite of their injuries—men who could unobtrusively infiltrate various levels of society when the need arises—and bring about the change we are hired to do."

"I never doubted ye—nor have me brothers or cousins. Nor ye, Tremayne. Ye've proven yerself time and again." Garahan had to clear his throat to continue, "Without yer holding Finn up beneath the scaffold...and me above...his neck would have snapped before Bayfield slashed through the rope with his saber."

Coventry and Tremayne tossed their rum back. "Now then, Tremayne," the captain said, "what have you discovered?"

Garahan watched Emma's eyes close and accepted the fact that the little one had him completely wrapped around her finger. "She's going to break hearts."

"Do you want me to put her in her cradle?"

"Nay. Let her sleep in me arms for a bit." He didn't admit *he* wasn't ready to let the wee lass go just yet. "I need to tell ye what I learned earlier, then return to Grosvenor Square. It'd be easier to tell the whole of it at once."

"After we hear what Tremayne has to say. Tremayne?" Coventry said.

"Our contact at White's heard Corkendale boasting that he would take down Wyndmere's house of cards...one at a time," Tremayne replied.

Coventry frowned. "I understand he married an heiress, and recently inherited a barony."

"Aye," Tremayne answered. "Married over the anvil in Gretna Green a year ago. As yet, there isn't a connection discovered between the baron and His Grace—or His Grace's siblings."

"What of the duchess?" Garahan asked. "Any connection to Lady Persephone?"

"None," Tremayne responded.

"Someone who recently ascended to the lowest level of Society could be out to elevate his position within the *ton*...by exposing the truth about the Duke of Wyndmere," Coventry said. "Although there is nothing to expose. The man has no skeletons. Therefore—"

"Mayhap the blackguard plans to *create* a truth that those who are envious of the duke would be willing to believe," Garahan said.

Coventry agreed. "Some will believe it of the current duke, because of his older brother's life of debauchery and depravity while he was the fifth duke. Good work, Tremayne. What did you find out at Tattersalls, Garahan?"

Garahan smiled when the babe in his arms scrunched up her face as she settled closer to his heart. He silently vowed to protect wee Emma with his life. "Apparently, a footman—we believe one of Corkendale's, though 'tis still to be verified, as me source's information is secondhand."

"Go on," Coventry urged.

"Vicious rumors, just as before, slandering Lady Calliope and Lady Aurelia."

"They have chosen two of the kindest, most compassionate ladies of the *ton*—obviously they do not know the ladies personally, as we do," Coventry said. "Otherwise, they would not deliberately try to tear their reputations to shreds. Any specifics—gambling, riding astride, showing their ankles in public?"

Garahan did not smile at Coventry's jest.

Coventry was immediately on alert. "Tell me all of it."

"The *on dit* is that neither of the two ladies' babes were fathered by their husbands."

Coventry shot to his feet. "Bloody hell!"

Emma woke and started to scream. Garahan shifted her so she was upright against his shoulder. He rubbed her back to quiet her. "There now, lass, don't fret. 'Tis just yer da." When Coventry reached for his daughter, Garahan handed the babe to him.

"Emma, love," Coventry soothed, "don't cry." When she quieted and closed her eyes once more, he asked Garahan, "Who is the culprit this time?"

Garahan met Coventry's gaze and said, "Me."

Tremayne snickered. "When in God's name would you have had the time?"

"'Twas me response to Burton, the head groom over at Tattersalls."

"Anyone who knows you, and the fact that you are the duke's first choice to fill in at his other estates whenever the need arises, would never link your name to such a deed," Coventry said with conviction. "In spite of the rumor and innuendo from the last attack against them, their reputations remain above reproach."

"I mentioned that as well," Garahan said.

"We'll have to advise His Grace, the earl, and the viscount of this latest salacious rumor."

Garahan wanted to track down the footman and beat him senseless for knowingly spreading false rumors about two women he greatly admired and respected. A thought occurred to him. "What if the footman was presented proof?"

"What proof could there possibly be?" Tremayne asked.

"A signed statement from the attending physician and midwife would exonerate Garahan—but could be forged," Coventry said.

"The viscountess and the countess live miles apart," Tremayne said. "Do we know if they used the same midwife and physician?"

"We need that information verified. I will pen the missives to the physician and midwife I believe they used," Coventry said. "I will wait a day or two before sending word to His Grace and their lordships—we should have more information then."

"Are ye sure ye should wait?"

Coventry nodded. "Remember what occurred last time?"

"Aye—the duel—and their ladyships defying their husbands by attending," Garahan said. "Ye may want to advise Lady Aurelia's uncle, Lord Coddington, as well."

"Excellent point, Garahan," Coventry murmured. "Tremayne, I need you to deliver a missive to King."

Tremayne nodded and smiled as Emma was passed back to Garahan while Coventry penned and sealed the notes.

Note in hand, Tremayne left.

Garahan handed the babe back to Coventry and asked, "Do ye want me to deliver the missives to Sussex?"

"No. I'll use our messengers. You'll need to deliver the missives to their lordships when and if we receive more information. You'd best return to the duke's town house and the lass waiting for you."

Garahan paused in the doorway. "I didn't mention a lass."

"Didn't you?" Coventry asked. "I must have just assumed a young woman was involved, otherwise you wouldn't be distracted."

"'Twas your darling girl that did the distracting. She's a beautiful babe, Coventry. Remember, ye have the whole of the duke's guard and yer own men to call on. Consider yer family under our protection. Call on us any time."

Coventry's green eye glittered with determination. "I can protect my own."

"That ye can, but as ye know, vermin have been known to climb up out of the gutter every now and again to try to destroy something pure—something good. We'll see to it that doesn't happen."

Coventry held out his free hand to Garahan.

Garahan shook it. "Watch yer back."

"Watch yours," Coventry said.

After slipping out through the door and closing it quietly, Garahan descended the stairs. With each step, his anger further threatened to erupt. Corkendale would pay for spreading lies about their ladyships. To use Garahan to tarnish the duke's reputation, after His Grace had worked so hard to restore the family name, was unconscionable. He clamped down on his jaw—and his anger—and unhitched his horse.

"There's a handful of oats waiting for ye, laddie. Take us home."

CHAPTER SIX

EMMETT WAS WAITING for Garahan when he arrived at the duke's town house. Garahan noted the protective stance his cousin had assumed. "Trouble?"

"Aye, but not what ye think."

"Is everyone inside for the night?"

"Aye. Before ye go inside, I need to ask ye something."

Emmett nodded to the two footmen standing guard at either corner of the home—they would remain at their posts until Emmett and Garahan returned.

When they reached the doors to the stables, Garahan asked, "What do ye want to ask me?"

Emmett grabbed a scoop and filled it with oats.

Garahan's gelding's ears pricked up at the sound. "Good lad, ye know ye're about to have the treat I promised ye." Garahan removed the horse's tack and settled him in his stall. Looking over his shoulder, he asked his cousin, "Well? 'Tisn't like ye to stall—must be a woman involved. Only reason ye'd be tongue-tied."

"As a matter of fact, there is."

"Do I know her? I may have been away from London for the last few months, but I have kept abreast of what's been happening at His Grace's estates—and what me cousins and brothers are up to. What's her name?"

Emmett waited a beat before answering, "Melinda."

Garahan's gut clenched. "Well, ye can untie yer tongue and get over her, because she's already spoken for."

"She didn't say she was spoken for."

"When would the two of ye have had time for a conversation?" Garahan demanded.

"You dropped her off and left in a hurry. There was plenty of time."

"Not when ye're on guard duty." He curled his hands into fists and then uncurled them. "Did ye have to go for the physician? How many ribs are broken?" He felt the blood drain from the top of his head to his feet. "Dear God, did her cousin do more than strike her face?"

"Aye, James," Emmett said, reaching for his cousin. "But 'tisn't what ye fear." His Adam's apple bobbed as he said, "Mrs. O'Toole wrapped her ribs—they were only bruised. The lass's back is in shreds—I did the best I could, but fibers from her chemise and gown were embedded in the lash marks. They're infected and had to be lanced."

Garahan's stomach rebelled—he clamped down on the urge to retch, spun on his heel, and sprinted toward the back of the house.

"Wait! Ye cannot disturb the lass," Emmett called out. "She needs to rest."

"Who was with her when ye examined her?"

"Who in the bloody hell do ye think?" Emmett asked.

Garahan paused with his hand on the doorframe. "Mrs. O'Toole and Mrs. Wigglesworth."

Emmett nodded.

"Did ye have to do the lancing, or was the physician summoned?"

"'Twas worse than we feared, even after removing the poultices and giving the lass the herbal draught."

Garahan nodded, understanding that they had *had* to send for the physician. "Did the physician prescribe laudanum for her pain?"

"Aye. Though he cautioned us to be very careful with the dosage, as she's a bit on the slender side for her height."

"And ye'd have noticed that as well, caring for her injuries."

"To be honest, I did not notice anything but the number of times that bleeding bugger must have struck the lass with the wooden rod she said he used on her."

Garahan dug deep—and deeper still—calling up his steely control to contain his anger. "How many times?"

Emmett grabbed hold of Garahan's shoulder. "She said she lost count after twenty."

"I'll need the exact amount. I'll be taking more than a pound of flesh off the bastard."

"Not tonight," Emmett warned.

"And why not?" Garahan demanded.

"The physician was determined to speak with Gavin King over on Bow Street about the matter."

"Well now, that's one of the few reasons, I would allow ye to convince me not to go after the bleeding bugger." He met Emmett's gaze and asked, "Do I have to tell ye how I feel about the lass?"

Emmett shook his head. "I see it clear as day in yer heart."

Garahan snorted, "Don't ye mean me eyes?"

"Being as how yer heart's in yer eyes, I suppose I do."

"I'm not some lovesick lad of four and ten," Garahan said.

"Nay, ye're a man three years older than meself, who has never lost his head over a lass before. I'm warning ye, if ye give the lass one reason to cry over the likes of ye—ye'll never know what hit ye."

Garahan inclined his head. "I can agree to that. Best know right now, I'm asking the lass to marry me."

Emmett shook his head. "Ye're daft."

"I just might be at that. Can ye come with me to see her? I want to be sure she doesn't need anything."

"Aye. I'll come with ye."

Garahan opened the door, and the pair walked down the hallway to the door to the servants' side of the town house.

Emmett paused with his hand on the doorknob. "Do me a favor?"

"What do ye need?"

"Don't be proposing to the lass tonight."

Garahan shoved his cousin inside. "Ye know I never make a promise I cannot keep."

CHAPTER SEVEN

BARON STEPHEN CORKENDALE stood with his hands clasped behind his back, staring into the fire. His plan had to work! He had to prove to the *ton*—and his wife—that the sixth Duke of Wyndmere had them all fooled. He and his family were cut from the same cloth as the fifth duke, who'd been shot in the back leaving his married lover's *boudoir*.

It would be easy. The blasted duke was vocal in the House of Lords, worked tirelessly to better conditions for military men returning from battle wounded—or not at all—and expediting funds owed to their widows and children. Another example of the duke's bleeding heart was his man-of-affairs—a one-eyed, limp-armed former captain in the Royal Navy.

Corkendale was in the process of interviewing prospects to fill the position of *his* man-of-affairs. He would pick someone who would promote the image Corkendale wished everyone to see. Strength, social position, and power.

Another count against the duke was the fact he did not have a mistress, or two, waiting in the wings for him. He was a family man—protecting not only his brother and sister, and their families, but also two of his distant cousins and their families! Who in the bloody hell would bother?

Not him! Corkendale's recent ascension to baron was tainted by a hasty marriage and the mysterious deaths of the previous baron and his baroness. The baron prior to that died without issue.

Stephen had known he was his cousin's heir for years, but until recently had no idea that there was a stipulation stating his cousin's heir must be married to inherit the title and the property entailed. He thought more coin would be attached to the barony.

His wife's constant complaints—her pitiful wardrobe allowance and his town house being too far from Mayfair to be considered fashionable—had him desperate to do something! He should have inherited the barony five years past, when he'd engineered the carriage accident that took the life of his cousin's wife. His cousin had survived the *accident*.

He strode to the crystal brandy decanter and filled a glass. Drinking deeply, he remembered how meticulously he'd planned his cousin's demise. The worry that the witness would go back on his word—despite the coin he paid the man—filled him. "There should not have been any witnesses!"

He threw the glass against the fireplace. For a heartbeat, the shards of crystal glistened in the firelight, before falling to the hearth, where they lay lifeless. The unbidden image of his cousin flashed in his mind—the moment when he was thrown from his horse. Corkendale had to ensure his cousin perished this time. He had hired two men to do the job—while he watched from a safe distance. What he had not counted on was anyone else witnessing the tragic *accident*.

"Stephen!"

The dulcet tones he'd hoped to hear for the rest of his life vanished the day he wed Lady Elizabeth. Her soft voice and infatuation with him ended the morning after he'd wedded—and bedded—her.

God help him! The harpy constantly badgered him, shrieking his name at the top of her lungs from wherever she happened to be in their town house.

If only he could rid himself of her, too…

He knew whom to hire to do the job. When and how depended upon how much longer he could stand his wife's constant complaining.

The shrew's voice drew nearer. Drawing in a steadying breath, he turned as the doors to his private study burst open.

"There you are! Did you not hear me calling you?" his wife demanded.

"Ah, my dove, I did not. Forgive me for woolgathering when I should have been waiting to attend to your every need."

She paused on the threshold to frown at him. "You do try my patience."

"Not my intention. What is so urgent that you would interrupt me in my *private* study? We were to meet this afternoon to discuss your social calendar, were we not?"

His wife hesitated. With her mouth closed, she was lovely—golden tresses, bright blue eyes, and the figure of a goddess. But once she opened that mouth…

"I do apologize, Stephen—" He glared at her, and she immediately apologized. "My lord," she corrected herself. "We finally received our invitation to the Hollisters' ball. It's all everyone is talking about and will be quite a crush. I simply must ask you to loosen your purse strings and allow me to have Madame Beaudoine create a ball gown worthy of the occasion."

Their very brief courtship had consisted of three dances and being discovered in a passionate embrace. God, must he truly pay for falling for the chit's obvious charms for the rest of his life? His mind raced as he considered various accidents that could befall his wife in her daily excursions to the shops on Bond Street, and afternoon tea with her lady friends at Gunter's, before she returned home to badger him with tales of her friends' gowns—bemoaning the ones he had already had designed for her…though not by the much-in-demand Madame Beaudoine!

Mayhap a new gown from the madame would shut her up long enough for him to achieve his goal of discrediting the duke and his family. He'd planted the first seeds of dissension, suggesting that one of the duke's private guard had fathered the duke's sister-in-law's babe and that of the duke's cousin's wife! It was time to plant the next seeds—the accusation that the duke's sister and her husband's house parties were a cover for the orgies that took place at their estate in the borderlands.

Pleased that the next steps would soon be rippling through the *ton*, he felt he could afford to indulge his wife...for the short remaining time they would be wed.

CHAPTER EIGHT

PAIN SHOT THROUGH Melinda's back, waking her. Her head felt woozy, but was nothing compared to the aches that had seemed to worsen overnight. Hadn't Emmett O'Malley warned her that with physical injuries, one or two days after receiving the injury, the pain may increase?

Desperate to sit up, she opened her eyes and gasped at the handsome face so close to her own. Her pain momentarily forgotten, she struggled to know where to begin thanking the man.

The intensity in his dark brown eyes had her wondering if he'd waited long—or was the intensity due to something else entirely?

"I've been waiting for ye to wake up, lass."

She stared at the dark-haired man who had rescued her. If she'd known what her cousin wanted her to do ahead of time, she'd have thrown herself on the mercy of the new vicar—or begged in the streets—before accepting her cousin's offer of a job and a place to live so far from the village she'd grown up in.

She licked her dry lips. "Do you think I could have a sip of water?"

"Aye. Let me fetch ye a cup."

James rose from the chair beside her, and she noticed he now wore well-tailored black clothing—similar to his cousin's. Mayhap this was a uniform they wore when in the part of London where those of the *ton* lived.

While she studied him, he poured a small amount in a cup and returned to her side. "I'm not sure how ye can drink this lying down. Can I help ye to sit up?"

Tears pricked the back of her eyes, but she refused to give in to them. "I'm not certain you should even be alone in the room with me...or am I beyond redemption, having worked in the stews of London?"

James set the cup on the small table by the chair. "Ye should not feel shame for the condition of the tavern ye worked in. Ye're a brave lass, who accepted yer own kin's promise of a job to work and a place to stay."

Tears welled in her eyes despite her resolve not to let them. "But I... He..."

James crouched down beside her, his face so close to hers, she could not help but notice the strong line of his jaw, his slightly crooked nose, and the cleft in his chin. "I'll not hear another word about it. Ye're safe here. Ye'll rest and get well. Do ye understand?"

Getting a bit of her gumption back at the command in his tone, she asked, "Is that an order?"

He did not answer her question. Instead, he surprised her by getting to his feet and striding to the doorway. "I'll be right back."

Having no other choice, she lay there...alone in a strange house, surrounded by the duke's servants and two very handsome men, members of the duke's private guard—James Garahan and his cousin Emmett O'Malley. How in the world would she be able to lift her head in public after being carried out of the tavern in James's arms, riding through the streets of London atop his horse, and finding herself captive in the Duke of Wyndmere's town house on Grosvenor Square?

Her throat tightened at her predicament. There was no way to save what little was left of her reputation.

Though James had delivered her to what he considered a safe place, it was his cousin who'd tended to her back. She shuddered remembering the lengths he and Mrs. O'Toole went to caring for her injuries. Her belly clenched as she remembered the physician's visit that followed. It had felt as if he flayed open the skin at her shoulders, the middle of her back, and low on her spine.

As well as the scars she'd have from the beating, the ones from lancing the infected welts would be far worse. A tear escaped at the realization that if she had somehow managed to return to her village, with no one being the wiser as to how she had spent the last six months—working from sunup until well past midnight—she might have had a chance at a normal life. But now, she could not return. She would ask Mrs. O'Toole or Mrs. Wigglesworth which agency to apply to for work as a scullery maid. She was not afraid of hard work.

Mrs. O'Toole bustled into the room, closing the door behind her. "Melinda, let me help you sit up." With a bit of maneuvering this way and that, Melinda found herself bundled and sitting up on the cot. "James said he left a cup of water on the table for you."

Melinda tried to steady her hands, but they were shaking so badly, she spilled the water. "I'm sorry."

"Not to worry. My fault for not realizing how difficult it would be after lying on your stomach for the last few hours—without a bite of food to eat."

"You did offer," Melinda reminded her. "But I was not certain I could keep it down."

Mrs. O'Toole wiped up the water on the floor, so no one would slip, then poured more in the cup and handed it to Melinda. "Now then, I'll help steady you."

Melinda met the woman's unflinching gaze and thanked her before taking a drink. She sipped from the cup until her parched mouth and lips felt moist again. "Thank you, Mrs. O'Toole. You've been so kind to me—a stranger thrust into your care. I'm grateful to you."

Mrs. O'Toole smiled, taking the empty cup. "How much pain are you in?"

Melinda bit her lip, but didn't answer right away.

"That much? We shall have to see if you are up to some beef broth and maybe a bit of bread soaked in the broth—and my specialty calves' foot jelly. An invalid's diet for you for the next week at least."

Melinda's stomach—obviously empty—rumbled in protest, and Mrs. O'Toole reminded her, "We want the broth and the rest to stay put, don't we?"

"Aye," Melinda agreed. "But I haven't eaten yet today."

"I thought you were able to eat where you worked?"

Melinda stared at the hands in her lap. "Only if I finished my chores to my cousin's satisfaction. He was very angry after I refused...after he tried to make me..."

Mrs. O'Toole reached out to grasp Melinda's hand in hers. "Our James and Lieutenant Tremayne were there in time to keep anything from happening to you. You are safe here." She released Melinda's hand. "Now then, James has asked if he could have a word with you—with your permission, of course."

Melinda wrung her hands. Instead of agreeing, she asked, "Does anyone else know that we were alone in this room?"

The cook sighed. "You have nothing to fear from the men in the duke's guard. They are honest, trustworthy, and will guard you with their lives. No one on the duke's staff would think to speak ill of you or James. He returned from his meeting and asked to watch over you while I prepared a meal for those who work here."

"Then no one will think I've ruined my reputation by—"

"My dear girl, you have been gravely mistreated, and your wounds treated by Emmett, and the duke's physician. Not one person in this household—nor the physician—would dare to comment other than to mention how brave you were through the treatment."

"Thank you, Mrs. O'Toole. It will be harder for me to find another scullery maid's position if a trail of rumor followed me to one of the agencies." Melinda paused, then asked, "Would you mind giving me the direction of a reputable agency? I need to find another position as soon as possible."

"We'll talk about that later. Right now, we need to get something warm in your belly. The physician did say if you were up to it, you could have weak tea—as long as you ate at every bit of the calves' foot jelly, broth, and bread."

"I'd be grateful for whatever you can spare."

"If you are in pain, please tell me. The physician left laudanum along with his diet instructions. You may have a dosage after you eat."

Relief filled her. "I think that may ease some of the discomfort. Thank you."

Mrs. O'Toole walked to the door and left it open, promising to return in a few moments.

James tried to step around her. "I need to see—"

The cook placed her hand in the middle of James's chest. "While Melinda is awake, you will not be alone with her. She will have the benefit of a chaperone—as is proper."

"But—"

"I'll not hear another word on the subject."

Melinda could not fathom the cook taking a man the size of James Garahan to task. He was broad through the chest and shoulders, and almost equal in height to Emmett. The way he did not argue with the duke's cook surprised—and pleased—her.

Though she had no idea what he could possibly want to speak to her privately about. She wondered if Mrs. O'Toole would unobtrusively sit on the other side of the room from them to give them a semi-private moment.

They returned a few minutes later, with James carrying a tray, and Mrs. O'Toole directing him where to set it down.

"Shall I help you—" Mrs. O'Toole began, only to be interrupted by James.

"Allow me. I'm sure ye don't want yer loaves of bread to burn."

The cook frowned, and James continued. "If ye leave the door open, and ask one of the footmen to stand outside the door, that should take care of propriety, should it not?"

Mrs. O'Toole sighed. "I do have to take the bread out of the cookstove." She leveled a stern look on James. "Do not say anything to upset Melinda," she warned. "Talk about the weather."

Melinda hid the smile that wanted to break free at the disgruntled look on James's face.

"Aye, Mrs. O'Toole."

The older woman inclined her head and swept from the room.

James carried the cup of broth to the table and set it down. "Would ye like help?"

"I think I can manage."

He handed Melinda the cup and didn't say a word about how badly her hands were shaking. "Emmett told me about yer back. Why did ye not tell me? I could have been more careful carrying ye and carting ye here on the back of me horse!"

Her eyes welled with tears. Before they fell, he leaned close and brushed them away. "Forgive me, lass. It's me frustration at having unintentionally caused ye pain. Give yerself time to heal. Until then, use yer head and let us help ye to eat and any other task that would put a strain on yer wounds. Ye don't want them to reopen, do ye?"

She shook her head.

"Well then, let me feed ye."

Heat surged up her neck to her forehead, but she would have to move past her embarrassment or go hungry—and the broth smelled heavenly.

"Thank you, James. I am hungry."

Her stomach growled, and he grinned. "That's fine, then. Have a bit of broth, lass, while I regale ye with the unusual weather we're having."

Eyes wide, focused on the handsome visage before her, she nearly choked on the first swallow.

"Easy, lass. It takes some getting used to, being fed."

While he gently blotted the broth from her chin, she asked, "When was the last time someone had to feed you?"

His cheeks flushed, and he shrugged. "'Twas not that long ago that I don't remember what it felt like being helpless to feed meself."

She sensed he would not be forthcoming with whatever his injury was or when it happened. Staring at his slightly crooked nose, she asked, "Was it when someone broke your nose?"

He chuckled. "Ah, now that is a tale worth telling. 'Twas nigh on a decade ago...maybe a bit longer than that. I was visiting me cousin Patrick's family in Cork and spied one of his sisters halfway up the rowan tree by their barn."

"How old was she, if she was climbing a tree?" She chewed and swallowed a mouthful and licked her lips.

James cleared his throat and glanced at the cup in his hand before answering. "A lass of just six years—stuck, she was. 'Tis easier to climb up than down, I'm told."

"But not for you?" she asked.

He grinned as he blotted her lips. "Nay, I'm not afraid of heights, but me wee cousin Grainne was frozen with fear."

He continued to feed her and blot her mouth as he told of climbing up the tree. It was when he was convincing the lass to let go of the branch and hang on to him that her elbow connected—hard—with the bridge of his nose, breaking it. By the time his tale was finished, so was Melinda's meager meal.

"Thank you for feeding me without making it more uncomfortable than it already is."

"The pleasure was all mine, lass."

"It's been a long time since I've tasted broth so savory or bread that delicious."

"Mrs. O'Toole is a wonderful cook. Wait until ye taste her cream scones, warm from the oven, with raspberry preserves and clotted cream—or plain. Me cousin and I are found of grabbing one or two on our way through the kitchen as we go on our rounds."

"They sound delicious, but I don't think they are on the physician's list of foods I am allowed to eat for the next sennight."

He winked at her. "Mayhap I'll sneak one in to ye."

"Everyone has been so kind to me. I am not sure how I will repay their kindness—and before you get angry with me, I was referring to lending a hand with the chores. I'd be more than happy to repay the kindness by working as a scullery maid once I'm able."

He frowned at her—not the reaction she'd expected. "We'll see what Emmett and the physician will have to say about yer progress healing. Until then, ye're to rest."

Their eyes met, and she could not look away. Something in the depths of his gaze pulled at her, urging her to lean close. When she did, she felt the brush of his lips on hers. Warm, soft, delicate—like the touch of an angel's wings.

"Ah, lass, ye have no idea what ye do to me when ye look at me like that."

She licked her lips. "Like what?"

His Adam's apple bobbed up and down before he answered, "Like ye want me to kiss ye again."

She sucked in a breath and then another before asking, "Would you kiss me again if I asked you to?"

His lips were a breath away, his eyes swirling with a mix of emotions—too many for her to interpret.

"Ah, I see you have finished your meal, Melinda," Mrs. O'Toole said, bustling into the room. She shook her head at James. "Do you see why I do not think it's wise for me to allow the two of you to be in here alone?"

James eased back from her and ran a hand through his hair. "Mayhap tomorrow. I can spare some time to feed ye yer morning meal, if ye wish."

"Thank you. I'd like that," Melinda said.

"Well then, until tomorrow morning." He paused in the doorway. "Try to rest, lass. Ye need it to heal."

"I'll try."

"She'll be needing that dose of laudanum, Mrs. O'Toole."

"I shall see to it. Thank you for sitting with her, James."

"'Tis me pleasure." He bowed and left the room.

Melinda felt empty inside watching him leave, and was afraid he'd taken her heart with him.

"If you can resist a fine man like James Garahan, you are a stronger woman than me," Mrs. O'Toole said.

"He kissed me."

"From the blush on your cheeks when I walked in the room, I thought he might have. He may steal a kiss from you, but would never think to do more than that. You can trust James."

Mrs. O'Toole helped her to use the chamber pot, then wash her face and hands, before giving her a dose of the medicine. She settled Melinda back down on the cot and drew a small bell out of her apron pocket. Placing it within reach on the table beside the cot, she said, "Ring if you need me. Close your eyes and try to sleep."

"I will, thank you." As the laudanum started to take the edge off her pain, Melinda closed her eyes and dreamed of the dark-haired, dark-eyed, handsome Irishman she wanted to trust. In her dreams, he swept her off her feet, then stole her heart, kissing her with a passion that left her breathless, aching, and yearning for more.

CHAPTER NINE

COVENTRY CRUSHED THE missive in his hand. "Of all the slanderous rumors levied against the duke and his family, this is by far the most vile!"

Garahan and Tremayne shared a glance, but neither wanted to interrupt before the captain told them what the missive contained...and more, whom it was from.

Coventry did neither. He tossed the crumpled ball of parchment onto the middle of the scarred mahogany table he used as a desk and strode over to the window that faced Lumley Street.

With Coventry standing with his feet spread and his hands clasped behind his back—he only wore his sling in public—Garahan could imagine the man standing on the deck of his ship, bellowing commands, while taking on fire amidships.

"Whatever it is, we will handle it," he said.

Coventry drew in a deep breath and blew it out. "Lady Phoebe has never harmed a soul in her life! Her behavior, which could be called hoydenish, was due to her penchant for racing through Hyde Park at dawn with her hair unbound, or walking down Bond Street and suddenly grasping the hand of her maid—or lady friend—to dance down the sidewalk. Never this."

Garahan was about to speak when the captain continued, "Good God, this will cut Jared and Edward deeply. They spent years keeping close guard over their younger sister—stifling her."

"More than necessary with a headstrong sister?" Tremayne asked.

"Aye," Coventry answered. "The fifth duke—their eldest brother, Oliver—was well known for his penchant for spending his time in the gaming hells and brothels in the very bowels of London. He'd bring his cronies home with him after a few nights spent in those gaming hells. His Grace had connections that would alert him that Oliver was headed home to the London town house. He and the earl would make a game of sweeping their young sister into the carriage and setting off at breakneck speed to Wyndmere Hall."

Garahan's stomach clenched. The brothers had gone to extraordinary lengths to protect their sister. They had stepped into the role of parents, and guard dogs, shielding her from their brother who had chosen the path that would lead him straight to hell.

"Who sent the missive?" Tremayne asked.

"It was anonymous," Coventry answered.

"Who delivered it?" Garahan asked.

"A young lad—poorly dressed. I believe I have seen him a time or two picking pockets on Hart Street. He hasn't been caught…yet."

"How young?" Tremayne asked.

Coventry turned back to face Garahan and Tremayne, pausing a moment before replying, "Could be ten or twelve summers, mayhap tall for his age, and only eight or nine summers."

"If the lad is trying to earn coin to put food in the mouths of younger siblings," Garahan said, "his mother could be a widow— maybe even one of your fallen comrades' widows."

Coventry nodded. "I've sent Bayfield around to see if he can locate the lad." Squaring his shoulders, he said, "Men, whoever is behind this atrocity has reached a new level of blatant disregard for the pain and suffering these rumors could possibly inflict on their target." The lethal gleam in his eye promised retribution.

Garahan knew the captain's history with the duke and his family.

He guessed Tremayne knew of it, too.

"I have known Lady Phoebe for more than half her life. She is like a younger sister to me. This coward must be found and made to pay!"

"We shall see to it," Garahan promised.

"Aye," Tremayne agreed. "The perpetrator has obviously not received the response he anticipated with the first sally—what was it, a sennight ago?"

"Just shy of," the captain said.

"Best tell us what he's said about Lady Phoebe," Garahan urged.

Before the captain could answer, Tremayne asked, "Does the slander include Baron Summerfield, as well?"

Captain Coventry rubbed the back of his neck. "Aye. 'Tis said Baron and Baroness Summerfield host house parties as a ruse."

"For what?" Tremayne asked. "Running a gaming hell in the borderlands?"

Coventry's green eye locked on Tremayne first, Garahan second. "The bloody bastard said Lady Phoebe and her husband host orgies—disguised as a costume ball where guests don Grecian or Roman garb! The detailed accounts are too outrageous to be believed, but disgusting enough that there will be those who will not be able to resist the urge to pass such an illicit *on dit* to their cronies."

Garahan walked over to the table and picked up the missive. He read the words without showing any outward reaction to them. The descriptions were beyond vile. Inside he was seething—a dangerous combination of anger and revenge bubbling beneath his surface calm. The silent monologue going on inside his brain was the only thing that kept his emotions from boiling over. He handed the missive to Tremayne.

"Although my first reaction is to toss it in the fire," Garahan said, "ye'll need to keep this as evidence, Coventry."

The temper in the captain's one-eyed gaze was telling—the man never showed what he was thinking, with one exception: if his family was nearby.

"Have ye alerted His Grace?"

Coventry frowned. "Nay, I received this missive moments before you arrived. I sent off an urgent message to the duke regarding the first offensive rumors, along with the information we have unearthed. Before you ask, I sent missives to the earl, and the viscount as well."

"Mayhap ye should send the missive concerning this latest verbal attack to me cousin, Patrick, at Wyndmere Hall. Ye can trust him to keep a level head when relaying it to the duke."

Coventry stalked over to the window again, slamming the flat of his hand against the window frame, rattling the glass. "Patrick is the only one who can stop the duke from saddling that black beast of a thoroughbred and riding straight to the borderlands to warn Marcus."

Garahan mused aloud, "The baron and the duke will try to lock Phoebe in her bedchamber to keep her from following them to London."

"Mayhap you should send reinforcements to Summerfield Chase," Tremayne suggested.

"Bayfield, Hennessey, and Masterson can leave at a moment's notice," the captain said.

Tremayne looked at Garahan, who added, "Aye. I'd trust yer men with me life—even this one."

Tremayne shoved Garahan with his shoulder. "Admit it, you could not have saved your cousin's life without me."

Garahan's throat tightened as he remembered how close it had been. "With ye lifting Finn from beneath the scaffold, and me adding me strength standing atop it—keeping the rope slack—he was spared a horrible death."

"Do you think this round of lies and innuendo ties into what oc-curred at Penwith Tower, captain?"

"Nay. I believe someone is trying to tarnish the Lippincott name, and the house of Wyndmere—again. But with our connections at all levels of society," Coventry said, "they will not succeed."

"Whoever is behind this could be a connection to the former duke," Garahan said.

Tremayne frowned. "Mayhap someone trying to ruin the duke by attacking the men of the duke's guard."

Coventry nodded. "Or both. I'll send Bayfield and the others to the borderlands."

"What do ye intend to do when their lordships arrive from Sussex?" Garahan asked. "Ye know the earl and the viscount will not sit on their laurels while the rest of us are following leads."

"The duke will remind them to stay close to their wives," Coventry said.

"There's strength in numbers," Garahan said. "They will either insist their wives stay put at Lippincott Manor or Chattsworth Manor. God willing, they'll listen this time."

"The guard will be doubled if they gather their wives and children in one place," Tremayne said. "Others can be hired from the village, if need be."

"Can you leave immediately, Garahan?" Coventry asked.

The image of Melinda's face tilted up to receive his kiss popped into his head, momentarily distracting him. Digging deep to ignore the need, he answered, "If ye send word to Emmett as to where I'll be."

Coventry nodded. "Tremayne, keep in contact with our man at White's and the groom at Tattersalls."

"Aye, captain."

Their orders received, Tremayne and Garahan exited the building. Outside, Tremayne turned to Garahan. "You have my word that I'll watch over Melinda in your absence. Emmett and the others will protect her. She'll be safe. Concentrate on your assignment."

Garahan groaned. "Thank ye. I'll be trying to talk the earl and the viscount out of leaving their families under guard while they head here."

"Do you think their wives would follow them?" Tremayne asked as he mounted his horse.

Garahan also mounted and then answered, "Me greater worry is that their ladyships will bundle up their sons and make the journey as soon as their husbands are out of sight. If they've caught wind of what is happening, I have no doubt they've already packed their bags and hidden them in their nurseries."

His thoughts turned to the brown-eyed lass he'd left in the care of Mrs. O'Toole and Mrs. Wigglesworth—guarded by his cousin. He had been looking forward to feeding her breakfast. By the time he returned, she'd have healed to the point where she would not need his help. Would she still seek his company?

"God, save us from strong-minded women."

Tremayne's words changed the direction of Garahan's thoughts. He snorted with laughter. "Don't ye mean, God, thank ye for placing feisty women in our path? Ma swears on our family Bible that they'll be our saving grace."

"I wouldn't bet on it," Tremayne replied. "Watch your back, Garahan!"

"Best be watching yer own!"

CHAPTER TEN

WHEN MELINDA WOKE the next morning, it was to discover Garahan was gone, with no word of when or if he would return. Though they'd only just met, she had come to rely on the stalwart member of the duke's guard. He'd treated her as if she mattered from that moment he'd entered the tavern where she worked. It was a heady feeling.

Unlike the other patrons, she did not have to dodge his hand reaching for her waist—or her backside—when she served him. He was kind, polite, and that smile of his…

A deep voice broke into her revere. "Good morning, Melinda."

She turned her head toward the door, and James's light-haired, green-eyed cousin, Emmett. Without thinking, she asked, "Are you related to James on his mother's side or his father's?"

The giant's smile was reflected in his eyes. "Well now, the connection is through marriage. Our uncle Sean married Eileen Garahan, cousin to James's father."

She smiled, and was about to push up onto her elbows when he stopped her. "Let me check yer back before you move and stretch the tender skin."

She sighed but did as he asked. The room wasn't as warm without the quilt, but she did not bother to mention that fact. The man was here to check her injury, not see to her comfort—James had done that.

Now that James was gone, the sooner she healed, the quicker she could look for a job and not be beholden to the kindness of others. Her gut clenched at the thought of never seeing James again.

She flinched when Emmett gently lifted one of the linen strips that covered her wounds.

"Sorry for yer pain, lass. 'Tis as I expected, not worse," he said, replacing the linen strips and covering her with the quilt. "'Twill be a few days more sleeping on yer stomach, but I'm thinking with help, ye can sit up in a chair for a bit." He crossed his arms and narrowed his eyes. "But only if ye don't lean on anything—'twill set ye back a few days' healing time."

"I would welcome the chance to sit for a change, and promise to be careful."

"Mrs. O'Toole will be in shortly with yer breakfast and to change the linen strips. If ye'll be sitting, she'll need to add a few more layers and then wrap a wide strip around ye to hold them in place."

He paused, staring off into space. "There might be a way that ye'd heal faster, if ye think ye're up to it."

That statement had her mind fully concentrating on Emmett, instead of letting her thoughts drift to James. "Whatever it is, I'll do it."

He grinned, and she was reminded of James's charming smile.

"Well now, it may sound a bit risky."

"Meaning it may not work?"

He laughed. "Nay, lass. Meaning it would involve leaving yer back exposed to the air, so yer wounds could dry in between treatments."

"You mean *risqué*?"

"'Tis what I said."

She did not want to argue with the man who had taken such good care of her. "Forgive me, I misheard you."

"Not a problem, lass. Now then. Shall I inform Mrs. O'Toole and Mrs. Wigglesworth of the change in yer care for the morning?"

"Just for this morning?"

"Aye, an hour or two with yer abused skin exposed to the air will help the healing along. Then again this afternoon—after ye rest, mind," he continued. "Another hour, I'm thinking."

"Thank you for taking care of me, Emmett. Please let me know if there is some way I can repay you."

He frowned. "Didn't I overhear me cousin raising his voice to ye about the subject just yesterday?"

She sighed. "You did. But I—"

"Will not bring it up again, as it troubles me cousin—and meself," he interrupted.

"I'm sorry," she said. "That was not my intention."

"Someone will be right with ye. If ye have need of me, tell either Mrs. O'Toole or Mrs. Wigglesworth."

"Thank you," she said. "I will."

He paused with his hand on the doorframe. "Ye haven't asked after me cousin."

She felt her cheeks grow warm at the question. "Mrs. O'Toole mentioned earlier that he's gone."

"Aye. He fills in now and again at the duke's other residences before the quarterly rotation ends. James is actually stationed in Sussex at Chattsworth Manor, until the next rotation of the guard."

Her heart sank. *Sussex?* "I see," she whispered. "He won't be coming back, then, will he?"

"It all depends on where he's needed. The next rotation is a few weeks off."

Keeping a tight rein on her emotions, she thanked him. She would do her part to do as he and the others asked, to speed up the healing process. If James would no longer be at the duke's town house, it would hasten her need to leave.

When Mrs. O'Toole returned, Melinda would ask again for the name of an agency. Feeling more secure with an attainable plan, she wondered if James would miss her.

In all honesty, he had not said anything that would lead her to believe he had more than a brief interest in her—rescuing her from an intolerable situation and spiriting her away to a safe place where she would have the time to heal.

But he had kissed her.

She sighed, rationalizing it would be best if he returned to his former post. She could heal, and do small tasks for the kindly staff in return for their care, until she was recovered enough to seek a position on her own.

In her dreams—daydreams and nighttime—she could live out her life the way she'd always planned to, in the tiny village of Peppering Eye, with the dark-haired, dark-eyed Irishman who'd stolen her heart.

Mrs. O'Toole rushed into the room with her bland meal and weak tea. "Are you ready to eat?"

"Yes, thank you. Did Emmett speak to you?"

The older woman smiled. "He did. I'm so glad you are agreeable. I know it will be uncomfortable to lie still with your back uncovered. But we'll place warm bricks wrapped in thick linens around you, so you won't catch a chill."

"You can go about your duties without worrying about me."

Mrs. O'Toole frowned at her. "Of course we'll worry. We care. Now then do you need help with the chamber pot?"

Melinda nodded, appreciating Mrs. O'Toole's matter-of-fact approach to what normally would have embarrassed her to the core. When she was finished, and a bit steadier, Mrs. O'Toole poured water from the pitcher into the ceramic bowl and handed Melinda a small round of rose-scented soap and a soft cloth so she could wash.

Relieved to have accomplished those tasks, Melinda was more than ready to sit and eat.

"Mind that you do not lean back."

"Emmett already cautioned me against doing so. If you have a needle and thread that I can use, I'll mend my gown. Once it's repaired, I won't have to borrow your nightrail."

Mrs. O'Toole smiled. "It's already been repaired, good as new." She held the cup of broth to help Melinda drink.

"I'm not as shaky as I was yesterday. May I try to hold it on my own?"

"Of course." The cook smiled, watching as she finished. "Would you care for a splash of cream in your tea?"

Melinda handed the empty mug to Mrs. O'Toole. "Am I allowed a pinch of sugar, too?"

The cook's laugh warmed Melinda's heart. "A teaspoonful, I think."

"Thank you."

Half an hour later, Mrs. Wigglesworth entered the room, followed by a footman who carried the wrapped bricks. After thanking the man, the older women shooed him out of the room and closed the door.

"Now then, lie down and we'll tuck these around you, and then tend to your back," Mrs. Wigglesworth said.

Surprised that it was not as painful as yesterday, Melinda relaxed listening to the two women talk about their years working with the duke's family. When they shared tales of the men in the duke's guard, she listened closely, smiling to herself at the affection in their tone.

Their voices sounded farther away as her eyelids closed of their own volition and her breathing evened out. In her dreams, she was the one James climbed the tree to rescue—not his young cousin. Clinging to him, she reveled in his strength and agility, making his way down, one branch at a time, until they stood on the ground once more.

When she thanked him for rescuing her, he answered with a kiss that robbed every last thought from her head. She sighed. Loving James Garahan came naturally.

She woke later to the realization that the feeling in her heart had not changed. Sometime between the first tankard of ale that she served him a few weeks ago, and the angel's kiss he'd pressed to her lips earlier, she had fallen in love with the handsome-as-sin Irishman.

CHAPTER ELEVEN

G ARAHAN COVERED THE distance between London and Sussex as expected, with no unforeseen delays, stopping along the way to change horses, and for a quick bite to eat. He was to deliver missives from Captain Coventry to Viscount Chattsworth and Earl Lippincott.

Normally Coventry would have entrusted the missives to the duke's messengers, but after what occurred recently in Cornwall, the decision was made to send messages with duke's guard—when possible. When it was not, one of Coventry's men. Until the crooked excise official's trial was over, and justice served, they would not use the young messengers other than in and around London, where they were based.

Garahan smiled and urged his horse into a canter as they rounded the curve in the road, recalling the tale of derring-do from his cousins Seamus Flaherty and Michael O'Malley. They had escorted Lady Calliope from Wyndmere Hall to Chattsworth Manor, riding on either side of her carriage, when the wheels slid on ice as they rounded the curve, causing the carriage to tip over and land on its side. He'd never doubted the ingenuity of his cousins, but had to admit he'd admired the way they rescued Lady Calliope and her maid, Mary Kate, working together to pull them from the carriage before righting it.

He had missed Mary Kate when she accompanied Lady Calliope to Chattsworth Manor, but it was nothing like the dull ache that had begun to plague him the moment he'd mounted his horse and ridden away from London hours ago. Should he have said something to the lass? Told Melinda how he felt?

Nay, he thought. 'Twas too soon. If one of his cousins had told him they were suffering pangs of loneliness being separated from the woman they loved, he would have thought it a tall tale. But the feelings were real, and the ache in his heart increased with each mile he rode.

He rubbed a hand over his heart and shook his head. He had no time for such thoughts. He had messages to deliver, and responses to wait for, before he could return to London. He hoped Tremayne would have more information about the footman spreading the ugly rumors—and the blackguard the footman worked for.

He'd wager a month's pay the footman's employer was the culprit behind the verbal assault. Lady Phoebe did not deserve to be at the heart of another scandal. He hoped to God she would not spiral back to the nightmares she had suffered.

The road straightened, and Chattsworth Manor came into view. A glance at the rooftop assured him that the duke's recent instructions were being followed to the letter, with extra guards atop the manor house and others guarding the perimeter. The viscount's tenant farmers had suffered several attacks a few months ago.

Lifting his hand in the air, he signaled to the rooftop guard, who answered in kind. Riding around to the rear of the manor house, he urged his mount to the stables, where they were greeted by MacReady, the viscount's valet—and sometime footman, when the occasion warranted it.

The old Scot was mumbling beneath his breath as he strode toward Garahan. "Something's happened."

Garahan lifted an eyebrow in silent question.

"You look like you're carrying a heavy weight," MacReady said. "With you, it usually means trouble."

Garahan shrugged. "I have a missive to deliver to the viscount. Then I'll be on me way."

"Do you have another message to deliver to his lordship, the earl?" MacReady asked.

"Aye. Both are important. I'm sure the viscount will fill ye in after he confers with me cousins. By the way, where are Michael and Seamus patrolling?"

"As it's Seamus who has the shift guarding her ladyship and her babe, your cousin will be trying to coax a smile out of her ladyship's maid."

Garahan stopped in front of the stall he'd been leading his mount to. "Mary Kate?"

"Aye. She was smart enough to eventually give up pining for you, once she realized you were avoiding her."

He had not wanted to hurt the lass's feelings. But it was easier to avoid her than to speak to her. Garahan rubbed a hand over his face. "She deserves to be happy. What I feel toward the lass is protective. If me cousin has had luck coaxing smiles from the lass, I'm happy for the both of them."

"As I heard it, you were the one who swept her off the sidewalk, though wasn't it one of your O'Malley cousins who hired a hackney to take her to the duke's town house?"

"Aye. That's where Mrs. O'Toole and Mrs. Wigglesworth cared for her—the same as they were taking care of Melinda now."

MacReady's bushy eyebrows rose in surprise at the mention of the lass's name. The canny Scot's eyes twinkled—a sure sign he would be repeating what he just heard.

"It's not what ye think, MacReady."

"Ah, so you've rescued another lass. Is she as pretty as Mary Kate? Was she forced from her job without reason—or her last wages?"

Garahan shook his head. He was torn. If he didn't tell the man something, the curmudgeon would make it up to add interest to his tale.

"*Bollocks!*"

"I'm thinking you're interested. Melinda, is it?"

Glaring at the Scotsman, Garahan grumbled, "You'll make up a story worth repeating if I don't tell you."

The old man grinned. "I will."

"Bloody hell! Fine, then. But ye'll only repeat what I tell ye to me cousins—don't embellish it."

MacReady agreed. "I'll only tell your kin."

"I'll have yer word on it, MacReady," Garahan said.

"You have my word. I will only share what you tell me about the lovely Melinda with your cousins."

Garahan nodded. "I was on assignment in a run-down tavern in the very bowels of London—and was surprised to find an angel working there." He frowned, not wanting to speak ill of the lass, or have those he worked with form opinions that would not be a true picture of her.

MacReady slapped his thigh. "I knew she was beautiful."

Garahan narrowed his eyes. "She'd been battered."

"The devil you say."

Garahan wished she had not been—but it was the bruises that had him taking a closer look at the lass. Would he have noticed her if not for that? "I thought if I offered her a job, with better working conditions, and a place to stay, she would willingly leave."

"She'd either have been working for family," MacReady mused, "or too frightened to leave."

"I returned to the tavern the other night in time to rescue her. I left her in the excellent care of Mrs. O'Toole and Mrs. Wigglesworth."

"The lass is taken with you," MacReady said.

Garahan snorted. "How would you know?"

"Your fatal Irish charm. The lassies cannot help themselves. Now, if it were myself in your situation, the lassie would have fallen for my

Scots brogue, strong back, and silver tongue." They were both smiling when MacReady added, "Aye, Melinda is taken with you."

Melinda. Her name was a benediction. Garahan rubbed a hand over his heart again.

"Indigestion?" MacReady asked.

"Could be," Garahan answered, hoping that what little he'd shared with the man would not backfire on him. "I barely had time to chew and swallow a bowl of stew during the last change of horse."

"A man needs to let his meal settle before climbing back on his horse." MacReady patted his stomach. "Proper digestion often requires a measure of good Scots whisky."

Garahan chuckled. "Well now, there's where ye'd be wrong then. Nothing tops off a meal like a shot of *Irish whiskey.*"

MacReady narrowed his eyes and glared at Garahan. *"Scots whisky."*

Garahan handed the reins off to the stable lad. "Would ye see that me horse gets a cup of oats, and mayhap an apple or carrot if ye have one?"

The young man smiled and promised to treat the horse like a prince.

"Ye should treat him like a king, lad," Garahan called out.

"The only horse treated like a king in my stables is Maximus—my thoroughbred stallion," a deep voice called out from behind Garahan.

He spun around and greeted the viscount. "Yer lordship. I've a missive for ye."

"Good to see you, Garahan. Are you staying with us this time?"

"It all depends on yer response, yer lordship, and that of the earl."

He did not need to speculate as to how their lordships would take the news of this latest attack on their families. Both the earl and the viscount had been under fire from the moment they began showing an interest in the women they later married. It was their accuser's mistake to underestimate the strength of the bond between the duke and his distant cousins, whom he treated like brothers.

The viscount's jaw clenched, and he squared his shoulders. "I'll read the missive now, where Calliope cannot see my reaction. She's exhausted from lack of sleep and tending our very hungry son."

"I'm betting the lad has grown since I was last here."

The viscount's jaw relaxed. "He has. Watches us like a hawk. Observing his facial expressions, you can see the babe is trying to reason out who is who in his world—other than his mother and me."

"'Tis as it should be." Garahan reached into his waistcoat pocket for the missive and handed it to the viscount, who paused to check the seal.

"I trust you, Garahan. I'm merely checking it as I've been instructed to. You can report to Coventry that it had not been tampered with before I read it."

"Not that that would likely happen. I wouldn't be handing it to ye with a broken seal if on the off chance some blackguard managed to snatch it out of me pocket. Though, faith, I'd have to have been clubbed on the back of me head in order for that to happen."

The viscount wasn't listening—he was intently reading Coventry's message. "There's more he isn't telling me."

Garahan noted it was not a question. "Aye."

"If it involves Edward and Aurelia—and their babe—I need to know."

Garahan locked gazes with the viscount. "Yer lordship, ye know that is not how the captain sees it." His gut burned with the need to tell the viscount the part of the threat that sickened him—his being accused of being the true father of the viscount's babe.

The viscount's expression hardened. "I do not give a bloody damn how Coventry sees it! This involves my wife, and no doubt Aurelia as well. She and Calliope are sisters of the heart. Whoever is behind this attempt to slander her good name again knows she considers Lady Aurelia as such."

"If ye like, I can allow ye time to mull over yer response to Coventry, while I deliver the earl's message. I can swing back and collect yer response."

The viscount considered the offer. "If you have a missive for Edward, did it contain a similar message?"

Garahan did not answer the question. The viscount knew that to do so would go against Garahan's oath to the duke and the captain.

"Did Coventry send word to Lord Coddington, Aurelia's uncle, as well?" When Garahan didn't immediately answer, the viscount commanded, "Just nod once for yes, damnation!"

Garahan did so. He had not verbally responded, which he knew followed Coventry's orders—though not to the letter. Bloody hell! Garahan felt the viscount and his wife needed to know. The couple, and Edward and Aurelia, had suffered from ugly rumors before. The viscount had taken a lead ball in the back—preventing a murder—during a duel defending Lady Aurelia's honor.

Just a few months ago, the viscount and his wife were targets once again. Garahan knew if the man behind the attacks was not connected to Prinny—and therefore above reproach, and the law—the attacks never would have happened.

"I shall wait for your return."

"May I borrow a horse?" Garahan asked. "I pushed me mount the last few miles to reach ye."

"Of course." The viscount motioned for one of the stable lads to saddle the gelding nudging Garahan in the shoulder with his nose. "It appears that someone wishes to take you to the earl."

Garahan chuckled and turned around to scratch behind the gelding's ear. "There's a lad. Ye'll take me to the earl and countess?"

The horse lifted his nose in the air and whinnied.

"Have MacReady or Hargrave let me know when you return."

"Aye, yer lordship." As the viscount turned and walked away, Garahan wondered how the man would react when he heard the full accusation involving Lady Calliope and Lady Aurelia. Would the viscount believe that Garahan would cuckold him—or the earl? Would he believe his viscountess—or Lady Aurelia, for that matter—capable of such a thing? He didn't think so, but love and jealousy were known to cause a man to temporarily lose his mind.

Lord willing, neither the viscount nor the earl would hear Garahan's name entwined with the salacious rumors before the situation had been resolved. If they did, he prayed they would not believe any of it.

CHAPTER TWELVE

GARAHAN RODE AS if the devil were nipping at his horses' hooves, but he recognized the emotion welling inside of him—'twas guilt.

Bollocks! *I should have told their lordships the whole of it!*

Leaning forward, he became one with his horse. Their movements in sync, he urged the gelding into a gallop. The need to outrace his earlier decision to hold back vital information—as instructed by Captain Coventry—warred with his conscience.

After a good run, he straightened in the saddle and slowed the horse to a canter. "We're going to be stopping soon. Ye've given me a good run, lad, when I should not have let ye continue at such a pace. Faith, we both needed that run, though, didn't we? I'll make certain there is a handful of oats, mayhap an apple, when we stop at the coaching inn up ahead."

A short while later, they arrived at the first stop—and change of horse. Garahan made certain the duke's horse received the promised oats and apple. Satisfied his mount was being taken care of by the stable lad, he sought out the stable master.

"Just the man I'm looking for, Walsh."

The old man smiled. "Garahan, I haven't seen you lately. Where have you been keeping yourself?"

"Well now, ye know I can't be saying. But I will tell ye the duke keeps me busy."

"Fair enough. Now, so I can do as His Grace requests—and since the family resemblance is great—I have to ask, which brother are you?"

Garahan snorted with laughter. "James. Me brothers would be impressed that ye think we look that much alike, but everyone knows I'm the best looking of the bunch."

Walsh shook his head as they walked past the stalls housing two sets of matched grays—used exclusively with the duke's carriages—and walked over to the stalls where a trio of the duke's horses were stabled.

Admiring the geldings, Garahan knew how fortunate he was to be among those working for the duke. Although posting inns had horses available, not all of them were equal to the duke's. His Grace took great pride in taking care of his family—and the private guard who worked for him—by stabling horses at strategic inns along the roads leading to his properties in the Lake District, borderlands, Cornwall, and Sussex.

"His Grace has a keen eye for horseflesh," the stable master said.

"Aye," Garahan agreed. He strode up to the first stall and said to the horse, "Are ye interested in a roundabout journey to London? I've two stops to make in Sussex first." The gelding eyed him with interest, but did not even twitch. "Has this lad been out recently?"

"Aye," the stable master replied. "He arrived yesterday."

Garahan did not bother to ask who had ridden the horse. The duke had recently added Coventry's men to the list of those who were authorized to use the stabled horses. The inns kept an accurate account, should the need arise to audit the records.

Garahan stroked between the horse's eyes and thanked him for his service to the duke. Moving to the next stall, he asked the same question, and this time the horse lifted his head. "Ah, this one's listening—but not a definite response. Well now, mayhap the next time I pass through this way." He scratched behind the horse's ear and continued to the last of the stalls.

The roan gelding's ears twitched as he watched Garahan approaching. "So 'tis yerself who's interested in a bit of a ride today." The horse's answering whinny was the right response.

Saddled and ready to ride, Garahan thanked Walsh and headed back in the direction he'd just traveled.

"They'll think me daft," he mumbled aloud. Wisely, his horse did not contradict him.

He started out at a steady, fast trot. But he could tell by the way the gelding was champing at the bit that he wanted to run. He urged his horse to a canter before giving him his head. Both man and beast reveled in the speed as hooves pounded along the road toward their first destination—Chattsworth Manor.

MacReady was there to greet him when he arrived. "What brings you back?"

Garahan dismounted and headed for the doors to the stable. "I need to speak with his lordship."

MacReady followed, waiting for Garahan to hand the reins to the stable lad.

Garahan felt the man's steady stare. In answer, he shook his head. He had to speak to the viscount first. A sense of urgency filled him. Time was not on his side. He had a gut-deep feeling that he could not shake—something was amiss, and that something had to do with Melinda. As soon as he delivered his personal messages, he would head back to London.

"I'll ask Seamus or Michael. They'll fill me in on what is going on." MacReady glared at him before asking, "Will ye be coming back to finish out the rest of this rotation of the guard?"

Garahan answered the question with a question: "Do you think the duke knows in advance where a problem will arise?"

MacReady held his tongue.

Garahan had never asked the duke which of the properties he would be moving to before now—he hadn't needed to. He'd been pleased to be the duke's first choice of man to handle whatever emergency cropped up at one of his estates. But now...now he had a reason to ask, for the sake of the wounded angel he'd had to leave behind at Grosvenor Square.

"Flaherty seemed pleased to be back here at Chattsworth, when first you left us," MacReady said. "I understand from Seamus that the duke has hired on men to join his London guard."

Garahan knew MacReady had more to say, so he waited for the man to finish speaking.

"What happened to the handful of Bow Street Runners, Gavin King's men, that have been here a time or two?"

"Ye know I am a man of me word, and there are things I'm bound by me oath not to speak of."

"That I do." The man's eyes were filled with merriment when he added, "And you know that I am a man who cannot resist needling you until you answer my questions."

Garahan snorted out a laugh. "Aye, ye wily old Scot! Now then, I need to speak to the viscount. I'm sure ye'll be hearing a bit of that conversation, if his lordship deems it necessary."

He strode to the back of the manor house. Heavy footsteps had him looking up, and smiling, as his cousin Michael O'Malley walked toward him down the long hallway.

Instantly on alert, Michael asked, "What brings you back?"

"I need to have a word in private with the viscount."

"We're both members of the duke's private guard," Michael reminded him. "There isn't anything ye should be keeping from me."

"I'll tell ye after I speak to the viscount...and then the earl."

His cousin stared at him for a few intense moments before inclining his head. "Ye'd best not try to leave Sussex without apprising me of the situation."

Garahan paused in front of the door to the servants' staircase. "I won't," he promised. He opened the door and looked over his shoulder. "If ye hear shouting, don't bother to investigate. I expect what I have to say will anger his lordship."

Michael's face was void of expression when he asked, "Do ye now?"

"If ye hear the sound of bodies being tossed about, ye may want to lend a hand."

Michael clenched his jaw. "Ye'd never strike the viscount."

"No, I would not."

"Then…" Garahan knew his cousin understood what he had not said when Michael replied, "Ye'll want me to interfere so the viscount doesn't beat ye bloody."

"I'd appreciate it."

"Why don't I accompany ye now?"

"Let me have a few minutes to explain first. As I said, if ye hear the sounds of an altercation, then come. Otherwise, that means his lordship is open to listening."

"Well then," Michael said. "I'll be waiting."

Garahan took the stairs two at a time. When he reached the top, he slowly opened the door, looked both ways, and stepped into the upper hallway. He strode to the viscount's private study door and knocked.

"Enter."

He opened the door, stepped into the room, and closed the door behind him.

Immediately on alert, the viscount shot to his feet. "What is the problem? Shall I summon O'Malley and Flaherty?"

"No. Yer family is safe. Ye're not under attack. I have more information to relay."

"Regarding the scathing *on dits* circulating about my wife—and the ridiculous notion that I am not William's father?"

Garahan drew in a breath for calm, knowing he'd need to remain so in order to reason with the hot-tempered viscount. "Ye may want to have a seat while I relay the rest of what I know."

The viscount frowned. "The part Coventry left out of his missive?"

"Aye, yer lordship."

"What is it?"

Best to tell him. Garahan met the viscount's irritated gaze. "I know the name of the man who supposedly cuckolded ye."

The viscount slapped both hands on his desk and leaned forward. "Give the man's name, so I can rip his heart out!"

Garahan sighed. The viscount was going to be difficult. "I'll give ye the name, if ye promise to leave the man's heart intact."

"I'll do no such thing! The man is claiming he is—"

"I know for a fact that the man being accused of this atrocity is not claiming a thing," Garahan interrupted, "except his innocence in this matter."

Rounding the desk, the viscount stood in front of Garahan, demanding, "Tell me the name."

"'Tis Garahan."

Shock had the viscount's voice dropping in volume as he said, "One of your brothers? I do not believe it!"

Righteous indignation filled Garahan. "My brothers are honorable men and would never think of doing such a thing!"

The viscount nodded, paused, and shoved Garahan back a few paces. "You? The bloody bastard is you?"

Garahan did not lift his arms from his sides when he answered, "'Tisn't me either, yer lordship."

The viscount shoved him again until his back hit the wall—hard enough to have a painting crash to the floor near their feet. The viscount did not stop there. He wrapped a hand around Garahan's throat and pulled his arm back, ready to deliver a jab.

Garahan's gaze never left the viscount's. He braced for the blow, expecting it, but was surprised when the violence left the viscount's eyes, and the hand around his throat loosened and dropped.

The viscount raked a hand through his hair. "Forgive me, Garahan." He stepped back. "I know you are as honorable as your brothers—and your cousins—and would never dishonor my wife."

"Or any woman," Garahan added, rubbing his throat. The feel of the viscount's hand reminded him too closely of that rope from long ago. "Ye're forgiven. I want ye to know that we've been working to uncover who is behind this verbal assault. One of Coventry's men, Tremayne, is continuing to follow leads, while I was sent to deliver the message to yerself and the earl."

"Then why in God's name did you not relay the entire message?"

Garahan met the intensity of the viscount's gaze and replied, "I did."

"Why was your name not included in the missive?"

"I believe Coventry expected ye to react this way, and tried to save ye from yer temper by leaving me name out."

The door burst open, and Michael stood on the threshold. "Yer lordship! What's going on?"

The viscount eyed Michael, glared at Garahan, then looked back to Michael. "Did you know of this claim?"

"What claim?" Michael asked.

"About Garahan being the father of my son!"

Michael's mouth dropped open.

"You've delivered your personal message, Garahan, and will have to answer to Coventry when you return for disobeying his orders and telling me the whole of it. I shall be sending a missive to the captain myself, demanding to be kept fully in the know in the future. The hell with his idea of only telling me half of what I need to know!"

"I must tell ye, on Coventry's behalf, the captain was more concerned yer wife would overhear the message—or learn of it otherwise—and follow ye to London."

"I had not planned to go to London, but I believe I will."

"Another possibility Coventry was trying to prevent, yer lordship. If ye leave, ye know her ladyship will try to follow ye. Do ye want her following after ye with yer babe in her arms, while ye throw down the gauntlet demanding satisfaction from whoever defamed yer wife?"

Michael added his opinion: "Lady Calliope will defend you to the last breath, yer lordship—and will follow you if she feels it necessary."

The viscount scrubbed his hands over his face. "Bloody hell! Coventry has the right of it, Calliope—"

"William—darling!" A breathless Lady Calliope rushed into the study and stopped short, a look of confusion on her face. "You are unharmed?"

"As you can see, my love."

She stared at him before glancing at Michael and then Garahan, who was still rubbing his throat. "Did you trip over a chair and injure your neck, James?"

Without missing a beat, Garahan agreed. "I thought the viscount was choking and, in my rush to aid him, tripped."

Calliope walked over to stand before her husband. She narrowed her eyes in suspicion. "Well?"

Michael spoke up. "His lordship was coughing. It sounded like he was choking, and Garahan came to the rescue."

Lady Calliope's gaze settled on Garahan, who shifted from one foot to the other. "I see. That would explain why my father-in-law's favorite still life of his hunting dogs somehow landed on the floor when you tripped on the chair that is still in its place by my husband's desk."

"Aye, yer ladyship." The lie burned in Garahan's gut, but he had no alternative. The viscount—and Coventry—would have his head if Lady Calliope learned of this latest attack.

A babe's cry was all it took to distract her from asking more questions. "If you'll excuse me, I need to see to our son."

The viscount pressed a kiss to her forehead, escorted her to the door, and closed it behind her. Standing with his back to the door, he said, "I appreciate the lengths you'd go to keep my wife from finding out the truth of what just occurred."

"I despise prevaricating, and only do it when absolutely necessary," Garahan said.

"There are times in life when a man needs to keep things from his wife, for her own good," the viscount added.

"Don't ye mean safety?" Michael asked.

"Aye," the viscount agreed. "Do you need me to accompany you to Lippincott Manor, Garahan? You may face a similar reaction to your news."

"'Tis best if ye remain here and keep an eye on yer wife."

"She won't suspect a thing," the viscount told him.

"I wouldn't count on that," Garahan replied.

⇛⤞⇚

CALLIOPE PULLED HER ear away from the door and rushed down the hallway. *I knew Garahan was not telling the truth!*

She entered the nursery, mumbling about hardheaded husbands and stubborn Irishmen. Picking up her son, she soothed his tears before changing him.

"There now, sweet babe, isn't that better?"

His eyes were wide as she brushed her nose against his, delighting a laugh from the babe. "I shall get to the bottom of what the men are hiding from me!" Picking him up, she cuddled him close and walked over to the rocking chair and sat. A voracious eater, he suckled as if it would be his last meal.

"Slow down, dearest," she crooned. When he did, she brushed her fingertip along the curve of his cheek, over and over. "That's it, slower now. You don't want a nasty bubble that would make your belly ache, do you?"

His eyes never left hers as he put a hand to her breast and suckled slowly. Awed by the powerful pull between mother and son, she pushed all thoughts from her mind save one—singing to him while he emptied her breast. She put him on her shoulder and coaxed a burp from him before switching him to her other breast.

He started out as if he hadn't just eaten his fill, then slowed down. "You are so beautiful, William."

"I know."

She jerked at the sound of her husband's deep voice. Looking over her shoulder, she frowned. "Is it your intention to curdle my milk?"

His eyes opened wide at the question. "I beg your pardon?"

"Haven't you listened to any of the instructions our midwife gave me after our babe was born?"

"I may have been a bit distracted." He walked over to stand beside her. "I was trying not to keel over after his exhausting birth."

She narrowed her gaze at him. "Exhausting for whom?"

He snorted, then coughed to try to cover the fact that he'd laughed. "You, my darling."

"Hmmm. Are you ready to tell me Garahan lied?"

"Garahan did not lie."

She shook her head. William had a twitch at the corner of his left eye when he prevaricated. "That was a lie."

He squared his shoulders and stared down at her. "I do not appreciate your calling me a liar."

"I do not appreciate being lied to." She unlatched their babe from her breast, covered herself, and put him against her shoulder to coax another burp out of him. When he had, she pressed a kiss to his cheek and stood.

Her husband was there to lend a hand, but she stepped around him to lay their babe in his cradle. "Until you are ready to apologize for lying to me, do not bother to return to our bedchamber."

The viscount towered over her, but she ignored his ploy to get her to back down. He'd used it before to no avail. He tried to reach out to grab hold of her arm, but she slipped around him and out the door.

She did not look back—it would weaken her resolve, and she did not intend to change her mind. She would get to the bottom of what the men had been discussing, and take whatever action she deemed necessary.

God help William if he tried to keep her under guard inside their home while he ventured to London on a quest to right a wrong he did not see fit to share with her.

"I followed him once!" she said aloud as she opened the door to their bedchamber. An ugly thought slithered into her mind. "He intends to challenge someone to a duel!" It was the only reason she could think of why he would not want her to hear whatever news Garahan had delivered from London.

She rushed over to the bellpull in the corner of the room and gave it a tug. Plans were already forming in her mind when she heard the knock on her door. She tugged it open, grabbed hold of Mary Kate's arm, and yanked her inside.

Her maid's eyes were round with shock. "What's happened?"

"Garahan returned and delivered a missive that had my husband responding physically."

"He left earlier. Why did he return? What could he possibly have said to his lordship to cause him to react in such a way?"

"They would not tell me. Garahan lied to me, too!"

"It must be serious, then," Mary Kate said.

"I have a feeling it has to do with whatever was in the missive Garahan delivered earlier. My husband refuses to tell me what it contained." Before her maid could respond, Calliope added, "I'm going to take our babe to London."

"But your ladyship—"

"I cannot leave him behind, and my heart tells me something is dreadfully wrong." Tears welled up in her eyes, but she dashed them away. "I will not let whoever is threatening my husband—or our family—think they can do so and not suffer repercussions!"

"Your ladyship, think of your son."

She reached for Mary Kate's hand. "I am. Remember how we slipped away the last time?"

Her maid frowned. "I remember trying to get up on a horse and falling off—three times."

Calliope could not contain her smile. "But we managed to leave using William's carriage."

"With the help of Seamus and James," Mary Kate reminded her.

The forlorn look on the maid's face had Calliope squeezing Mary Kate's hand before letting go. "Seamus seems to be going out of his way to speak with you between his shifts—and whenever he is on duty protecting us from inside the manor house."

"He always makes me smile when we have those few moments to speak to one another."

"Have you noticed how Seamus's eyes light up whenever he sees you?"

The maid tilted her head to one side. "Do they? I hadn't noticed."

Calliope nodded. "I think he's done waiting for you to get over your infatuation with James."

"I have gotten over James," Mary Kate said. "How could I not, when every time he returns, he goes out of his way to avoid speaking with me? I know he cares for me—but have come to realize it is in a brotherly sort of way."

"Exactly!" Calliope said. "Now then, Seamus, on the other hand..." She let her words trail off, hoping they would sink in and take hold. It was past time Mary Kate stopped pining for a man who had never showed more than a friendly interest in her.

"Do you really think Seamus admires me?"

"What's not to admire?" Calliope asked. "Your violet eyes and soft brown hair are the first thing I noticed about you."

"Thank you, your ladyship, but standing beside you, who would notice me? I'm a head shorter and a stone or two heavier."

Calliope shook her head. "What I would not give to have your curves, Mary Kate!" Looking down at herself, she brushed at her skirts and sighed. "Even after giving birth, I could never hope to attain such a womanly figure. I'm built like a stick."

Mary Kate frowned. "You are wand-slim, your ladyship, with slender curves that add to your ethereal beauty. I'm built more like a milkmaid."

They stared at one another for a few moments before bursting into laughter. "We are a pair," Calliope remarked. "We should be grateful for the gifts the Lord has given us instead of bemoaning our shapes and height."

"My mum would say the same," Mary Kate added.

Calliope waited a beat, then said, "About our plans…"

The two put their heads together and began to formulate how and when they would leave with Calliope's son. They had to evade the viscount—and the duke's guard—or the plan was doomed to fail.

Half an hour later, they had a plan. All that was left to do was get word to Lady Aurelia!

CHAPTER THIRTEEN

EARL LIPPINCOTT SHOWED Garahan into his private study. "What brings you back so soon? Did something happen along the road to London?"

"Nay," Garahan was quick to answer. He did not relish another man's hands wrapped around his throat, but would brace himself for it.

"What, then?" the earl asked.

"There's more to the missive from Coventry—something I think ye should be made aware of."

The earl's expression showed intense interest. "Did you already relay similar information to the viscount?"

There was no use in Garahan's pretending he had not, when the earl and viscount knew their wives were included in this latest vindictive *on dit*. "I just came from Chattsworth Manor."

The earl studied him closely, waiting for him to speak.

"I know the name of the man accused of cuckolding ye."

The earl took a step closer. His eyes were a dark, deadly blue. "Tell me!"

"His name is Garahan."

The earl blinked. "A distant cousin of yours, or no relation?"

Relieved that the earl had not immediately assumed it was a blood relation of his, Garahan answered, "Neither, yer—"

The lightning-fast jab to his chin had his head snapping back and his head ringing. Thank God he'd already had his feet braced apart, or he'd have fallen backward against the wall. An all-too-familiar feeling.

The earl stalked over to where Garahan still stood and demanded, "What in the bloody hell does that mean? You would never dishonor my wife—or your vow to my brother!"

Garahan moved his jaw from side to side. "Nice jab, yer lordship. If I hadn't been blessed with a chin of granite, ye'd have knocked me senseless."

The earl shook his head as if to clear it. "Forgive me, Garahan. I acted without thinking."

Garahan chuckled. "'Tis the truth that I expected ye to. If it makes ye feel better, the viscount grabbed me by the throat and shoved me against the wall in his study hard enough to knock a painting to the floor."

The earl's eyes narrowed. "The still life of his hunting dogs?"

Garahan snorted. "Aye. Not to worry, only the frame's a bit damaged."

"I did not mean to punch you."

"Didn't ye now?" Garahan asked. "From the way yer eyes darkened a split second before ye let yer fist fly, I'm thinking ye did."

It was the earl's turn to snort with laughter. "To be honest, I'd have struck whoever delivered such news."

"Then 'tis glad I am that I was the bearer of the news, and not some poor young messenger boy."

"I believe I understand why Coventry did not wish you to relay the name of the man who allegedly fathered my son. If my guess is right—because you have yet to answer my question—he is also allegedly the father of the viscount's son."

"Coventry was more worried about Lady Aurelia and Lady Calliope following ye."

The earl nodded. "Given their history, they probably would."

"Tremayne is currently following leads as to who is behind this, while I was tasked with delivering the messages."

"But without mentioning your name," the earl supplied.

"Coventry was adamant that I not tell yerself—or his lordship."

"I see."

"Coventry is trying to prevent anyone in the duke's family from coming to harm—whether it be verbally…or physically."

The earl sighed. "I know that he is, and I appreciate it. However, I must insist that you explain to Coventry that I will not tolerate having vital information being held back from me."

"Aye, yer lordship." Garahan touched his chin and winced. "Yer jab is on par with me cousin Patrick's."

The earl grinned. "Thank you. I've been practicing with William."

"Faith, it's a fine thing, then, that he pulled his punch instead of following through, or I might not have been able to stand up long enough to deliver the rest of yer message."

"Do you have time to meet with Chattsworth and myself?"

"Nay. I should have kept going once I delivered Coventry's messages. I have a bad feeling something happened in me absence. I need to be going."

"Very well." The earl held out his hand to Garahan, who took it. "Thank you for being willing to take a fist to the chin to speak the truth—and for protecting my family."

"'Tis an honor, yer lordship."

The earl accompanied Garahan to the stables and saw him off.

Neither man saw Mary Kate stealthily entering the side door to the manor house, or they would have been on alert that the earl's wife—and the viscount's—were up to something.

TWO HOURS LATER, Calliope and Aurelia had exchanged messages through their lady's maids.

The women agreed to pack one bag each with clothes and nappies for their babes. They planned to travel light, and did not need more than a change of clothing and basic essentials. Whatever else they needed, they would purchase it after they arrived at Grosvenor Square.

What worked before would work again. Calliope and her babe would sneak out of her home, with Mary Kate's help. Aurelia and her babe would do the same, with the aid of her lady's maid, Jenny.

Fingers crossed, they waited for their husbands to leave before they put their plan into action.

CHAPTER FOURTEEN

MELINDA OVERHEARD TWO of the footmen speaking, and although she tried not to listen, it couldn't be helped. Their deep voices carried into the room where she'd been staying since James carried her there a sennight ago. Their words had worry creeping into her soul. James had been called away to Sussex—where another young woman he had rescued was working for a distant cousin of the duke.

She had no claim on James, though her heart said otherwise. It was no use waiting around for the man to return. She'd heard enough talk about how he was the duke's first choice to send to his other properties when urgent matters arose. What those situations might be, she certainly did not know, and it wasn't her place to ask.

It was ridiculous to feel such a strong connection with a man she'd barely had the time to get to know. But she'd felt the pull, and thought James had, too. Was she mistaken? Had her gratitude to the man colored her thinking where the handsome Irishman was concerned?

The last time she'd seen James, he had told her he would help her eat breakfast. But the next morning, she'd woken to find him gone. The days had passed slowly, but eventfully. She had followed Emmett O'Malley's instructions, and with Mrs. O'Toole and Mrs. Wigglesworth's ministrations, her back was healing.

Although both women had insisted Melinda rest, they eventually gave in to her pleas to allow her to help with small tasks to fill the time. She was looking forward to the day she was healed enough to dress normally and do more than lend a hand around the duke's town house.

Today was the day she was to resume a normal routine. She would get dressed for the first time in a sennight—and she fully intended to find her way to one of the reputable hiring agencies Mrs. O'Toole had recommended when she pressed her yesterday.

She could not wait for James to return. He had done so much for her already. It would be rude of her to expect him to do more.

The knock on the door had her looking up expectantly.

"Are you ready to get fully dressed today, Melinda?"

She smiled as her two favorite women among the duke's London staff entered the room. Mrs. O'Toole carried a deep blue gown and pristine white chemise. While Mrs. Wigglesworth carried stockings and a pair of serviceable half boots.

Melinda's eyes filled. She could not remember the last time she'd had new clothes to wear. Her stepfather had neglected so many things after her mother died. The spark in his eyes had dimmed along with his zest for life.

Blinking, she dismissed those thoughts to concentrate on the possibilities that lay before her.

"One more look at your back," Mrs. O'Toole said. "Although I only expect improvement daily from here on out."

Once that was done, they wrapped her ribs. Mrs. Wigglesworth shooed her toward the dressing screen in the corner of the room. "Why don't you go behind the screen and try these on?"

"If you need assistance, we are right here," Mrs. O'Toole added.

Melinda did as they bade her and stepped behind the screen. After carefully removing the oversized nightrail that she slept in, she placed it on top of the screen and donned the soft-as-a-cloud chemise. It felt wonderful against her skin.

"Everything all right, dear?" Mrs. Wigglesworth asked.

"Yes. Fine, actually." Melinda slipped the gown over her head and brushed her hands over the delicate material. "Oh, the gown is lovely," she said, stepping out from behind the screen. Holding the gown out to the sides, she turned to the left, and then to the right. "It's beautiful. I haven't owned a gown so fine in longer than I can remember."

Before she could continue, Mrs. O'Toole held up a hand. "You are not to mention one word about repaying us."

Melinda blinked back tears and nodded.

Mrs. Wigglesworth looked down and laughed softly. "I do not think you will get past His Grace's guards with bare feet. Do you need help putting on your stocking and boots?"

Melinda smiled. "I was so excited about the gown, I just had to show you." She twirled in a circle and then slipped behind the screen. Once she was fully dressed, she returned. "Better?"

The two older women took in her appearance from head to toe. "Lovely. All that is left is to help you put your hair up," Mrs. Wigglesworth remarked.

"Oh, Melinda," Mrs. O'Toole said with a sigh. "You will add a ray of sunshine to any room you enter, my dear."

Melinda hugged both women and then drew her fingers through her waist-length hair to untangle it, while the ladies discussed the best way to pin it up. "I normally braid it, then coil it atop my head."

"Such soft, fine hair. Do you have any idea how lovely you are?" Mrs. Wigglesworth asked.

Melinda stared at the small looking glass Mrs. O'Toole had brought in with her a short while earlier. "If my previous employer allowed me to have sufficient fresh water daily, I would never have looked such a sight."

"Now, now," Mrs. Wigglesworth said. "No use harboring ill will toward someone who will be sorely missing you. From what you've said, the only thing he did was pour ale, drink with his cronies, and cast aspersions against your moral character."

"The man should be horsewhipped," Mrs. O'Toole added.

"Tell me the man's name," a deep voice boomed from the open doorway, "and I'll take care of it!"

Emmett O'Malley asked permission to enter and was granted it. He walked over to stand in front of Melinda. If his smile was any indication, she must look much better than she had.

"Lass, ye're a sight a man would be honored to see of a morning."

She could feel her face heat and knew her cheeks were flushed. "Thank you. I was just mentioning to Mrs. O'Toole and Mrs. Wigglesworth that a pitcher of clean water daily will work wonders with one's appearance."

He frowned. "Yer former employer was stingy with fresh water?"

She did not want to anger the man, when Emmett had been such a tremendous help during her healing. "I...uh...must have exaggerated."

"There is no need to protect the blackguard," Emmett said. "Since me cousin has yet to return, it'll be me pleasure to have a word with the man."

Melinda placed her hand on Emmett's forearm. "Please do not— you have no idea what kind of man he is." Worry filled her. "He cannot be trusted."

"Ah, lass. I already knew that from the marks on yer fair face, and the beating ye suffered at his hands." His eyes flashed a dark and dangerous green. "He'll be wishing he hadn't...by the time I get through with him."

Fear bubbled inside of her as she remembered being struck from behind. Bile rushed up her throat when she recalled the way he manacled her wrists, to hold her still while he used that wooden rod on her back. "Emmett—don't go!"

"Well, now. I see me cousin's replaced me in yer affections, lass. That happened quickly," Garahan said from the doorway.

His handsome face had her heart stuttering in her breast, while his words slashed at her heart and pricked her pride. "You're back?"

"As ye can see." His clipped tone, and the disdain in his dark brown eyes, raked her from head to toe. "From the roses in her cheeks," he said with a nod to his cousin, "'twould seem ye've taken good care of the lass while I was away."

Emmett did not answer him. Instead, he turned to Melinda and offered his arm. "Allow me to escort ye to the kitchen. I believe Mrs. O'Toole has yer breakfast waiting for ye."

Garahan stood fuming in the doorway. It bothered her that his first words to her upon his return would be harsh when she had done nothing to deserve them. "Thank you, Emmett. I am hungry."

➤➤➤◄◄◄

EMMETT SHOVED HIS cousin out of the way with his broader shoulder. Garahan seethed, adding the physical differences between himself and his cousin to the list of reasons he planned to beat him bloody.

Garahan intended to follow behind them, but Mrs. O'Toole grabbed his sleeve and tugged hard. "How dare you come in here and strip away the confidence Mrs. Wigglesworth, Emmett, and I have been rebuilding while caring for Melinda's injuries?"

He opened his mouth to speak, but closed it again at the flash of anger in the woman's eyes.

"That poor young woman just admitted that her employer refused to give her fresh water to wash with," Mrs. Wigglesworth said. "How does one exist in such deplorable conditions?"

Garahan stiffened at her words. "I suspected it might be the case, but did not have the chance to ask."

"I doubt she would have told you if you asked in the accusatory tone you used just now," Mrs. O'Toole said. "I'll not be serving you one bit of food until you apologize to the lass."

Garahan looked from one frowning woman to the other before he turned and walked out of the door.

Following along behind him, Mrs. O'Toole whispered just loud enough for him to hear her, "I do believe our James has finally met his match."

Mrs. Wigglesworth linked arms with Mrs. O'Toole. In a clear, audible voice, she said, "It's about time James has to put forth an effort to win a young woman's affections. He has had it far too easy, if the tales his cousins have told are true. Simply smiling at the lasses and expecting them to follow him willy-nilly."

Garahan's fists itched to strike something. Having to witness the woman he'd rushed back to London for speaking to his cousin—in a way Garahan considered more than friendly—curdled his empty stomach. Listening to the two older women he'd come to care for as if they were favorite aunts speak of him as if he were not right in front of them was a direct hit to his pride.

He ignored his gut, vowing not to be led about by the young woman he'd all but pledged himself to before leaving on assignment.

"Not our Melinda," Mrs. O'Toole said. "As long as she is a guest in this house, no man will speak to her like that again, or I'll be lodging a complaint with His Grace."

"Melinda deserves to be courted good and proper," Mrs. Wigglesworth added. "We shall see that she is."

Garahan would later swear the two old biddies were trying to make him feel guilty for the way he'd spoken to the lass. He'd think about it, after he'd had a word—or mayhap traded a punch or two—with his cousin.

He entered the kitchen in time to see the tender look in Emmett's eyes as his cousin briefly touched his hand to Melinda's shoulder.

Mine! was all Garahan could think as he took two steps and tossed the first punch. Emmett sidestepped the blow and laughed. "If Mrs. O'Toole were here right now, she'd toss ye out on yer *arse!*"

"If Mrs. O'Toole were here," Garahan said, "I wouldn't have

punched ye."

"Tried," Emmett reminded him. "Ye missed."

"What do you two hardheaded Irishmen think you are doing—in *my* kitchen?" Mrs. O'Toole demanded.

Emmett shrugged.

Garahan hated seeing the censure in the cook's gaze. He looked at Mrs. Wigglesworth and saw the same expression on her face. He had violated one of Mrs. O'Toole's strictest rules—no fighting in her kitchen.

"Out! Both of you!" the cook commanded.

"But—" Emmett began.

"I did not—" Garahan started.

Mrs. Wigglesworth cut them off, saying, "You know the rules. No fighting in the kitchen, or you lose kitchen privileges."

"Ye know ye cannot ban us from the kitchen," Emmett said. "The duke would not expect us to work without food."

Mrs. O'Toole stepped right in front of Emmett and glared up at him. "This is my domain. In here, I am queen…and that outranks the duke!" She glared at Emmett and then James, raised her hand in the air, and said, "I declare you two shall be banished!"

⟫⟫⟩⟨⟨⟪

MELINDA'S EYES WELLED with tears. She was the reason the men had argued, though it had not been her intention. Because she had let her fear tangle with her gratitude for Emmett's care and kindness, it was her fault they were being banned from the kitchen. Members of the duke's private guard should be able to have full access to the kitchen—and whatever meals Mrs. O'Toole prepared in it.

"Please, don't banish them, Mrs. O'Toole," Melinda begged. "It was because of me that they disagreed in the first place. James has just arrived back from wherever he has been—and I know Emmett has been on the overnight guard shift. I should not have tried to talk him out of speaking with my former employer."

Garahan's stomach clenched at witnessing her plea for himself and his cousin. The mix of emotions clear as day on her face—fear tangled with guilt—unmanned him.

Melinda glanced at Mrs. Wigglesworth, and Garahan recognized the lass's silent plea for help before she looked back at the cook and asked, "Won't you please reconsider? I'll leave now, so they can eat. It will only take me a moment to roll up the gown and shoes I arrived in, and I will be on my way."

Mrs. O'Toole looked up at the ceiling—something he'd seen his ma do more than once when dealing with his brothers and cousins. The cook's sigh even sounded like Ma's—a very loud, put-upon sigh.

"Very well," Mrs. O'Toole said. "Emmett and James may eat—after James apologizes to you for his manner of speaking." She nodded to Emmett. "Emmett, you and James must promise never—and I mean never—to even think about fighting in this kitchen again."

"Aye, Mrs. O'Toole," Garahan said.

Emmett bowed to the cook and thanked her.

"I shall call you when Melinda has finished. This is her first meal sitting at a table in a sennight, and Mrs. Wigglesworth and I mean to see that she only has polite conversation while she eats." She put her hands on her ample hips and frowned up at the cousins. "Do I make myself clear?"

"Aye, Mrs. O'Toole," Emmett said.

"Ye sound like me ma," Garahan said. He thought he saw a hint of a smile in the cook's eyes, and quickly added, "Aye, Mrs. O'Toole. There's just one thing I need to clarify with the lass first."

He could tell from the exasperated look on the cook's face that she was about to refuse. He quickly added, "'Tis about the lass's safety."

"Very well. Then let the poor thing eat in peace."

"Ye'll not be going anywhere yet," Garahan told Melinda. "I have to make me report to Captain Coventry. I only stopped here because I had a feeling..." He could have kicked himself in the head for saying what was in his heart.

"You had a *feeling?*" Melinda asked.

He cleared his throat. "There's times when I get a sense of foreboding," he answered. "I needed to stop and see if ye were all right." He wasn't going to admit to anything else with the three faces staring at him expectantly.

"I agree with me cousin," Emmett said. "Men such as the one ye worked for are not known for their forgiving ways."

Garahan nodded. "Or forgetting. Until we know for certain that he won't try to track ye down and drag ye back, ye'll be staying here."

Melinda shook her head. "I need to find work, and intend to do so today. Mrs. O'Toole has given me the names of two reputable agencies where I can apply for work as a scullery maid."

Garahan and Emmett shared a glance, and Garahan knew he and his cousin were in full agreement when Emmett said, "Ye aren't setting one foot outside this house."

She got to her feet, lifted her chin, and brushed past the two of them. "Watch me!"

"Ye *eedjit!*" Garahan said.

Emmett frowned. "She's leaving!"

"No, she isn't!" Garahan chased after her.

There was no way he would let her leave when he had not had the time to send out feelers to find out if the bloody blackguard she worked for was trying to locate her. Ignoring the ache in his heart at the thought of never seeing the lass again, he concentrated on what he would say to convince her not to leave.

Lord, help me find the words!

CHAPTER FIFTEEN

M ELINDA HEARD THEM arguing and ignored them as she dashed out of the room.

Her hand was on the knob to the rear entrance to the town house when she felt a large, callused hand cover hers. Staring at the hand, she marveled at the warmth—and strength—in it. She sighed. She did not want to leave, but how could she stay? She was no longer incapacitated. There was no reason to. Time to make her way alone in the world once again.

Gently lifting her hand from the knob, Garahan tugged on it. "Lass, don't leave."

She didn't pull against him, simply placed her other hand on the doorknob. Melinda drew in a breath—and then another—desperately afraid that when she met his gaze, her heart would break in two. She gathered her courage and turned around, but did not raise her head. Staring at the middle of his broad chest, she asked, "Why? You brought me here to have my injuries tended to. They have been."

"I made a promise to ye, lass, that I intend to keep. Did ye forget the promise of a job?"

Though the soothing sound of his deep voice called to her, she did not give in to it. How could she, when she wasn't sure if she could look him in the eye without tearing up? Digging deep for a calm she did not feel, she said, "In case no one told you, today is the first day I have been able to dress in something other than the nightrail I borrowed from Mrs. O'Toole. Emmett, Mrs. O'Toole, and Mrs. Wigglesworth took such good care of me while you were away." Resigning herself to never seeing the handsome man again, she rasped, "It is time for me to find work. I cannot expect to live off your charity—and that of His Grace—any longer."

He pulled her closer, but she still could not bear to see what she feared was in his gaze—pity. They stood in silence for a few moments before he asked, "How do I know ye're not going to suffer a relapse?"

The hitch in his voice had had her looking up at him. Dark brown, mesmerizing eyes held too many emotions for her to separate. One crucial emotion was not there, which surprised her. He did not pity her.

Holding that to her heart, she shook her head and answered, "One doesn't have a relapse from a fist to the face or a whipping."

He winced at her words and placed his free hand to her waist, urging her closer. "'Tisn't safe for ye to be in London on yer own, lass. Ye're safe here."

Again, she disagreed. "I have been on my own for nearly a year now. I am capable of making my way in the world."

"Oh, aye." His voice roughened as he said, "And a fine job ye've been doing of it!"

She tugged her hand from his and stepped back from him. "How dare you belittle how hard I worked for my cousin! I did the work of two men, and that of the serving lass who worked there before me."

The lid blew off his temper. "And why did the lass leave?"

Her face crumpled. She did not want to tell him. He would use it as leverage against her, as proof that a woman alone faced trials in life a man did not.

"Yer employer convinced one of his patrons she would accept coin for her favors, like he said of ye, didn't he?" Garahan asked.

She blazed with indignation. "Yes, but he lied then, too!"

He closed the distance between them and growled, "Aye, the bastard lied, and admitted it before we left the tavern."

The humiliation swept up from her toes, but worse—she felt her nose start to itch. A prelude to tears she knew she would not be able to control. "Let me go, James. Please? I do not know where I belong, but I know it is not here—in your world."

"There's where ye're wrong, lass. Ye belong here—with me." Her mouth opened in shock as he pulled her into his embrace. He kissed her forehead, one cheek, and then the other. "Stay, lass."

"If I stay here, rumors will start, and I'll be labeled a woman with no moral character."

He clenched his jaw, lifted his chin, and pinned her to the spot with the determination in his gaze. "Stay, then, and be me wife!"

Her eyes filled, and a tear slipped past her guard. He brushed it away and placed a kiss to the end of her nose. Tipping her chin up, he pressed his lips to hers. Softly, tenderly.

"I'll protect ye with me life, lass. No one will ever harm ye again."

SHE CLOSED HER eyes, and he wondered what she was thinking. He did not want to push her into agreeing, but needed her to accept his offer. How in the bloody hell could he protect her if he had no idea where she was?

She opened her eyes, and the sadness in the soft brown there opened a hole in his chest. Her next words widened the wound. "I cannot let you marry me because you feel beholden to protect me, James." The depth of emotion in her gaze added to her plea. "Please, let me go."

Heavy footsteps coming closer broke through the shock of her refusal. Garahan knew he could not force her to stay. He released her to rake a hand through his hair.

He turned around in time to see Emmett's fist a split second before it connected with his nose. The solid left cross to his face stunned him for a few moments before pain rocketed through his face to the back of his skull.

"Whatever ye did to make the lass cry, ye'll apologize for it. Now!" Emmett thundered. When Garahan just stood there staring—and bleeding all over the floor—Emmett grumbled, "Bugger it!" He dug in his waistcoat pocket for his handkerchief, handed it to Garahan, and then chased after Melinda. "Melinda, wait!"

Garahan cursed. Holding his cousin's handkerchief to his broken nose, he followed them. It hurt like bloody hell to run. His head pounded in time with his footsteps. By the time he'd made it to the entrance to the alleyway, Emmett was speaking to Melinda.

Garahan froze. He knew he could not take one step out of the shadows where he could be seen by passersby. The complication of one of the duke's personal guard arguing—while bleeding profusely—with another member of the guard over a woman would only add to the current rumors.

Garahan's duty was not only to uncover the source of the scathing *on dits* circulating about the duke's family, but also to keep more rumors from surfacing. He fought against the need to rip Emmett's hand away from Melinda's, knowing he had no choice but to keep to the shadows. The sight of him chasing after Melinda and Emmett had the potential to tarnish the lass's reputation—and that of the guard! He would not do that.

Keeping his eye on the couple, he felt relieved when they started to walk toward him. The blood begin to soak through his cousin's handkerchief, so he tugged his own from his waistcoat pocket and pressed it to his nose. "Bloody hell, that aches."

"Serves ye right for making the lass cry."

He glared at his cousin, then shifted his gaze to the lass. Her eyes *were* rimmed red, and tears clung to her long eyelashes. If not for the distress lingering in their depths, he'd have remarked at how pretty they were. Instead, he said, "I did not think me proposal would make ye weep, lass. Forgive me?"

"Is it so hard for you to listen, and understand, why I must find work on my own?" Melinda asked. "I need to prove to myself that I am capable of earning a wage—one that I can live on—working for a reputable employer."

"Why refuse help, then, when it's given with no strings attached?" Garahan asked. "Unlike that bastard ye used to work for."

"The fact that you'd even ask is proof that your mind is closed and you will never understand."

"I understand that ye want to find a position without a helping hand from those who have yer best interests at heart," Garahan said.

"You know that is not true," she said. "I told you I asked Mrs. O'Toole for the names of agencies she trusted, and she gave them to me. Why can you not just let me go?"

"Ye haven't had breakfast," Emmett interrupted. "Ye cannot expect to make a good impression on an empty stomach."

Garahan noticed the way she narrowed her eyes at his cousin, and was pleased that she appeared angry with the both of them.

Her words confirmed it. "And you cannot make a good impression when you haul off and punch someone in the face without provocation."

"Are ye daft, lass?" Emmett asked. "Me *eedjit* of a cousin made ye cry! That's reason enough in me book."

Garahan stifled a snort of laughter and moaned. "I could use a hand. This seeing double's turned me stomach."

Instantly on alert, Emmett grabbed hold of Garahan's arm and ordered Melinda, "Go to the kitchen, lass, and have Mrs. O'Toole make up a poultice for me cousin's face." When she stood and stared at the two of them as if they'd lost their minds, Emmett urged, "Hurry now! He may have injured his brain."

Garahan would have laughed if he didn't already know it would hurt too much. The two Melindas shifted into one, and then back into two. His last thought as the world around him went from gray to black was the O'Malley bastard got one over on him.

GARAHAN CAME TO swinging.

"Easy now, lad," Emmett warned. "Ye've a grand follow-through with that jab and might end up rolling off the cot and onto the floor."

"*Shite!* Why in blue blazes did ye have to break me nose? Wasn't it enough yer little sister broke it when we were lads?" Garahan said.

Emmett slowly smiled, the *amadán!* He was probably remembering the blood and Grainne crying.

"As I recall," he said, "ye gave me a fat lip."

"Ye happened to be handy at the time, and I couldn't very well hit yer little sister. 'Twas an accident hitting me nose with her elbow while rescuing her from that tree."

Garahan was only seeing one and a half Emmetts at the moment. Feeling his oats, he motioned for his cousin to lean closer.

Concern marred Emmett's brow as he did as his cousin bade.

Garahan waited until he was in just the right spot...

"Bloody hell!" Emmett bellowed, holding a hand to his split lip.

The sight of his cousin—the nose breaker—stanching the flow of blood from the massive split in his lip courtesy of himself—*thank you very much*—had Garahan laughing.

Mrs. O'Toole stood in the doorway, hands on her hips, frowning. "What *is* going on in here?"

Garahan noticed one of the duke's recently hired guards stood poised and ready to interfere, should that be necessary. Obviously the man did not know the O'Malleys and Garahans were kin and should never be interrupted when they were arguing. To keep the fight where it belonged, between himself and his cousin, he pasted an innocent look on his face—one that always had his ma sighing with exasperation. "Just thanking me cousin for his help convincing Melinda to stay."

The cook stared at them and shook her head. "She's gone."

Emmett let go of Garahan's cravat and shoved him back onto the cot. "When did she leave?"

Mrs. O'Toole answered, "She left as soon as you hauled James in here over your shoulder."

Emmett glanced at Garahan and said, "Do not even think about following the lass. I'll bring her back."

Garahan didn't heed his cousin's edict. "Ye aren't the boss of me, lad." He sat up and swung his legs over the side of the cot—and promptly fell off. Twisting at the last moment, he landed on his shoulder. "Bloody hell, that hurts!"

Mrs. O'Toole stepped aside as the man behind her rushed into the room. She wrung her hands in agitation as she was remonstrating the cousins. "You should know better than to strike Emmett, James—he is your cousin, for Heaven's sake!"

Emmett coughed to cover his laughter before saying, "Mrs. O'Toole, surely with such a grand Irish name ye'd understand 'tis part of being kin. Ye're allowed to punch one another—on occasion."

He squatted down and tried to slide his hands beneath Garahan's arms. Garahan swung at him. "Leave off, will ye?" Emmett said. "'Tis bad enough ye have Mrs. O'Toole scowling at us."

Doing his best to glare at his cousin, Garahan got onto his hands and knees, grabbed a hold of the edge of the cot, and pulled himself to his feet. Noticing the guard he had yet to meet was staring at him, he grunted. "Don't just stand there! Give a man a hand, and fetch a handful of the linens Mrs. O'Toole has stacked on the table beneath the cabinet."

"Is your cousin always like this, O'Malley?" the new guard asked.

Emmett grinned. "Findley, ye best be knowing it now—ye're in over yer head, lad."

The dark-haired guard grabbed the linens. Pausing in front of Garahan, he said, "Do you need me to straighten your nose for you?"

Garahan took the man's measure. He was built like himself and his cousins—tall, broad through the chest and shoulders, with the height to carry it off. Not a bad-looking sort, he thought, studying the slashing scar on the underside of the other man's jaw.

Accepting the proffered cloth, he pressed it to his nose. Tipping his head back, he asked, "Have ye had occasion to straighten a broken nose before?"

Findley laughed. "On myself, more than once."

Garahan snorted, then moaned. It hurt like blazes to laugh.

"Mrs. O'Toole," Emmett said, "is the poultice ready?"

She spun around and rushed back to the kitchen. A few moments later, she returned with the poultice.

Shifting the cloth on his face to see, Garahan noticed the cook's look of concern. Her words confirmed it. "Emmett, see if you can catch up with Melinda. She said she was going to apply for a position with Samuelson's Agency."

"What about me cousin?" Emmett asked. "I've yet to set his nose."

"I won't be needing yer help," Garahan said. "Findley here will see to the task. And, in case ye're worried, I won't be telling yer ma that ye broke me nose and left me to fend for meself."

Emmett snorted with laughter. "She'd never believe a Garahan over her favorite son."

Garahan ignored him and said, "Go after the lass, Emmett. I need to ask her again."

Emmett paused in the doorway. "Ask her what?"

"To be me wife," Garahan rasped.

"She'll refuse ye again, ye know," his cousin told him.

"Ah, but the third time's always the charm. I'll be asking her until she realizes she cannot live without me."

Emmett shook his head. "Ye'll be old and gray before that slip of a lass agrees to pledge her troth to ye."

"We'll be wed before Sean's babe arrives!"

"But Mignonette is due in a matter of weeks," Emmett reminded him.

Garahan lifted his chin, pleased that he only saw one Emmett now. His vision had cleared. He knew then he was not concussed. "Faith, I have not forgotten. 'Tis all our cousin talks about." He motioned with his hand to get Emmett to move. "Ye'll see. Melinda will not be able to hold out against me charm and me good looks."

Mrs. O'Toole took the bloody cloths from Garahan. "Let Emmett find Melinda first, then the two of you can boast and brag all you want—once she's back where she will be safe."

Garahan glared at his cousin, demanding, "Don't just stand there, go after the lass!"

Emmett left, and Findley walked over to the pitcher and poured hot water into a bowl. Garahan watched the man wash and dry his hands before asking, "Do ye have any brothers?"

"Sisters," Findley answered.

"Any that would be of interest to me cousin who just left? He needs a woman of his own—he cannot have mine."

"Only one is of marriageable age, though I doubt my parents are willing to let her wed just any man." Findley grinned. "I'd have to know more about O'Malley before I even think about introducing one of my sisters to the man. Tell me everything I need to know."

Garahan used the warm cloth Mrs. O'Toole handed him to wash his face. With a nod to Findley, he lay on the cot. "After ye put me nose back where it belongs, I'll share a bit of the whiskey in me flask while I tell ye the tale of me cousin Emmett, the healer."

CHAPTER SIXTEEN

CORKENDALE MUMBLED TO himself as he paced the floor.

"Do you want me to meet with the duke's stable lad?" his footman asked. "I could ask about the young woman rumored to be staying at the duke's town house."

The baron paused to consider the idea. "Are you certain this servant is not connected with the duke's private guard?"

The footman assured his employer, "Aye. I overheard he worked for the duke, and followed him to find out more. He'll do anything for coin—his mum's sick."

Corkendale nodded. "Speak to him. Find out if there are any new serving girls hired recently. I need to know what is going on in the duke's household. I could add to the current *on dits* circulating."

The footman was about to leave when Corkendale said, "One more thing, Huggleston!"

He stood at attention, waiting.

"Make certain the stable lad is not trying to extract information from you about me!"

"Aye, your lordship."

Corkendale walked over to the brandy decanter and poured a glass. Swirling the contents to warm it, he considered all of the possibilities. One thing was certain—he did not believe Huggleston's claim that his young contact was working against the duke.

He lifted the glass, drained it, and set it on the sideboard. Although he did not want to tip his hand, sometimes one had to do one's own dirty work in order to get the answers one required.

"Arthur!"

His bellow was immediately answered by his butler, a stout man on the far side of sixty.

Corkendale had not had the coin to replace more than one or two staff members. He fully intended to get rid of them all! They were loyal to his late cousin.

"Yes, your lordship?"

"Have my carriage brought 'round—I am going to pay a call on the Duke of Wyndmere."

"But your lordship, everyone knows the duke is not in residence."

"Well then, when I arrive, they will no doubt relay that very information to me." Corkendale was not about to share the purpose of his visit with his butler. The man bordered on senile—in Corkendale's opinion. When the man continued to stare at him, he let his temper show. "I'm leaving in five minutes, and if the carriage is not ready and waiting in front of this town house, then by God—"

The older servant moved with surprising speed for one so rickety.

"That's more like it," the baron said to himself. "By the time I clean house of senile servants, I will have been through the proper mourning period, after losing my dear wife, and will be in search of a new baroness."

His plan formed quickly in his mind. Corkendale left his town house in an uproar in his bid to demonstrate his control over everyone who owed their livelihood to him.

Pleased with the results—two maids in tears, the butler and housekeeper pale with worry—Corkendale embarked on a mission to extract information from the horse's mouth: the Duke of Wyndmere. In the duke's absence, the next best thing was the head of the duke's London guard—Seamus Flaherty.

>>><<<

"GARAHAN, THERE'S A gentleman demanding to see Flaherty."

Garahan lifted the poultice off his face and blinked at the butler. How long had he had the blasted thing on his nose this time? "Did ye tell him Flaherty's not here?"

"Aye. In Flaherty's absence, he's asking to speak to you."

"Do we know the man, Jenkins?"

"No, although he presented himself as the Baron Corkendale."

Corkendale! The name arrowed through Garahan's aching head. That was the moniker they'd unearthed when searching out the name of the footman heard spreading rumors about their ladyships.

Mopping his face with a clean handkerchief, he raked his hand through his hair while Jenkins patiently waited. "How bad does me face look?" Jenkins studied him long enough to have Garahan blowing out a breath. "Never mind. The duke won't be pleased if I greet anyone with me face like this. Did ye tell him I was here?"

"I told him you were in a meeting. After seeing the condition of your face, I believe I shall tell future callers that you are not to be disturbed—handling the duke's urgent business."

Garahan nodded. "Aye. 'Tis the best we can do until this bloody bag of herbs takes the swelling down. Nothing I can do about me two black eyes for a bit, though."

"Anything else?" the butler asked.

"Nay. Tell the man I'm in a private meeting, and that I asked ye to have him state his business and leave his bloody card."

When Jenkins turned to leave, Garahan added, "See if ye can extract a bit of information from the man."

The staid butler's eyes lit with purpose. "Very good, Garahan."

A few minutes later, Jenkins returned with a scowl on his face, immediately alerting Garahan to trouble—Jenkins rarely showed emotion.

"What is it?"

"The baron was not happy to hear you were not to be disturbed, nor was the man inclined to state his business. We had a bit of a standoff—the young whelp thought he could intimidate me with his rank, when I work for His Grace!"

Garahan stared at the butler for a few moments, digesting the fact that he'd never heard the man utter that many words at one time.

"—until Findley appeared," Jenkins was saying, "and escorted the man to his carriage, watching it until it was out of sight."

"Good man, Findley," Garahan said. "I'll have a word with him."

"He said he would find you after O'Malley returned."

Garahan's gut clenched. "I thought I heard my cousin's voice earlier." While he was under Mrs. O'Toole's strict orders to lie down and let the bloody poultice reduce the bloody swelling. "Did he leave?"

Jenkins inclined his head. "He was here briefly, then left again."

Garahan knew he would not like what he was about to hear. "Tell me, Jenkins, and don't leave anything out."

"It appears that Miss Waring was hired straight off. The position of scullery maid had just come in. She'll be working in a town house near Mayfair."

Garahan was watching Jenkins like a hawk and noted the hint of worry in the man's eyes. "Whose household?"

"Baron Corkendale's."

Garahan strode to the door, bellowing for Findley. When the guard appeared, he relayed the news, then said, "I'll send word if I run into any difficulty."

"Have you seen your face in a looking glass?" Findley asked.

Garahan shrugged. "Not this time, but I won't be forgetting what it looked like the last time one of me cousins broke me nose." He did not add that it was little Grainne O'Malley.

Findley's lips twitched, but his expression quickly changed to one of concern. "You cannot show up on anyone's doorstep looking like you've been in a fight—or ready to start one."

"The hell I can't!" Garahan had his hand on the doorknob when Findley grabbed hold of his elbow and spun him around.

"Your face is a mess. Coventry made it clear when he hired me that we were not to appear in public in a state that would call our duties to the duke in question."

"Bugger it!"

"I will go in your stead. Is there a message you want me to deliver to Corkendale?"

Garahan wanted to punch something, but buried the need deep. He needed to remain calm in order to think clearly. "Aye—tell the man that there has been a mistake at the agency, and Miss Waring still has a fortnight left to serve in the duke's household."

"What if he does not accept my word?" Garahan cracked his knuckles, and Findley shook his head. "I refuse to strike the man without provocation...and even then, not with so many witnesses who will be only too happy to embellish when they pass along the gossip."

"I wasn't going to suggest ye do that. I was cracking me knuckles, imagining how it would feel to knock the man's teeth out."

"A bit on the painful side," Findley said.

"Aches a bit, does it?" Garahan asked.

"You could say that," Findley admitted.

"Well then, encourage the man to listen to reason, and if that does not work, advise him that ye will return with Gavin King of the Bow Street Runners to escort Miss Waring to Grosvenor Square."

Findley frowned. "That's your plan?"

"Aye. I'll send one of the footmen with a missive for King now."

"What if Miss Waring does not wish to return here?" Findley asked.

"Tell her that I'm out of me head in pain."

Findley shook his head. "You're out of your head, all right." Before

Garahan could insist the guard deliver his message, Findley continued, "From what I've observed of Miss Waring, she is a woman of great courage and fortitude."

"And well I know it." Garahan shoved Findley toward the door. "Hurry back!"

He turned around to find Jenkins waiting to speak to him. "Well done, Garahan."

"Thank ye, Jenkins. I'll be doing me rounds while we wait for me cousin, Findley, and the lass to return."

Armed with the knife in his boot and a pistol tucked in his waistband, Garahan motioned for one of the other guards to follow him. When the guard nodded, Garahan said, "I'll take the north alley; ye take the south. We'll meet back here in two hours—if not sooner, depending on whether or not we see the whites of Emmett and Findley's eyes, or if we receive word that all hell has broken loose."

Garahan nodded to the man and strode down the long hallway to the side door, murmuring a prayer. "Lord, I can deal with either outcome, but would prefer the former—if it be *Yer* will."

Two hours later, Findley returned alone.

CHAPTER SEVENTEEN

MELINDA SMILED AT Mrs. Elston, the elderly housekeeper, reining in her worry that she'd be shown the door as soon as someone found out that her last position was in the worst part of London.

She'd never had the opportunity to give the name of the tavern to the woman who interviewed her at the agency. The woman was overjoyed that she had a qualified, presentable young woman to fill the spot quickly for a lord who was known to have very little patience.

"Right this way, Miss Waring," Mrs. Elston said. "I'll introduce you to our cook, Mrs. Lewis. Work without complaint and you will get along just fine."

They walked into the kitchen. "Mrs. Lewis," the housekeeper said. "Good news—the agency was able to fill Lord Corkendale's request immediately. Miss Waring has experience and the recommendation of Mrs. O'Toole, the Duke of Wyndmere's cook."

Mrs. Lewis set her rolling pin aside, brushed her flour-covered hands on her apron, and looked appropriately impressed.

Melinda wondered if everyone knew the duke's household staff. Unsure if she should say anything or not, she merely nodded.

"Well," Mrs. Lewis said. "I've known Mrs. O'Toole for years. If she recommended you, it wouldn't matter if you worked in the stews of London before stepping into the duke's kitchen. Her word is all I need to know that you will be a wonderful addition to the staff."

Melinda swallowed against the lump in her throat. She wanted to tell the cook and the housekeeper about her last position, but Mrs. O'Toole had cautioned her against it. Mrs. O'Toole and Mrs. Wigglesworth both added their praise to the letter of recommendation the duke's man-of-affairs had penned when Jenkins sent the request the day before. The cachet of the duke's name would never be questioned.

On her half-day off, Melinda would go to Grosvenor Square and inquire after the captain and ask if they would send her thanks to him. Until then, she had best keep her head down and perform every task given to her.

SHE WAS SCRUBBING the pots and pans Mrs. Lewis had used to prepare the midday meal when a bellow echoed in the hallway from the other side of the town house. She froze, waiting for the angry baron she'd been warned about to storm in through the kitchen door.

"He's not like the last baron," the cook said, "God rest his soul. The previous baron never raised his voice to the staff. He paid our wages on time, and insisted we take our full day off."

Her matter-of-fact tone soothed the edges off Melinda's worry enough for her to ask, "I thought it was a half-day?"

"Things changed once the new baron inherited the title," Mrs. Lewis said. "Lots of things. Best finish washing those pots before—"

Her words were cut off as the kitchen door burst open and slammed against the wall, and a tall, thin, angry man stormed into the room. "Where is she?"

Mrs. Lewis took up a defensive stance in front of Melinda. "Who, your lordship?"

"The new scullery maid." He reached around the cook and grabbed Melinda by the arm, demanding, "Why did you leave the duke's employ? Were you dismissed?"

Fear curled low in her belly, but she had survived more than anger before—she would not let the baron know she was afraid of him. She tugged on her arm, but he did not release her.

She kept her voice devoid of the emotions roiling inside of her as she answered, "I was not dismissed."

He seemed surprised that she did not quiver and cry before him. He studied her before letting go of her arm. It ached from his cruel grip. She had no doubt he had bruised her arm. "Why else would you leave? The duke is known to pay overinflated wages and treat his servants like family."

She tried to remember what Mrs. O'Toole and Mrs. Wigglesworth had offered as reasons, should her new employer ask why she left. Before she could form the words, he closed the distance between them. She took one step back, and then another, until he pushed her against the wall by the dry sink.

The unholy look in his eyes reminded her of the man who'd torn her gown the night James rescued her. "I've heard all about you," he sneered, pressing his body against hers—leaving no doubt as to his intentions.

The intimate feel of him had her fear trebling until it nauseated her, but she would not give him the satisfaction of knowing he'd succeeded in his bid to terrorize her.

"Every one of the duke's guard had you on your back with your legs spread—"

"Your lordship," the butler interrupted as the baron grabbed her by the shoulders. "There's a man named O'Malley demanding to speak to you." When the baron didn't respond, the butler added, "He works for the Duke of Wyndmere."

Melinda sent up a silent prayer of thanks for the timely interruption, but dared not let it show on her face. She'd dealt with men like the baron while working at the tavern. Keeping her tangled emotions and thoughts hidden had served her well then, and it would do so now.

The baron's lips curled upward—though she wouldn't call it a smile. "After I get rid of him, I'll be back to continue our conversation."

As soon as the door closed behind him, Mrs. Lewis bustled her out of the kitchen and into the servants' hallway. "Hurry now! You do not want to be here when the baron returns."

"But my job—"

The cook moved faster than Melinda could give her credit for, urging her forward. She had the rear door to the town house open, and was apologizing as she pushed Melinda through it. "No job is worth what that devil plans to do to you!" She shook her head. "The last two maids... Never mind. Go! Carefully now—do not let him see you leaving."

Melinda knew she would have to do as she was told, but what would she do now? Where could she go? Not back to the agency, as they would demand to know why Baron Corkendale sent her packing so quickly. She had no doubt his shouted slurs would be repeated, and she would never be able to refute his claims. The baron had damaged her reputation beyond repair.

She'd left without her reticule and the few coins Mrs. Wigglesworth had given her earlier—along with her shawl and the only other gown she owned. Well, she'd brought this situation upon herself. Her pride would not allow her to live off the kindness of the duke's staff and a certain dark-eyed, handsome Irishman. The need to prove she was capable of finding work on her own had landed her in her current situation. Now it would be up to her to decide how to resurrect her reputation while keeping her virtue—and pride—intact.

James's words came back to haunt her as she crept along the side of the town house, waiting in the alleyway until she heard the front door slam closed. She had been doing tolerably well on her own—until she'd refused to give in to the demand that she entertain the taverns' patrons in the back room. Mayhap she should seek work without the aid of the agency and Captain Coventry's letter of recommendation.

The sound of horses' hooves against the cobblestones had her wondering, was Emmett leaving? Mayhap it was someone else on the street in front of the baron's town house who happened to be riding by. She needed to leave, but had to be certain no one was waiting to stop her when she left the safety of the alley.

With her back to the wall, she continued to make her way toward the front of the town house. Bile rushed up her throat at the thought of what the baron would do if discovered her trying to leave. She had no doubt what the man intended. There would be no reasoning with a man like him. She'd heard more than one tale of young women being violated. Rich or poor did not matter—men determined to take what was not offered never listened to reason.

But she couldn't stay here long—the baron was bound to return to the kitchen and find her gone. What would he do to Mrs. Lewis? Her worry for the kindly woman she'd just met filled her. *Lord, please don't let him hurt the cook!* She was only trying to help her escape an all-too-common fate of young serving girls.

She inched closer to the street. Drawing in a calming breath, she peeked around the corner. Strong fingers wrapped around her wrist, yanked her onto the sidewalk, and into a hackney.

Dear God, she would never escape this time!

HUGGLESTON LOOKED AROUND furtively as he approached the back entrance on Grosvenor Square. As he'd been told to, he waited at the back of the stables for his contact to meet him.

"Huggleston?"

His stomach settled as he recognized the voice. "I'm here!"

He stepped out from where he waited to greet the young stable lad he'd met at Tattersalls a few weeks ago. When he'd first overheard the young man mention his ailing mother, he sensed he could use the lad for his own purposes. When he heard the boy worked for the duke, he'd followed, observed, and listened as the boy told of his mother's illness and the coin they owed the apothecary—a tale too close to his own.

Huggleston sensed the boy would be the solution to finding out more information about the duke and his household, as well as a way to earn a bit more coin from his employer Baron Corkendale. He had to, for his sister's sake.

The boy's downcast look had him asking, "Anyone give you trouble sneaking away to meet with me?"

"Nay. Are you going to give me the coin you promised? My mum needs more of the headache powder. They plague her something fierce."

The boy looked more uncomfortable than the last time they'd met. "Do they watch you closely here? Will you be missed?" Huggleston asked.

The boy shook his head. "They trust me to do my job. I take good care of His Grace's horses."

Huggleston doubted the lad did more than shovel out the stalls. But, needing the boy for the information he could supply, he nodded. "What news do you have for me today?"

The boy looked over his shoulder and leaned in close to say, "The young lady who was staying here left this morning."

"Do you know where she was going?"

The boy glanced to the left, and to the right, before answering, "Some agency."

"Agency?"

"Aye, to look for work."

Huggleston frowned. "Isn't that why she was here? To work?"

The boy shook his head. "They carried her in a week or so ago. She was in a bad way."

Interest piqued, Huggleston asked, "Ill, was she, or was it something else?"

The boy scuffed the toe of his boot into the dirt before meeting Huggleston's gaze. "Something else. I heard they sent for a physician."

"Did anyone go after her?"

"Aye, O'Malley and then Findley."

"Who's Findley?"

"One of the duke's guard, like O'Malley and Garahan."

"Garahan?"

"Aye, he's the one that brought her here on his horse."

Huggleston nodded. "And you took care of his horse for him."

The boy puffed up his chest. "I did. Fed him a cupful of oats, too. Garahan had come a long way and wanted to make sure I gave his horse extra attention."

Huggleston hoped the information he was gathering would be enough for the baron to elevate his position within the household to butler, like he'd been promised. He desperately needed the blunt. "Did he come from the Lake District?"

"Closer," the boy told him. "Sussex—Chattsworth Manor."

Huggleston knew the baron would need this information as soon as possible. "Did you hear any other names mentioned?"

The boy was starting to grow restless and uneasy. "I've been away from my duties too long. The stable master will come looking for me."

"If you want that coin I promised, you'll answer the question."

The boy took a step backward, and then another, but answered, "Lippincott."

Huggleston tossed a coin at the boy, who caught it on the fly before disappearing inside the stables. The scent of horse and hay drifted toward him but, just as abruptly, dissipated when the door closed behind the boy.

Confident he would get what he deserved, Huggleston didn't bother to scan the perimeter before walking along the edge of the alleyway.

He never saw the man dressed in black step out of the shadows and follow him.

➤➤➤◄◄◄

GARAHAN PULLED JIMMY into the safety of the stables. Holding a finger to his lips, he watched one of the duke's newly hired men follow after Huggleston. He needed to wait for Emmett to return before he began searching for Melinda.

Jimmy whispered, "Well?"

Garahan patted the young lad on the back. "Ye did grand, Jimmy. It sounded like he believed yer tale."

The boy shuddered. "I hope he doesn't find out and come back looking for me."

"Ye know we'll protect ye with our lives, lad, so quit worrying over it and tell me how yer ma is feeling."

The boy's face lit up. "She's sitting up and able to eat. Said she'd never be able to thank ye for sending Mrs. O'Toole's mixture home with me." He grinned and confided, "She said the herb tea tastes like *shite!*"

Garahan chuckled. "Well now, there's nothing wrong with yer ma's sense of taste. I've had to down a bit of that healing tea in the past and can say it does taste like *shite*."

Jimmy's eyes widened as he leaned forward and asked, "Horse or dog?"

Garahan's booming laugh had the horses leaning over the top of the doors to their stalls, whinnying and whickering. "The lads behind ye are telling ye their *shite* doesn't taste bad—'tis dogs' that does."

The boy's giggle lightened Garahan's heart and was the distraction he needed waiting for Emmett to arrive. If his *eedjit* cousin hadn't plowed his fist into his nose, Garahan would have been the one to go after Melinda. As it was, he'd been waiting for hours now.

He trusted his cousin with his life—and it gutted him to admit that his jealousy had caused him to wonder if he could trust Emmett with Melinda.

Reaching into his pocket, he pulled out a handful of coin and handed it to the boy. "Remember what I said. Take this home to yer ma and make sure she stashes these in a safe place. We don't want anyone thinking ye picked some lord's pocket over on Mayfair."

"I promise." To Garahan's surprise, the boy threw himself at Garahan, wrapping his arms around his waist. "Thank you!"

Garahan was Irish enough to allow his eyes to fill with tears. "Best get on home now, lad, and make sure yer ma drinks every bit of that tea until she's used up the herbs. We can get more when she needs it."

Jimmy released his hold on Garahan, bade the horses goodbye, and was gone.

Taking his time to speak to each one of the geldings, Garahan scratched behind their ears and gave each one a slice of apple. "That'll hold ye until it's time for yer evening meal."

He slipped out of the familiar scents and sounds of the stables and into the chaos of an argument raging in the kitchen.

"What in blazes happened?" he demanded, entering the fray.

"She's gone," Emmett told him. "I have reason to believe she was at Corkendale's town house when I demanded to speak to the baron. But by the time I muscled me way into the entryway and the kitchen, she was gone."

Garahan's gut iced over. "Where did she go?"

Emmett's worried gaze met his. "Faith if I know. The cook said the baron spouted insulting things...insinuated we'd all had our way with the lass."

Garahan felt the heat of his anger ignite. "That bloody bastard."

"Me arrival was timely, the cook told me. It interrupted when the baron had the lass's back against the wall. By the time I walked into the kitchen, she was gone and the cook didn't know where. Said she shoved Melinda out the door, warning her not to return after the way the baron set his sights on her."

"We have the cook to thank, then," Garahan said.

"Aye. The baron was fit to be tied, started spouting about making her pay and coming after us." Emmett shook his head. "What do ye think ails the man? We've never met him before."

"What ailed the others?" Garahan asked. "Without provocation, they set out to destroy the duke and his family. What's to say that isn't the case with the baron as well."

"More like, those wanting what they don't have," Emmett replied, "and not afraid to toss those that have more beneath their heel while they grind their reputation to shreds." He paused, then added, "Mayhap they were dropped on their heads as babes."

Garahan added another to his list of those that he would see to it paid for their treatment of the lass. So far, it was the tavern owner, the man who'd accosted her in the back room, and now the baron. He could not wait to collect what they owed.

"I'll be heading out, then," Garahan said. "Have ye sent word to Gavin King or Coventry?"

"Aye, and I stopped on Bow Street to check in with King. He has two men currently in the area who will be on the lookout for the lass."

"Why did she not return here?" Garahan asked. "She was safe here."

Emmett's shoulders slumped. "Damned if I can figure out the workings of the female mind. Me da reminds me he's still trying to follow along with how Ma thinks. He's only been at it for twenty-five or so years."

Garahan sighed. "Me da's often said the same. They've more years on us, boy-o. I'm thinking they have the right of it." Locking gazes with his cousin, he asked the question plaguing him: "Why do ye love the lass?"

Emmett was quick to respond, "'Twas her courage and ability to handle the pain and not complain while we tended to her back. Whenever I spoke to the lass, 'twas like stepping into the sunshine."

Garahan nodded. "For meself, 'tis all that and more. I admire her tenacity and ability to continue to work in an untenable position with no hope of improvement because she had no choice. Her pride more than matches me own. But 'tis her endless capacity for compassion and the way she trusted me without question in the worst of circumstances."

Emmett was silent, and Garahan knew his cousin was taking in all that he'd said. Finally, Emmett rasped, "Ye never mentioned her warm brown eyes or dark brown hair, or the way her lips lift when she smiles."

Garahan shrugged. "Those are only the beauty she carries on the outside. 'Tis the beauty within the lass that called to me from the moment I laid eyes on her."

Emmett sighed. "I will not compete for the lass's affections, James."

Relief filled Garahan. He had not wanted to have to go up against his slightly taller, broader cousin. The lasses tend to fall at the feet of the O'Malleys for reasons Garahan and his brothers could not fathom.

"Ye'll watch yer back," Emmett ordered him.

"Aye, and me nose," Garahan said. "I'll not be wanting to bump into anything for the next little while. Else Coventry'll be on me back about showing me battered face in public while working for the duke."

"Ah, but the captain will let ye venture into the underbelly of London until yer face heals."

Garahan snorted in agreement.

"If ye don't return in a few hours," Emmett said, "I'll send out a search party."

"*Bugger it!*"

"There's the James I know and love. I meant what I said. Send word if ye need me."

Garahan paused to look at his cousin, who knew him like a brother, and nodded.

"I'd check the tavern, if I were ye," Emmett said. "What's to say that bastard didn't have ye followed and has been waiting to snatch the lass from us, forcing her to return to work for him?"

Garahan nodded. "'Twas me plan to return there—and to take Tremayne with me."

"A sound notion."

Garahan gave him a hard stare. "Don't wait up for me."

"I won't."

As Garahan rode off into the night, he asked the Lord if he was too busy for the likes of himself, or had another plan entirely?

He wasn't surprised when the Lord didn't answer.

CHAPTER EIGHTEEN

ELINDA SHRANK BACK into the corner of the carriage. She'd never expected her cousin to come after her. What a fool she'd been! How could she not have seen the blackness eating away at his soul? The first time he'd hit her, she noticed the darkness creeping into his eyes. She'd seen the evil in his gaze—and nothing else—right before he brought the thin wooden rod down across her back.

She vowed not to show her fear to her cousin. "You cannot abduct a woman off the streets of London and expect to get away with it."

He stared at her from where he sat opposite from her. Why did he seem more menacing in the dim interior of the carriage? When didn't he answer her question, she asked another: "Why did you come after me?"

"Why do you think?"

Undeterred by his answering her question with a question, she asked, "Where are you taking me?"

He chuckled. "Where do you think?"

The first hint of fear speared through her. "This isn't a game!"

"That depends on whether you are the prey," he told her, "or the predator."

"I refuse to be drawn into your twisted games!" she said. "Just as I refused to be sold to the highest bidder at your tavern!"

She reached for the door, and he grabbed hold of her wrist, crushing it in his grasp. "You do not have a say in the matter. You are coming with me, and you will do as I say—with whomever I choose."

The lack of inflection in his voice chilled her far quicker than his words. He still planned to sell her body as he'd threatened.

Dear God! How could she possibly escape him now? Her thoughts swirled around and around until her head swam. She'd left the safety and comfort of the duke's town house, and the man who'd rescued her—the man who'd asked her to marry him! The man who turned her head and had her thinking that he might truly care for her despite her awkward limp and reduced station in life.

Even if she did not want to marry James—which, to be honest, would be an unattainable dream—she should have stayed where she was safe. Why did it not occur to her that her cousin was desperate enough to come after her when she had done the work of three people? And what did she receive in return? A lumpy pallet filled with old straw, questionably clean water, and one small meal a day.

He'd gone back on their agreement that first month she worked at his tavern. Cutting back on her meals the first time she refused the attentions of a customer. When she continued to refuse his customer, fresh water was replaced with what had to be the water she'd washed the glasses, pots, and pans in.

Still she did not complain—she'd known early on that if she left the village and the life she no longer had, there would be no turning back. Lord how she prayed for a savior to come and rescue her. If she worked hard enough, prayed hard enough, surely the Lord would send someone, wouldn't he?

Warmth filled her heart as the realization dawned. He *had* sent someone… He'd sent James!

And what did she do? The moment she felt she was well enough, she'd left the safety and security of the duke's town house. She was bacon-brained, had attics to let…was dicked in the nob! Worse than that—she had tossed the man's marriage proposal back in his face and run away from him without saying goodbye. Had she even thanked him for all he'd done for her? For the life of her, she could not remember.

Even if, by some slim chance, James managed to discern who had snatched her off the street and kidnapped her, he would never willingly follow the woman who'd given him so much trouble. The woman with the twisted leg and scarred back had tossed his good intentions, along with the offer of his name, back in his face.

A dark thought nearly consumed her—her life would be over the moment she set foot in that tavern again. Without a doubt, her cousin had already taken coin for the first of the men to be *entertained* by her. She would not submit willingly. She would fight tooth and nail...starting now!

Squaring her shoulders, meeting his evil gaze with her own, she vowed, "I will never do as you ask—no matter whom you accepted coin from." She felt the carriage slowing down. Without looking away from her cousin, she reached for the door, opened the latch, and flung herself out of the carriage.

Airborne, she crossed her arms over her face. She landed on her side and felt something give inside of her. She sucked in a breath as she rolled over and rammed her shoulder into something hard.

A nearby shout of alarm had her digging deep for the strength to push away from the curb with one arm and crawl onto the sidewalk. Horses whinnied in alarm. A coachman shouted a curse. The sound of footsteps drawing closer had her struggling onto her hands and knees. She had to move!

Small, strong hands grasped her by the arm, pulling her to her feet and into an alleyway, hidden from view in a darkened doorway.

"Don't make a sound," the raspy voice urged. "I'll hide you."

Her stomach lurched as the pain in her side and shoulder began to make itself known. "How do I know—"

"That I mean you no harm?"

She turned toward the voice and had to look down in order to look into the eyes of her rescuer. A well-dressed woman—somewhere around Melinda's age—studied her. "Who are you?"

"Michaela," the woman said. "It would be best if you do not know my full name. I cannot afford to have my family discover my mission."

"Your mission?" Melinda asked. The soothing tone of the woman's voice eased the worst of her worry.

"I rescue young women off the streets of London."

Her eyes widened. "Oh, but I'm not a… That is to say, I don't… I've never—"

Before she could finish, a harsh voice bellowed, *"Melinda!"*

Michaela put a finger to her lips, reached behind her, and knocked on the door with one sharp rap. The door opened behind them, and impossibly large hands pulled the women inside before quietly closing the door.

Michaela nodded to the big man who stood behind them. "Thank you, Alasdair."

"I see ye've brought another lassie into yer fold, Miss Michaela. I canna imagine where she'll be sleeping this night."

Melinda studied the big man. "You sound like someone I know. But your accent is different."

His low chuckle eased one of the knots in her stomach. "Name's Cameron—Alasdair Cameron."

She stared at the huge man, surprised that she felt no fear. In the faint light of the lantern he held, she saw his eyes were kind, though his face had been scarred by a blade at some point in his lifetime— reminding her of Tremayne, the man who'd been with James the night he rescued her. "Melinda Waring. You're not Irish, are you?"

His eyes narrowed, and though his irritation was evident, she sensed she had nothing to fear from him.

"Nay," he answered, lifting his chin. "Scots."

"Hurry," Michaela urged as she tugged on Melinda's arm.

Pain shot through her shoulder to the waist. She bit her lip—hard—to keep from making a sound. She let herself be led, though her feet dragged, and her body seemed to have a mind of its own. When she stumbled, she was lifted high into arms as strong as James's had been, held against a heart that beat steadily—not one that pounded as James's had.

"Quickly, Alasdair!" Michaela said. "She could have hurt her ribs or broken an arm. The way she landed on the street, and the sound when she hit the curbstone…"

"How did she end up on the street, Miss Michaela?"

Cognizant that she needed to speak for herself in order to keep control of the situation, Melinda answered, "I jumped out of the carriage."

What sounded like a rusty chuckle rumbled beneath her ear before the Scotsman asked, "Well now, lassie, was it moving at the time?"

Melinda nodded. "I could not let him take me back to the tavern."

"Did he plan to abuse ye?" Alasdair asked.

Her throat tightened at the thought of the beating—and the healing—she'd suffered through. "He did, but I'd rather let him beat me bloody again before I let any man force himself on me!"

Alasdair's voice deepened as he asked, "Again? The bastard beat ye?"

Michaela opened a door leading to the second floor. "No more questions. We have to see how badly she's injured and then decide how we can help her."

"I can walk."

"I'll set ye down in the attic room."

True to his word, as soon as they entered the room where Michaela stood waiting for them, Alasdair set her on her feet.

She locked her knees to keep them from buckling and lifted her chin high. "While I thank you for taking me in, Michaela—and for your help, Alasdair—I decide my own fate!"

Michaela's lips twitched. "Well, I see your pride is intact. Let's see about those ribs."

Alasdair was staring at Melinda's left arm. "I dinna want to worry ye, lassie, but ye damaged yer arm when ye landed."

"But it's my shoulder that pains me," Melinda replied.

"If yer shoulder hit the curb with enough force, that would explain why yer arm looks like it's dangling a bit. 'Tis likely pulled out of the socket."

She glanced at her arm, and sweat broke out behind her knees and on the nape of her neck. It looked as if it wasn't connected to her shoulder at all! She shook her head at the thought. Not possible—if that were the case, there would be copious amounts of blood. There wasn't any that she could see.

"If it pains ye now, best brace for it, lassie," Alasdair said. "Once the shock wears off, it'll hurt like a son of a bi—"

"Language, Mr. Cameron," Michaela cautioned.

She urged Melinda onto a chair and carefully placed Melinda's hands in her lap. Starting at the injured shoulder, Michaela announced, "You are right, Alasdair."

"I know." He frowned at Melinda. "Best have a look at yer arm as well. With any luck, 'twill just be bruised—not broken." She flinched when he palpated the lump on her arm. "'Tis a bruise to the bone—not broken."

"You are very fortunate that you did not hit your head," Michaela added, "or you might not need our help at all."

Melinda's stomach roiled at the notion that she could have been killed leaping from the carriage. "I'd do it again," she quietly told them. "At least I'd be in charge of my own fate."

"What's done is done," Michaela said. "I found you, and Alasdair and I are quite capable of fixing your shoulder—though I have to warn you, the pain will be almost as great as when you knocked it out of alignment."

"I won't complain," Melinda assured her.

"You are fortunate that I happened to be nearby and heard the commotion and could bring you here. Alasdair served in the King's Dragoons before he suffered the injury that nearly took his life."

Grateful to be distracted from thinking about injuries, she said, "I know of a man who served in the dragoons. He has a similar scar. Were sword slashes to the face a common injury?" Alasdair didn't answer, which had her worrying she'd insulted the man. "I mean no disrespect, Mr. Cameron, and must thank you for serving our king and suffering what had to have been an extremely painful injury. Please forgive me? I am truly sorry if my question was too personal to ask."

Alasdair frowned down at her. "Did anyone ever tell ye that ye talk too much?"

"Alasdair has a gift for healing," Michaela told her.

"I know a man who has the same gift, although he was not the one in the dragoons, nor is he a trained physician. Are you?" Melinda asked.

Alasdair shook his head and glared at Michaela. "Tell the lass, if ye must, but do it while we reset her shoulder. Prolonging what's necessary will only add to the pain and healing time."

Glancing up at the man, Melinda wished she'd kept her mouth closed. "I'm sorry. I tend to rattle on when I'm worried."

Michaela smiled. "Of course you are worried. You are in a strange place, with people who are telling you they mean you no harm, and are about to render aid to you for your injuries. I would be worried, too."

Melinda looked into Michaela's eyes and felt her stomach settle. "I don't know you, Michaela, but somehow I feel that can trust you."

"And Alasdair?" Michaela asked.

Melinda looked at the giant standing next to Michael and answered, "And Mr. Cameron."

"'Tis Alasdair, lassie," the Scotsman said. She noticed in the lamplight that his eyes were dark blue—the color of the sky at midnight. "Are ye ready, lassie?"

Unable to speak past the lump in her throat, she inclined her head.

"Do ye want a bit of rope—or wood—to bite down on while I reposition your shoulder?"

"Have you done this before?" Melinda asked.

He held her gaze while squatting down next to her. "Aye, lassie. Too many times to count. There's more than one way to see to the task. Depending on if ye can brace yerself for the pain, fast is best. If not, we can have ye lie down on yer stomach on the bench over there and let yer arm hang down. Then we'll—"

"Quick would be best," Melinda interrupted. "Less time for me to worry about what you have to do."

"Very well then, lassie. Close yer eyes and relax yer shoulders and arms. 'Tis necessary for yer shoulder to pop back into place."

"Pop?"

Alasdair hesitated and glanced at Michaela. "Mayhap slower would be better."

"Nay," Melinda said. "I'll close my eyes and stop asking questions." She closed her eyes and tried to relax. But no matter how hard she tried, she could not seem to relax until a certain Irishman slipped into her mind.

"That's it, lassie. Easy now—'twill be over by the time ye count to five."

Melinda obliged him by counting aloud. "One, two—" Her eyes shot open in shock, and her breath whooshed out as her shoulder slid back into the socket.

"'Tis done, lassie. Breathe," Alasdair commanded.

After he demonstrated breathing in and out twice, she was able to do so.

Clearing her throat, she found her voice. "Thank you, Alasdair. I know all about bones that don't heal right—but I wasn't sure about this type of injury to my shoulder."

"Ye've broken a bone before?"

She nodded. "My leg...when I was young. I have a permanent limp."

"Ye'll have the full use of yer arm and shoulder. It'll only be sore for a few days. The longer it remained out of the socket, the longer it would've taken the muscles and tendons that stretched to heal."

"It actually feels better—even though it is sore."

"Ye're a brave lassie, Miss Waring. A bit of the herbal draught, I'm thinking," he said to Michaela.

Michaela brushed a strand of hair from Melinda's forehead. "Is your stomach still turned upside down? We can hold off on the herbal draught until after we check your ribs."

Melinda hated feeling weak and injured, having spent a fortnight that way after James swept her off her feet and onto his horse, taking her to safety—safety in his arms.

"Miss Waring? Did ye not understand Miss Michaela's question?"

She cleared her throat before answering, "Yes. I understood. I was trying to decide."

"In that case, we'll hold off on the drink," Alasdair said. "We need to see to her ribs."

"We'll need you to give us a bit of privacy," Michaela said.

Alasdair turned to go, stopped, and looked over his shoulder. "Ye're a courageous lassie...for a *Sassenach*."

"*Sassenach?*"

"Aye. An Englishwoman." With that, he left the room and closed the door behind him.

"He may seem a bit gruff at first."

Melinda sighed. "I don't mind. He reminds me of the healer I mentioned. Both the healer and his cousin—the man who rescued me—are similar in size and build to Alasdair. Just as gruff."

While Michaela helped Melinda remove her gown and chemise to examine her ribs, Michaela asked about the healer and the rescue.

Melinda glossed over the tale, but from the look on Michaela's face, the other woman sensed there was far more to the tale than Melinda admitted to.

"There are old bruises, as well as new, but no movement when I apply pressure to your ribs. You will be sore for at least a fortnight, maybe longer," Michaela cautioned.

"You've studied under a physician, Michaela," Melinda said. "Haven't you?"

Michaela wrapped Melinda's ribs—if she noticed her scars, she did not mention it. Helping her dress, she said, "My father is a noted physician. After my mother passed away, it was a comfort to the both of us for me to assist when my father treated his patients. He quickly realized that I had the aptitude and was adept at healing."

"You were not allowed to study further," Melinda said, "were you?"

"I was not," Michaela answered as she fashioned a sling to immobilize Melinda's injured shoulder. "My father may have an inkling that I am using what I learned at his side to help others, but he chooses to turn a blind eye to it. My family believes I am attending a musicale this evening."

Melinda could only marvel that Michaela's father had been willing to teach her. It was sad the lengths the woman had to go to continue doing what she felt called to do, in order not to face the ridicule of her family and society. "I will never be able to repay you or Alasdair for your care—and for sheltering me."

"We do not expect payment for what we do." Michaela paused at the knock on the door. "All finished, Alasdair. Please, come back in."

"Cracks?" he asked, entering.

Michaela shook her head. "Bruised and sore."

Melinda noticed Michaela did not mention the faded bruises.

"I wrapped them," Michaela said.

"Snug, but not too snug?" he asked.

She huffed out a breath. "I do know how to treat ailments, *Mr.* Cameron."

Melinda laughed then immediately sucked in a breath as pain radiated through her side.

"Ye'll not want to be laughing for the next little while, lassie. I have the herbal draught ready."

He handed her the cup. While she drank, Alasdair asked, "Is there anyone we can send word to? Someone worried about ye, Miss Waring?"

She finished the herbal concoction and handed the mug to him, thanking him. Should she send word to James? Would he care? Would he come after her? "I'm not sure if I should."

"Well now, what of the man I heard ye speaking of—the healer?"

She shook her head.

"Ah," Alasdair said. "It's the man who bears a scar like me."

Again, she shook her head.

Michaela finished straightening up the supplies they'd used and said, "It would have to be the man who rescued you."

Melinda's eyes filled. "Aye."

Alasdair sat down on the chair opposite Melinda and nodded. "If I had rescued a fair lassie, such as yerself," he said, "I'd wonder why she'd run away from me. Did he do or say anything to have ye lose yer trust in him?"

A tear slipped free. "Nay."

"Why did you leave?" Michaela asked.

"I was healed and could not continue to live at the duke's town house—" Her hands covered her mouth.

Alasdair's thick eyebrows shot up. "Duke, is it? I happen to know one or two honest men who work for the Duke of Wyndmere."

Surprised, she asked, "You do?"

"Aye, and if the former dragoon is acquainted with the duke's guard, then I believe I know who the man with the scar is, too." He paused, then said, "Tremayne."

She nodded. If he knew Tremayne, then he might know James, too. "I left in a hurry," Melinda said. "I cannot impose upon them again."

Alasdair stood. "Now then, if memory serves, there are cousins and brothers employed by the duke. O'Malleys, Flahertys, and Garahans. Who was it?"

She answered, "James Garahan."

"Ah. If I were Garahan, I'd be tracking ye to the tavern he and Tremayne rescued ye from, searching for ye." His dark blue gaze pinned her to the spot. "Dinna let yer pride get in the way of good sense, lassie."

"Wait!" she said, watching him open the door. "Where are you going?"

He did not bother to turn around when he answered, "I'm sending word to Garahan, O'Malley, and Coventry."

Astounded that the Scotsman would know the captain too, she asked, "How do you know Captain Coventry?"

"Not many will look past our injuries to what we're capable of, now that we've mustered out of our service to His Majesty. Captain Coventry has, and he helps those of us who have suffered as he has by finding us work."

Melinda digested that bit of information. Mayhap she had let her pride get in the way. "Thank you for your aid tonight, Alasdair."

He nodded and walked out the door.

"Thank you, too, Michaela. I'm not sure what I would have done if my cousin found me."

Michaela's eyes narrowed. "Your cousin?"

Melinda answered, "By marriage—he's my stepfather's nephew."

"You'll be safe here until Mr. Garahan comes to fetch you."

Melinda sighed. "I doubt James will come for me. I'm grateful if I can stay the night, but will need to leave in the morning."

"And go where?" Michaela asked. "I will not permit you to leave here to wander the streets we rescued you from! What of the wounds we tended?"

Flabbergasted by the vehemence in the woman's tone, Melinda blinked. "I do not need anyone's permission to leave."

Michaela glared at Melinda, put her hands on her hips, and said, "If I have to tie you to that chair to keep you here until Garahan arrives, I will!"

Melinda believed she would.

CHAPTER NINETEEN

G ARAHAN RECEIVED WORD from Coventry and King as he was leaving to search for Melinda. King's men verified the rumors as truth—Corkendale *had* been overheard slandering Viscountess Chattsworth and Countess Lippincott at Tattersalls! Coventry confirmed Corkendale's boast at White's that he would take down the duke, from three trusted sources. Garahan had one of the duke's new men follow Huggleston, Corkendale's footman, earlier and knew he would have one more confirmation.

They now had more than enough verified proof, in Garahan's opinion. It was time to take the first step to silence Corkendale, by taking out his bloody mouthpiece—Huggleston.

He approached the baron's residence on Mayfair, keeping to the shadows. It was too soon to show his hand. He did not want anyone to know he was waiting for the footman to leave the town house. Emmett's intelligence from King had told of the footman's nightly forays to one of the poorer sections of London.

"Either spending his hard earned coin…or paying for his pleasure," Garahan mumbled beneath his breath as the man he'd been waiting for materialized out of the dark. Before the man reached the side entrance, Garahan had him in a headlock, covering the man's mouth with his free hand. "Make a sound, and I'll slit yer throat."

Huggleston stilled. "That's better. If yer a smart man," Garahan said, dragging the man around the back of the stables, "ye'll have been expecting me." When he was certain no one else was about, he spun the footman around and warned, "Make one sound other than to answer me questions, and ye die."

The pale light of the moon was enough to see the worry in the other man's eyes. "I've a few questions for ye. Give me the wrong answer and ye'll be meeting yer Maker. Understand?" The footman nodded and Garahan lowered his hand. "I hear ye were spreading tales slandering Viscountess Chattsworth and Countess Lippincott."

Huggleston, opened his mouth and snapped it shut and Garahan chuckled. "Smart man, but if ye don't answer me questions, ye'll still be meeting yer Maker."

The footman's strangled gasp was music to Garahan's ear. "Faith, I'm thinking ye finally understand. Ye either tell me what I want to know, or—""

"You slice my throat."

"Aye." Garahan decided to ask a question he already knew the footman was not guilty of. "I've information that ye we the one to spread the heinous rumor that Baron and Baroness Summerfield were hosting orgies."

"No!" Huggleston rasped. "I told Baron Corkendale that I would not repeat such a thing!"

"Yet ye'd spread the lie that the viscountess and countess cuckolded their husbands and each one birthed another man's babe!"

Huggleston hung his head. "I knew their husbands to be fair men, rumored to be in love with their wives and would protect their wives rather than believe the rumors."

"And that excuses yer slandering their husband's name, and by family connection, the duke's?"

Huggleston raised his head and glared at Garahan. "I needed the money for my sister! She'll waste away to nothing if I don't earn enough coin to pay the apothecary!"

At last, Garahan thought, the truth. "Well now, so ye're a selective liar."

Huggleston clamped his jaw shut. Wise move, Garahan thought. "Are ye willing to accept me challenge?"

"What challenge?" the footman asked before he snorted with laughter. "That rumor that you wanted to challenge me in a bare-knuckle bout was the truth?" When Garahan stared at him, the younger man boasted, "You'll never survive two rounds against me."

"Well now, I've been known to dabble in the fine art of bare-knuckle fighting. I'll be wiping yer slate clean if ye accept me challenge."

Huggleston shook his head. "My sister has a terrible fever—she'll die. I cannot risk it."

Garahan's heart went out to the man. Anyone who would do whatever it took to take care of their family deserved a second chance. "On me honor, Huggleston. If ye agree to the bout, I'll see that the apothecary is paid." When the footman didn't respond, Garahan added, "I'll send word as to when and where and until then—"

Huggleston rubbed his throat. "Corkendale will sack me. You may as well slit my throat now—but only if you agree to sell my body to one of the men known for procuring fresh bodies for medical students—and promise to give the money to my mum for my sister."

"Let Corkendale sack ye. Ye can help us unmask what Corkendale has rumored to have done to his cousin and his cousin's wife."

Huggleston stared at Garahan. "I thought that was speculation."

"Ah, so ye've heard, then. From what we know of yer employer, it's likely more than speculation." When the footman hesitated, Garahan urged. "I don't have the time to convince ye now. I've an important search to continue."

"Regarding Miss Waring?"

Garahan grabbed the man by his lapels. "What do ye know?"

Huggleston shrugged. "Only that Mrs. Lewis helped her escape the clutches of the baron. There's talk among the staff that he'd violated two other maids, who were sent packing. I planned to give my notice as soon as I had enough coin to pay the apothecary."

Garahan released him and patted his shoulder. "Agree to help bring down Corkendale, and I'll be letting ye go."

"And you won't have me followed?"

Garahan snorted with laughter. "Would ye believe me if I said I wouldn't?"

"No."

"Well then, yer the smart man I thought ye to be. Stop by the duke's town house on Grosvenor Square and ask for Jenkins. He'll be expecting ye."

"What about my sister?"

"Jenkins'll have the coin ye need." Garahan paused, then added, "Trust me."

Huggleston held out his hand. "Thank you for saving my sister's life, Garahan. I'm in your debt."

Garahan took it and gave it one swift shake. "We'll talk about debts later. Right now ye've information to extract from Corkendale, and I've a lass to find."

"Good luck!" Huggleston rasped as the two men went in opposite directions, each with a woman to rescue and a duty to fulfill.

GARAHAN FIGURED HE was an hour behind where he wanted to be in his search for the lass. It had been more than two hours ago when he and Tremayne had decided to divide and conquer—agreeing they would be able to cover far more ground that way and hopefully find Melinda. He hoped to God the former dragoon was making better progress than he was. At this rate, the leads were growing cold.

He swore as he came up against another dead end. The raw feeling in his gut was not a good sign. Time to reevaluate what had happened in the last twenty-four hours. Going over everything he knew—and had found out from the duke's stable lad and the hiring agencies Mrs. O'Toole had suggested to Melinda—he realized he had to go back further, to the night they'd rescued Melinda.

He fought to keep his anger in check as it surged through his veins. He knew for a certainty where the lass was. "That bloody, buggering bastard has her!"

Vaulting onto his horse, Garahan gave him his head. They slowed whenever they came to a busy intersection or thoroughfare blocked with the dearth of carriages.

Bloody waste of time, he thought as they paused to let a carriage go by. The quality would soon be standing around in groups, sipping champagne, and discussing how dull their lives had become, while spreading rumors that had no truth to them. Now that King and Coventry had the information he needed, they could put a stop to the vile rumors. He looked forward to confronting the baron with the information he knew Huggleston would uncover for them—after the lass was safe.

If his gut wasn't telling him something had happened to the lass, he'd be on Corkendale's doorstep right now—despite convincing the man's footman to leave his employ and work for the duke. He'd drag the bastard baron to Bow Street so King could interrogate the man. But his gut was never wrong—the lass needed him. He had to find her!

Halfway to the tavern, Tremayne caught up with him. "What kept ye?" Garahan asked.

"I received a missive from Coventry—"

Garahan interrupted, "About Corkendale?"

Tremayne shook his head. "A lieutenant I used to serve with. Cameron's his name. He's been in talks with Coventry about joining the captain's growing force of retired, injured military men."

"If that's all," Garahan bit out, "save it for later."

"Garahan—"

He didn't want to hear what Tremayne had to say, so he kept talking. "I've got to get to the tavern to save the lass!"

"But Coventry said—"

"Even if she doesn't want me to. By all that's holy, I'm saving her...again!"

"Bloody hell, Garahan!"

He finally glanced over at the man riding alongside him. He should be telling Tremayne about his meeting with the baron's footman, but his gut was shouting that Melinda was in trouble. He was frustrated that he couldn't haul off and club the dragoon in the face—Tremayne would no doubt return the favor, and they'd be no closer to rescuing the lass. "What's got yer smallclothes in a twist, Tremayne?"

"Either shut up, or go off on a wild goose chase, while *I* save Miss Waring."

Garahan abruptly pulled back on the reins. His horse snorted in reaction. "Where is she?"

"Not far from where Coventry lives."

The pair turned around and rode toward the building on the corner of Hart and Lumley. It wasn't run-down, by any means. On the fringes of the wealthier part of London, those who were able to carve out a decent living and support their families lived there.

Riding down Hart Street, Tremayne pointed. "That building," he said. "The one on the corner."

They came to a stop in front of the building, quickly dismounted, and tied their horses to the hitching post.

"The windows are all dark," Garahan said.

Tremayne nudged him with his elbow. "There's a faint light in that window—on the third floor."

Garahan tried the door and found it locked. Urgency had him pounding on the door with his fist, hoping against hope that Melinda was indeed somewhere inside the building. But was she being held against her will, or had she entered of her own volition?

"Did ye get the address wrong, or is Coventry's information wrong?" Garahan asked.

Tremayne shoved him out of the way. "When has the captain's information *ever* been wrong?" He knocked once, paused, knocked once, paused again, before giving two sharp raps. The door swung open, and a bear of a man equal in width to Tremayne—and Garahan's O'Malley cousins—stood frowning at them.

He locked gazes with Tremayne before glaring at Garahan. "Didn't yer *máthair* teach ye how to knock politely?"

"I don't have time to be polite," Garahan told him. "I'm searching for a lass who I believe has run into trouble."

"Are ye?" Glancing at Tremayne, the Scotsman gave a slight nod before asking Garahan, "What brings ye to my door?"

Garahan's Irish was up, and he ignored the Scotsman's question. "Her name's Melinda Waring. She stands about five feet eight, dark brown hair, and eyes the color of a just-turned field in early spring."

The man fell silent, irritating the hell out of Garahan.

"Have ye seen the lass?"

"If ye answer my question, I'll answer yers."

Garahan curled his hands into tight fists then slowly uncurled them. He could punch the man...after he had the information he needed. "I'm searching for the lass. She'd been under me protection until she got a maggot in her brain to leave without saying goodbye, or saying where she'd be going."

"I'd be interested in why the lass left yer protection. Was it something ye said...or did?"

Garahan shoved the man back into the building. "I don't have time for questions. I'll see for meself if Melinda is here."

The Scotsman grabbed the back of Garahan's frockcoat. Garahan never buttoned his coat, so he simply shifted one shoulder and then the other. The other man was left staring at the hand that held

Garahan's coat.

"Come back here!" he roared, chasing after Garahan, who'd already reached the door to the staircase and thundered up the steps.

"Melinda! Are ye here, lass?"

MELINDA'S MOUTH DROPPED open. When James called her name a second time, she shot to her feet as the door burst open. "James?"

He rushed toward her and jolted to a stop. "Dear God, lass, who did this to ye?"

Melinda was so relieved that he had come in answer to Alasdair's missive that she couldn't find her voice. She was afraid if she tried to speak, it would be inaudible.

He took a step closer and brushed the tip of his finger along the curve of her cheek. "Tell me his name, and I'll make the man pay for hurting ye."

Alarm filled her at the thought. He stood before her with two black eyes and a swollen nose, and he was ready to track down whoever had hurt her and make them pay? "No one," she finally answered.

"Ye cannot protect yer cousin, if he's the blackguard who injured ye. I still owe the man a beating for whipping ye and trying to force ye to…"

Thank goodness he didn't finish what she suspected he was about to say. Just the mention of it curdled the second dose of the herbal draught she'd had. She ignored the roiling in her belly, refusing to retch the foul-tasting herbal. She knew Michaela would stand over her until she finished another dose—and kept it down.

"I take it you are Mr. Garahan."

Melinda admired Michaela's calm. It soothed her, and obviously had an effect on James. She watched him look at her savior and hoped he would not discount the petite woman standing by a table on the other side of the room.

"Just Garahan, if ye please, ma'am. And who might you be?"

"Miss Michaela," she answered. "I'm so glad you've come. Miss Waring did not believe you would."

He turned and stared at Melinda, demanding, "And why they hell not?"

Melinda shrugged and had to pause to take deep breaths, waiting for the pain in her shoulder to subside. When she could breathe normally again, she looked at James. The play of emotions on his face soothed the worst of her worry. She could not explain the unreasonable fear that he would come to find her only to leave her later. Why *had* he come?

From his expression, he was frustrated—not angry. She knew the man needed answers.

She'd start with the easier ones. "I left when you and Emmett were arguing."

"Why?" Hurt flashed in the depths of his dark brown eyes for a second.

"You had already done so much for me," Melinda answered. "I didn't want you to feel responsible for me."

"But I do feel responsible for ye, lass. The first time I entered the tavern, I knew ye needed protecting. I want to be the man to protect ye."

She could not hold his gaze. The intensity in his eyes confused her. Was it her imagination, or was it desire that she'd seen a heartbeat before? Embarrassed to even think it, given the weak leg she'd struggled to hide since childhood, she said, "I can manage on my own."

"'Tis yer pride talking," he told her. "What about me offer? Do ye not think me pride suffered a blow after ye turned me down flat?" The man did not give her a chance to respond before continuing, "Yet here

I am, ready to bring ye back to the duke's town house. What will it take for ye to come with me? Shall I promise ye work?"

Her tongue got tangled at the glimpse of emotion swirling in his dark gaze.

"I'll not badger ye to accept the protection of me name," Garahan said, "as yer pride won't let ye."

Tears welled up and spilled over.

"Ah, lass, forgive me for speaking harshly, when ye've been through so much since last I saw ye. Tell me what happened to ye."

The door behind them opened, and Tremayne and Cameron entered.

She sighed, and then confessed, "I jumped out of a carriage."

His eyes rounded in surprise, and she noticed Tremayne was shaking his head.

"Aye, the plucky lassie jumped out of a moving carriage," Alasdair said. "'Tis how she bruised her ribs, and her arm, and pulled her shoulder out of the socket."

Garahan and Tremayne winced. "I can guess who forced ye into the carriage," Garahan said.

"Your cousin," Tremayne said.

She nodded.

"Where did he find you?" Tremayne asked.

She had to force herself to look away from Garahan to answer. "The cook at Baron Corkendale's town house had just rushed me out the back door. She told me it wasn't safe to stay...that I had to leave immediately. I made my way along the side of the house and waited until I heard the front door closing. I thought it was the baron who had left, and that it would be safe to step onto the sidewalk."

Garahan stiffened. "Yer cousin was waiting to grab ye, wasn't he?"

Her stomach ached at the memory of his painful grip. "He grabbed hold of my wrist and pulled me into a hackney. I tried to get him to release me...but he was too strong." The black look on Garahan's face had her trembling, though she knew it wasn't directed at her. "When he started threatening me with entertaining his customers, I waited for the carriage to slow down, grabbed the handle, opened the door, and jumped."

"Ye've either got the heart of a warrior, or ye've lost every bit of common sense ye were born with, lass."

Michaela chose that moment so speak. "Mr. Garahan, I'd like to introduce you to my right hand, Alasdair Cameron."

The Scotsman glared at him, and Garahan grumbled, "We've met."

"You should be grateful he was here with me when I pulled Miss Waring to safety," Michaela said. "Lieutenant Cameron served in the King's Royal Dragoons, and is an accomplished healer. He realigned her shoulder. It would have taken me twice as long to do so—and that would only have added to Miss Waring's pain."

Garahan blew out a huff of impatience and held out his hand to Cameron. "Ye have me eternal thanks, Cameron." When the Scotsman shook his hand, Garahan added, "If ye ever need anything— someone to guard yer back, a family member or friend in need—ye've but to ask. I'll be there."

The Scotsman nodded once before releasing Garahan's hand. As their hands dropped to their sides, he said, "I'm thinking the lassie isn't convinced ye want to marry her for more than protection. Then again, the Irish were always a bit slow in the head when it comes to women." Garahan took a menacing step toward Cameron, who held a hand up in front of him. "The lassie has seen, and suffered, enough violence in the last few hours. Soften yer tone, and mind yer words, or we'll be taking this discussion out back."

The man's words must have had their desired effect. Garahan fell silent. Melinda hoped he would get control of his temper. She did not fear James, but the sharp edge of his words made her uncomfortable. He was nothing like her cousin, who used a verbal assault first, then the physical. James would never treat her that way or raise a hand to her.

She was about to say as much when he said, "The last time I let me pride take hold of me brain, I ended up with a noose around me neck."

Shock stole her breath. She couldn't seem to exhale the breath she'd just drawn in.

"Breathe, lassie!"

Alasdair's words penetrated her fear, as those same words had earlier when he was putting her shoulder back in the socket. This time, too, she did as he bade her. When she could speak again, she asked, "What happened?"

"'Tis a tale for another time, and one I'll only be telling me bride, as she'll be the only one I'd trust to hold me heart in her hands," James said.

Melinda felt the warmth of his words wash over her. The desire in his eyes, and the sincerity of his words, called to her. How could she condemn the man she deeply cared for, by allowing him to marry her? A woman who had such a huge imperfection—a permanent limp— that others noticed, and discussed, much to her dismay. Her heart sank. She could not do that to James.

"Are ye done having a conversation with yerself, lass?"

She looked up and locked gazes with James. "How did you know what I was doing?"

"'Tis plain as day, and the expressions on yer face give it away."

Taking her uninjured arm, he helped her to sit. He went down on one knee beside her and said, "Lass. If I've held back what I was feeling for ye, it was to spare yer feelings. I'll not have ye thinking 'twas only yer face and form that I was attracted to."

"Face and form?" She couldn't credit that he would even think such a thing. "What about my crooked leg? Surely you noticed my limp."

His engaging smile had her staring at his lips.

"I confess, I wasn't looking at yer limp, lass."

She watched the words form, and heard him speak, but could not quite believe she'd *heard* him. Had she wished it to the point where she imagined words he had not said? Confusion filled her, and she sought to separate the truth from longing. "It is very pronounced, especially after a long day on my feet. What else could you be looking at?"

Tremayne snorted, and Cameron chuckled, then just as quickly fell silent.

Garahan sighed. "Ye're going to make me say it, lass, in front of those two *eedjits*?"

"Never mind," Melinda said. "Maybe I'm not ready to hear."

He reached for her hand, brought it to his lips, and pressed a featherlight kiss to the back of it. "Lass, me heart recognized ye the moment ye walked toward me with a smile on yer angel's face and kindness in yer eyes. I was in the tavern to gather information—not find the other half of me heart."

Wonder mixed with hesitation. "The other half?" She had to tell James what was in her heart, afraid that if she didn't, she'd never have another chance.

Swallowing against the tight feeling in her throat, she whispered, "When you smiled at me, a shiver raced from my toes all the way to my nose. My heart was beating so fast, I thought I would faint. I could not let you see how you affected me, because I did not believe that you would ever be interested in someone like me."

"I'm more than interested in someone like you, lass. I want ye to be me wife—not just for the protection of me name, but to share a life with ye. A future...mayhap children. I want to see yer smile when the sun rises, and when it sets, for the rest of me days."

She never dreamed someone as handsome, courageous, and caring as James would offer for her hand. Truth be told, she'd never thought *anyone* would want her. But did she have the right to saddle the poor man with her imperfections?

Her heart urged her to accept his proposal, and not to turn him down a second time. Her head urged her to be cautious, to compromise. "Do I have to answer you right away? May I think about it?"

He held her hand to his heart. The wild pounding told her that his calm exterior hid his uncertainty. Lifting her hand to his lips once more, he turned it over and brushed a kiss to the inside of her wrist, where her own pulse beat a rapid rhythm that matched his own.

"I beg yer pardon for asking ye without thought to how much pain ye must be in, lass. I'll not withdraw me question, so worry not. But I warn ye now, I'll only be asking ye one more time. Nothing will change me mind then," he warned her. When she stared at him, he added, "Not even if yer eyes fill with longing for me, like they are now—and well they should."

She started to tell him that she did not long for him, but knew it would be a lie. He saved her from the falsehood by holding up a hand. She closed her mouth.

"I won't be moved to change me mind, though I know yer heart skips a beat at the sight of me handsome self. Ye can throw yerself into me arms, and beg me to forgive ye—which ye should, but I'll only grant ye one more time to accept me heart and me love."

He rose to his feet, and still she found herself unable to speak. Her emotions were rioting inside of her as his gaze held hers. His words had her questioning her need to think over his proposal, when her heart desperately wanted to accept it!

Garahan bowed to Michaela. "Thank ye for taking care of the lass. If ye find ye have need of a strong back, or of me protection, or that of me cousins, ye have but to ask."

Michaela smiled. "I have heard bits and pieces about the duke's guard through Alasdair. Through his contact with the captain, I know that Captain Coventry holds you and your family in the highest regard. I will be more than happy to add you to a very select few whom I count on in times of need."

She held out her hand to James, and Melinda watched him take it and bow over it. The relief that speared through her, upon noting James did not kiss Michaela's hand, surprised her. She could not recall ever feeling jealous of another woman in her life.

James's gaze met hers over the top of Michaela's head. From his knowing smile, she knew James saw and understood the emotion slithering inside of her, squeezing her heart. She sighed. The man had the answer he sought.

She had fallen in love with the aggravatingly arrogant, exceedingly handsome, kind, and protective man—the duke's hammer!

CHAPTER TWENTY

C AMERON ARGUED WITH Garahan, and in the end, Garahan gave in to let the Scotsman hire a hackney so as not to add to Melinda's injuries on the ride back to Grosvenor Square.

"I'll be riding in the carriage and holding the lassie in me arms to keep her from moving about," Cameron said. "Some of these hack drivers are ham-handed and don't know a horse's head from its *arse*."

Garahan saw red, and was about to speak when the other man's eyes twinkled with laughter. He calmed enough to tell him, "*I'll* be the one riding in the carriage with Miss Waring."

"What about your horse?" the Scotsman asked.

"I'll be leaving me horse here," Garahan answered. "I'll send someone by to collect it for me."

With that matter settled, Cameron left to hail the hackney, while Michaela discussed the instructions the Scotsman had obviously gone over in detail with Melinda earlier. Mayhap when he was realigning her shoulder. Just the thought of it had agony ripping through Garahan. He'd separated his own shoulder years ago, and he hoped to never have to suffer through the like again.

Brave lass, he thought, watching the way she listened to the much smaller woman with respect and awe. He'd make a point of speaking to Coventry about Miss Michaela—who had not divulged her last name—and her good works. He doubted her family knew she rescued women off the streets or London—or that she had a fierce protector in the former soldier in the King's Dragoons. Mayhap her father knew and had arranged for her protector.

The connection between Captain Coventry and the men of the duke's guard was strong. Their vow to protect the duke and his family was their bond. His brothers and cousins shared an overriding need to protect the innocents of this world with Coventry. All agreed that they would champion the less fortunate from those who were wealthier, of a higher station in society, and sought to wield their power over those they felt were beneath them.

Finally, Melinda and Michaela finished their conversation. Miss Michaela handed Garahan a small bag. When he accepted it, the scent of crushed herbs filled his nostrils. "Mrs. O'Toole has similar herbs in her medicinal stores."

"Mrs. O'Toole?" Michaela asked.

"The duke's cook has been doctoring our lesser injuries since we hired on to work for the duke."

"What about more serious ones, like Miss Waring's?"

"Me cousin, Emmett O'Malley, has the gift of healing. If he cannot help ye, ye'd best be praying until the physician arrives."

Melinda added, "Mr. O'Malley was the one who tended to my back." She glanced at Garahan for a moment, then away.

"From what me cousin told me," Garahan added, "the poor lass suffered a terrible beating. Since her wounds went untended, they festered."

Michaela's brow furrowed. "You are lucky that you had them tended to, Miss Waring. The poisons from an infection could spread through one's body. You could lose a limb—or your life!"

"Another cousin, Sean O'Malley, nearly lost an arm months ago to a knife wound that flayed him open to the bone." A glance at the lass had him realizing the topic was upsetting her. "I'll be thanking ye again, Miss Michaela, and remind ye to send word if ye need me."

"I will, thank you, Mr. Garahan."

"Just Garahan," he reminded her.

Tremayne bowed to Miss Michaela, bade her goodbye, and led the way downstairs. "Wait here," he told Garahan. "I'll see if Cameron has managed to find a hack. They're usually busy this time of night."

"Aren't most people at home and settling in for the evening?" Melinda asked.

Tremayne and Garahan shared a brief look before Tremayne answered, "Unless you're a member of the *ton* and moving on to the next entertainment on your calendar for the evening."

Melinda seemed surprised by his answer. "How many could you possibly attend in one night?"

"More than I'd have the stomach for," Garahan admitted. "There's Cameron now."

The door opened, and the Scotsman motioned them outside. Frowning at Garahan, he murmured, "Best hold tight to the lassie," he warned. "Dinna let her arm or shoulder bump into anything, or ye'll undo what Miss Michaela and I did for her."

"Ye have me word, Cameron." When he nodded, Garahan added, "Ye know where to find me if Miss Michaela—or yerself—have need of me."

"Aye. Best get moving—the lassie is near to dropping with exhaustion and pain. She'll need another dose of the herbal I asked Michaela to send home with you."

"I'll see to it," Garahan said. Looking down at Melinda, he was mesmerized by the way the lantern light highlighted her beauty. The lass had no idea as to her appeal. Clearing his throat, he added, "I'll make certain she drinks every drop."

Cameron inclined his head. "Go. Quickly now!"

"Ye'll see to me horse until—"

"God save me from Irishmen who never know when to shut up!"

Tremayne snorted with laughter, while Garahan thought about

getting one quick jab in, but the small hand on his forearm had him reconsidering. Now was not the time. He had to get the lass back where she belonged, where he and Emmett could watch over her—at least until she decided to accept his proposal and marry him.

Bloody hell—she'd best be answering him soon. The wait would mess with his concentration, and he could not allow that to happen.

He gently lifted her into his arms, holding her securely, but not so tight as to cause her pain, and carried her over to the hackney where Tremayne stood, holding the door for them. "I'll be riding behind you," the lieutenant said.

Garahan nodded, leaned into the carriage, and gently set the lass on the seat. He joined her, settling her in his arms once more. When she shivered, he eased her head beneath his chin. He nodded to Tremayne, who closed the door and tapped on the carriage.

Cradling the lass close, he wondered why she refused his offer. Could she not see the depth of his feelings for her?

She sighed and relaxed in his arms. The soft sound of her breathing as it slowed had him admitting—silently—that his feelings went as deep as they could go.

He loved the lass.

CHAPTER TWENTY-ONE

ANGER FLASHED IN Emmett's eyes as he rushed over to the hackney. "Dear God in Heaven! Lass, what happened to ye?"

Garahan was grateful for his cousin's reaction—it would add fuel to his plans to make her cousin pay. He'd be discussing it with Emmett after the lass was settled in. He stepped down from the carriage and, with an intense look, told his cousin, "Later."

Emmett held the door while Garahan leaned inside the coach to gently lift Melinda into his arms. "I beg yer pardon now, in case I accidentally jostle ye, lass. 'Tisn't me intention."

Her gaze met his, and he knew she was suffering, though she hadn't complained. "It cannot be helped," she said. "I understand."

He wanted to clench his fists in anger. Yell at her for leaving the safety of the duke's town house. Demand she promise never to leave without being accompanied by one of the duke's guard. He glanced down at the woman he held to his heart and cursed beneath his breath.

She immediately apologized.

"Don't," he warned.

"Don't what? Apologize for your having to rescue me again, when I'm certain you have other duties to attend to?"

He bit back what he wanted to say. Harsh words spoken in the heat of frustration and temper would not undo what the lass had suffered since she left his protection. His ma's voice whispered in his head, *"Let the past be. Regrets only sour the stomach. Search yer heart and do what's right—'twill have an effect on the future."*

He tore his gaze away before he gave in to the temptation of Melinda's sweet lips.

Emmett stepped around him to open the side door to the building. "Jenkins!"

Melinda jolted, then moaned. Garahan's heart ached for the pain she must be in. "We'll fix ye right up with the herbal Michaela sent along. Ye'll see. It'll set you to rights, lass."

Then he'd hunt down her cousin and thrash the man within an inch of his life. If the bastard hadn't grabbed her off the street in front of Corkendale's town house, this never would have happened.

If she'd trusted Garahan and stayed put, she'd never have been at Corkendale's residence in the first place!

Jenkins moved quickly for a man of his years. His face expressionless, his posture erect, the duke's butler took control of the situation, as he had on so many occasions since Garahan and his kin had joined the duke's household.

Jenkins turned to the footman who followed in his wake. "Alert Mrs. O'Toole and Mrs. Wigglesworth that Miss Waring has been found and is gravely injured."

"Jenkins?" Mrs. Wigglesworth called out, approaching them. "What has hap—Oh, you poor dear." The housekeeper's flash of concern was immediately replaced with a serene expression.

Garahan knew with the duke's most trusted servants in charge, the lass would be tucked into a comfortable bed and cared for.

Between Emmett and himself, they would see to it that she would have protection—around the clock. The hell with whatever else happened. His sole focus was threefold: protecting the lass, hunting down her cousin, and flushing out Corkendale to end his attack against the duke's family.

The problem was immediately obvious—he couldn't be in three

places at one time. He'd have to ask for help.

"Bring her upstairs—" Mrs. Wigglesworth began.

"Can I please stay in the room off the pantry?" Melinda interrupted. "It was just down the hallway from the kitchen, where I was out of the way. Besides, it wouldn't be seemly for me to be in one of His Grace's guest rooms." When neither the housekeeper or Garahan answered, she added, "Please?"

"Did anyone ever tell ye that ye drive a man to drink?" Garahan asked.

She bit her lip, and he worried that she'd think he was upset with her... Well, he was, but he had to remember not to startle the lass—she needed gentling. "I was just teasing ye, lass. Don't mind me odd sense of humor."

"All of the Garahans have a queer sense of what is funny," Emmett told her as he opened the door to the servants' side of the duke's town house. "The rest of the family try not to hold it against them."

Garahan grunted as he walked past his cousin. There wasn't anything he could say to counter Emmett's words, so he bent his head and whispered, "Ignore me cousin. Aunt Eileen dropped him on his head when he was a babe."

"I heard that. Ye'll be swallowing yer words later," Emmett promised.

"I'd like to see ye try," Garahan challenged.

"What's all the commotion?" Mrs. O'Toole's eyes widened. Taking in the situation, she motioned for Garahan to take Melinda back to the tiny room off the pantry. "I changed the bedding and restocked the herbs and linens earlier. I'll just whip up an herbal that will keep her fever at bay."

Garahan looked over his shoulder to frown at Emmett, who followed them. "We don't need yer help."

Emmett glared at him. "Shut yer gob."

"Gentlemen," Mrs. O'Toole warned.

Garahan sent his cousin a look that promised they'd be settling this later. "Miss Michaela and Mr. Cameron helped Miss Waring after she'd been injured—they sent a bag of herbs to be made into a draught." He paused to take the bag of herbs Michaela had given him from his pocket. "Smells familiar—like the herbs ye use."

She opened the bag and sniffed. Nodding, she handed it to Emmett, who did the same before handing it back to her. "I've got the kettle on and will prepare this for you, Melinda. I'm afraid it's back to your invalid's diet. Nothing too heavy in your stomach for the next few days."

Garahan heard and approved. "Promise that ye'll stay while ye heal?"

Melinda sighed before answering, "I will."

"Promise," Garahan grumbled.

"I promise," she said.

"Fine, then. Are ye wanting to sit up so ye can have the herbal first, and then the broth, bread, and calves' foot jelly?"

She winced, and he wondered if it was from the pain—or the thought of calves' foot jelly.

"I would, thank you, James."

He set her on the chair in the small room, grabbed the quilt from the cot, and tucked it around her legs. When she shivered, he slipped off his frockcoat—glad he'd remembered to snatch it back from the Scotsman—and laid it across her shoulders, mindful of her injuries. "Better?"

She smiled at him—a weary smile, but a smile all the same. "Yes. Thank you, James. I'm grateful that you answered Michaela's missive."

"Actually, 'twas from Cameron."

"Would you have come," she asked, "if it was from a woman?"

"What in blazes do ye think?" he demanded.

"Ye'll lower yer voice, and speak in a respectful tone," Emmett warned, "or I'll ban ye from the sickroom."

"I'd like to see ye try."

Emmett drew in a deep breath, squared his shoulders, and assumed what Garahan recognized as his cousin's battle stance—on the balls of his feet, ready to spring into action.

Garahan did not want to tangle with Emmett in front of the lass. He planned to do that later—without witnesses. "Fine, then. Begging yer pardon, Melinda."

"Miss Waring," Emmett reminded him.

The need to whack his cousin in the back of the head had Garahan's hand curling into a fist before he reined in his temper and repeated his apology. "Begging yer pardon, *Miss Waring.*"

She looked from Garahan to Emmett and back to Garahan before replying, "You are forgiven."

"Here we are." Mrs. O'Toole bustled into the room with a small tray. She placed it on the long table beneath the shelving and handed Melinda a small mug. "Drink every drop."

Watching the delicate way Melinda's lips met the rim of the mug carved a hole in his gut. When she licked the drop of herbal from her bottom lip, he had to dig deep to keep from moaning aloud.

From the worry in the lass's eyes, he knew she had no idea the effect she had on him. An innocent—who'd nearly been violated *twice* now. Garahan had a feeling that her cousin's greed would not allow the man to let her go without one last try. He had encountered men like Melinda's cousin too many times to count over the years. His kind had only one religion—a leather purse filled with coins.

Garahan wished he could have been the one to see to the lass's every need, but he was not the one with the gift for healing. Emmett was. What he needed to do was to gain the lass's complete trust. For some convoluted reason, she did not believe he would be interested in her. Some blather about her limp and not being good enough for him. He'd have to go slowly, and show her with his actions...and his words.

She'd come around. She had to. He wouldn't be taking no for an answer when he asked her to be his bride for the third and final time.

"I need to have a word with Emmett, lass. Will ye be all right if I leave ye in Mrs. O'Toole's care?"

Fear flashed in the depths of her warm brown eyes, but she didn't hesitate to answer, "I'll be fine. Thank you, James."

He bowed to her, which seemed to surprise her. "I may have to leave for a short while, but ye'll be protected."

Her eyes held his for long moments before she said, "Be careful."

"Always, lass. Rest now."

With that, he and Emmett left.

As soon as they were out of earshot, Garahan said, "We'll send word to Coventry."

"Aye," Emmett agreed. "He has one or two men that can look into the situation at the tavern."

Garahan inclined his head. "And whatever he can discover about the lass's family." He stopped short. "Bloody hell."

"What?" Emmett asked.

"I never asked the name of the village where she'd been living with her stepfather."

"Do ye want me to go back and ask?"

Garahan would rather be the one to speak to her, but knew she'd be a distraction when he needed to keep his head on straight and focus on his duty to the duke.

"Aye. That might be best."

Emmett must have sensed the turmoil Garahan hoped he'd hidden, as he asked, "Why don't ye ask Jenkins to send a message to the viscount and another to the earl, letting them know we have proof Corkendale is behind the rumors?"

"Shouldn't we wait until Coventry and King wrap the culprit up in a bow and toss him in a cell at Newgate?" Garahan asked.

"Ye know they're liable to appear on the doorstep—with their wives and babes following along behind them."

Garahan frowned. "Ye're right. We'll need to ask King to supply a few men to Sussex to add to their protection."

Emmett paused with his hand to the door. "If their ladyships were to come to London—babes in their arms—they'd be accompanied by their maids."

"And personal guards," Garahan finished. "Like as not, the earl will have a plan for something like this. Leaving Sean O'Malley in charge at Lippincott Manor. Your brother, Dermott, and me brother, Aiden, would escort Lady Aurelia, her babe, and her maid."

"The viscount would have arranged for Michael O'Malley to stay behind," Emmett said, "leaving Seamus Flaherty to do the same with Lady Calliope, her babe, and her maid—Mary Kate Donovan."

The way Emmett said Mary Kate's name put Garahan's back up. "And well I know it. 'Tisn't a problem as far as I see it, unless the women don't travel in the same carriage."

"After the last time their ladyships chased after the viscount when he went to London to fight that duel, do you honestly think they would travel alone?"

Garahan thought about it for a moment—still perturbed that his cousin would suggest that having Mary Kate show up in London would be a problem. He could handle her if she arrived.

He hoped Seamus had spoken to the lass about the feelings his cousin carried for her—and had since he'd rescued the lass from the overturned coach.

"Ye worry about getting the name of the village from the lass," Garahan said. "Let me worry about handling things if—and when—their ladyships arrive with their babes in arms."

The men parted, each holding out hope that the women they'd protected off and on since being hired to work for the duke would listen to reason and do as they were told.

Garahan was still holding on to that hope that night when the earl and the viscount arrived on horseback.

CHAPTER TWENTY-TWO

GARAHAN GAVE ONE sharp, shrill whistle and waited for his cousin to appear. Emmett burst out of the side door to the duke's town house, ready to attack—or defend. The cousins and their brothers had learned that skill at a young age.

When it was evident they were not under attack, Emmett joined Garahan on the sidewalk. Watching two men riding toward them on horseback, he groaned. "Their lordships."

"Aye," Garahan agreed. "And ye know what that means."

"We should expect their ladyships in a few hours' time."

Garahan's gut was never wrong. "Where one goes...trouble follows. If our luck runs high, mayhap they'll be arriving tomorrow."

Emmett grinned. "'Twill be grand to see their ladyships. It has been some time."

"'Tisn't a social visit," Garahan grumbled. "They'll be following along behind their husbands because of their odd notion that only they can protect them."

Emmett crossed his arms in front of him and nodded. "They have been a help in the past."

Garahan snorted. "Help? Are ye out of yer mind? They made our job of protecting Lord Coddington, and the viscount, nearly impossible when they showed up at the duel thinking to *help*."

"As I wasn't at the duel between Coddington and Chellenham, I couldn't say for certain," Emmett admitted. "Ye have to admit, their hearts are always in the right place."

"God save us from well-intentioned females."

He stared at Garahan. "I'm thinking he's placed one directly in yer path, cousin. Best ye be certain to treat her well, boy-o, or ye'll answer to me."

Garahan fought the need to punch Emmett in the face, and conquered it, as the viscount and the earl reined in and dismounted in front of them. "Yer lordships," he greeted them. "What brings ye to London?"

"Lack of information," the viscount answered.

"Answers," the earl replied.

"Bugger it," Garahan whispered to Emmett, who coughed to cover up the fact that he was laughing.

The earl narrowed his eyes at Emmett as he strode toward him. "I heard that."

Garahan elbowed his cousin in the side. While Emmett was rubbing the spot, Garahan asked the question that needed to be asked—and answered: "How long before their ladyships arrive?"

The viscount glowered at him, then sighed, admitting, "You know them too well. I suspect they overheard Lippincott and I discussing our plans to leave and were packed and ready to follow behind us shortly after we rode out."

"Ah, so we do not have another day before they arrive, then," Emmett said.

"Mayhap hours?" Garahan asked.

The earl sighed. "Knowing how determined Aurelia and Calliope can be when they set their minds to something—"

"Hours," the viscount interrupted.

The front door opened with a flourish and Jenkins emerged. "Your lordships! Wonderful to see you. Let's get you settled. That will give us time to prepare extra rooms for the rest of your party."

The earl walked over to the duke's butler. "Thank you, Jenkins. My wife will undoubtedly arrive with our son and her maid."

The viscount joined him, adding, "Mine will be arriving with our son and her maid as well."

Garahan and Emmett brought up the rear, with Garahan mumbling, "They'd best have three or four outriders accompanying them."

"And arrive in *one* coach," Emmett added.

The viscount and the earl entered the town house, handing over their top hats, overcoats, and gloves to Jenkins.

Mrs. Wigglesworth approached the two lords with a beaming smile on her face. "Welcome, your lordships! Are we to expect their ladyships to arrive as well?"

"No doubt they will ignore our demand that they remain in Sussex," the viscount answered.

"Do we need to ask one of the footmen to bring down a second cradle from the attic to put in the nursery?" the earl asked the housekeeper.

"Their Graces insisted we have four cradles in the nursery at all times," Mrs. Wigglesworth answered. "They know what close friends their ladyships are and suspected they would be traveling together more often than not. If Their Graces are in residence, it would save time—and the footmen from carting the cradles up and down the attic stairs."

"Thick as thieves," Emmett murmured to Garahan.

"I heard that," the earl said.

Garahan noted the earl sounded as resigned as the viscount when discussing their wives.

"If there is nothing else," Mrs. Wigglesworth said, "I'll see to your rooms and have two others prepared. Do you think your wives would prefer to have their maids nearby, or shall I have rooms readied in the servants' quarters?"

The earl and viscount shared a look, and the earl replied, "Nearby,

I would think."

"Very good, your lordships." The housekeeper turned to see to their requests.

"Jenkins, would you have hot water sent up for Chattsworth and myself?" the earl asked.

"At once, your lordship. Shall I send Turner as well?"

"Yes, thank you, Jenkins."

"I'll not require the assistance of the duke's valet," the viscount said, "but would appreciate the opportunity to wash off the dust of our travels."

Garahan spoke up. "Shall I send word to Coventry and King that ye wish to meet with them?"

"Aye," the viscount answered.

"As soon as possible," the earl added.

Garahan bowed and left to speak to Jenkins. Two footmen were assigned to deliver the messages to save time.

That chore having been seen to, Garahan stepped into the servants' side of the town house. He had not spoken to Melinda since early morning. He hoped she was resting.

Entering the kitchen, he heard Mrs. O'Toole humming as she pulled a tray of berry tarts out of the oven.

He drew in a deep breath and sighed. "Those smell divine, Mrs. O'Toole."

She smiled as she set the tray on a rack to let them cool. She brushed her hands on her apron and asked, "Is there anything you need, James?"

"I thought I'd take a bit of tea and maybe a scone or two to the lass."

Mrs. O'Toole beamed at him. "I think she's a bit lonely—with her movement restricted and her being a bit on the warm side since midmorning."

Worry grabbed him by the throat. He did not recall if there was a risk of infection and fever when a bone slid out of place. It was usually with a broken bone—especially one that pierced through the skin. "The lass has a fever?"

"A smidge of one, nothing to worry about. She's been drinking the herbal as she promised. Let me prepare a pot of weak tea and add a plate of scones. Will you be joining her?"

"For a quick visit. I'm sure ye've heard by now their lordships arrived and that we'll be meeting with Coventry and King shortly."

"I am preparing their tray now. Captain Coventry prefers cream tarts to berry, and Mr. King will eat any sweet I prepare."

"Mrs. O'Toole, ye're a marvel the way ye look after everyone."

She beamed at him. "It is my job, after all."

"Ah, but ye do it with love, and ye can taste it in every bite of yer baked goods."

"If you think to turn my head with compliments so I'll forgive you for brawling in my kitchen, James, I already have." With a nod at the tray of already cool scones, she told him, "Make sure you wrap the extra scone or two you'll be placing in your pocket. It's extra work washing the crumbs from them."

He felt gratitude for her forgiving nature. Filling a plate, while she prepared the tea, he said, "Ye're a daily reminder of home and me ma, Mrs. O'Toole." He brushed a kiss to her cheek as he took the teapot from her and placed it on the tray along with the pitcher of cream, sugar, cups and saucers, and a plate of scones.

He stared at the pot of raspberry jam and the one with clotted cream long enough to hear the kindly cook huff out a breath. "Fine, then, take the jam and clotted cream, too."

"Thank ye, Mrs. O'Toole."

She shook her finger at him. "Do not let Miss Waring have more than a thimbleful of either, do you hear?"

"Yes, ma'am."

"We are stretching her invalid diet a bit already, giving her scones."

"But you said yourself that the lass needs a bit of sweet with her tea to lift her spirits."

"Off with you!" The cook shooed him out of her kitchen.

As he walked down the hallway, he heard a sound. He paused and shook his head. "Hearing things." As he took another step, he heard it clearly now—someone was sniffling. Was the lass in pain and crying?

Striding toward the room off the pantry, he entered in time to see her wiping her eyes with one hand.

"Are ye in such pain, lass? When was the last time ye had yer herbal?"

⟫⟫⟫⟨⟨⟨

MELINDA LOOKED UP, and the object of her daydreams stood before her in his finely tailored black frockcoat. The embroidered Celtic harp and the word *Eire*—a symbol of his homeland—were prominently placed over his heart.

She wondered how he managed to get through the day without even a speck of dirt on his clothing. The breadth of his chest and shoulders caught her attention, distracting her as he drew in a breath, and they seemed to expand before her eyes.

Garahan set the tray on the table beside her chair and squatted down beside her. "Lass, I cannot help ye if ye do not answer me questions."

Questions? Had he asked her any? "I'm sorry, I was woolgathering. What did you ask me?"

He frowned at her, but repeated his questions.

"No, I'm not. Two hours past."

"Do ye always use an economy of speech when ye're rattled, lass?"

The man saw too much, watched her too closely. Was it part of the close protection he'd promised her, or did he truly care for her?

She took her time answering. "I'm not rattled. I'm tired, my shoulder aches—but no more than it has—and I'm hungry."

He slowly smiled. "Well now. I convinced Mrs. O'Toole to part with a few scones—and a bit of jam and clotted cream. If ye're nice to me, and let me see if yer fever is any higher, I'll be adding a bit of both to yer scone."

Surprised by his claim, she asked, "When haven't I been nice to you, James?"

He took hold of her hand and brought it to his lips. "When ye refused me offer of marriage—twice."

She stiffened. "I only refused you one time—I'm still thinking about your second offer."

"It's been more than a day, lass. Yer lack of answer is as good as a no."

Before she realized his intention, he placed the back of his hand to her forehead. Frowning, he mumbled something. She didn't quite catch what he said but, from the look on his face, was not certain she *wanted* to know.

He rose to his feet and walked over to the table, his confident walk captivating her. His movements measured and sure, he added a splash of cream, and a dash of sugar, to her teacup and handed it to her.

"Thank you, James."

"Me pleasure, lass."

He placed two scones on the small plate, then added a dab of raspberry jam and a dollop of clotted cream on top. "Here ye are. Small bites now, mind?"

She would have thought a man of his size would be clumsy, but the more time she spent in his company, the more she realized her supposition was completely wrong. His strength, size, and economy of movement were masculine and graceful at the same time.

Staring at the plate he'd prepared for her, she nearly wept at the thought of savoring another of Mrs. O'Toole's delectable scones with a cup of tea—even if it was weak tea. But she managed to gain control of her emotions. "Thank you, James. I promise to take my time."

"Small bites."

She sighed. "And take small bites."

"That's it, lass—'tis better to savor the sweets when ye have them."

She took a bite, chewed slowly, swallowed, and closed her eyes. "Mmmm." When she opened them, it was to find James's dark brown ones staring at her mouth. "Have I got jam on my lips?" She licked them.

He looked away, then back, before clearing his throat to answer, "Aye. 'Tis gone now."

She blotted her lips with the linen napkin Mrs. O'Toole had provided. "Aren't you going to drink your tea?"

He picked up the cup—but not the saucer. When he shifted the cup so he cradled it in his hand to drink from it, she realized the teacup handle was much smaller than his fingers. It would be impossible for him to hold it any other way without dropping it—or spilling the tea.

"I know 'tisn't the correct way to hold me cup."

"I wasn't thinking that at all," she assured him. "I was wondering why no one has thought to make the teacup handles larger. Surely you are not the only man who has difficulty holding the handle of your cup."

He grinned. "'Tis a fact I usually don't bother with a cup at all. I prefer using a metal mug—it holds more tea, and I'll only dent it if I drop it."

"I wonder why Mrs. O'Toole didn't offer you one of the mugs she has in the kitchen. She sends the herbal mixture in one."

"I'm thinking she wanted to prepare a special tray for ye, lass. She said ye were feeling a bit lonely." Their eyes met, and he added, "I wish I could spend more time with ye, but I have to see to me duties." He polished off his scones and his tea. Setting his cup down, he told her, "I've a meeting to prepare for."

She looked at him, wishing there was a way she could know for certain he didn't offer marriage to give her the protection of his name. Could he really not be put off by her limp? Her shoulder would be well on the mend in a few days—no chance of it healing twisted, like her leg.

She dipped her head and stared at the floor.

The touch of his fingertip beneath her chin caught her by surprise. "Look at me, lass."

She did as he bade and was surprised by the depth of emotion swirling in his gaze. Admiration, concern, caring—or was it more than caring? Could he truly feel more for her than she thought possible?

"If I had the choice, I'd spend me time here—with ye. Know that. Remember that."

She was about to reply when his lips captured hers, and every thought in her head evaporated like morning mist over the farmers' fields back home.

His lips lingered, as if he were savoring the kiss. Completely lost, she nearly tumbled out of the chair when he ended the kiss, but his quick reflexes prevented her from falling on her face.

"Easy now, lass. Ye'll not be wanting to add a broken nose to the rest of yer injuries."

She looked at the fading bruises on his face. "It hurts something fearful, doesn't it?"

"Aye, lass."

He gathered her teacup, saucer, and plate and returned them to the tray. "I'll take me leave of ye, but promise to return later. I cannot say for sure what time it might be. All depends upon the outcome of our meeting with Coventry and King."

"Did I hear Mrs. O'Toole mention guests?"

"Aye, their lordships arrived a bit ago, and we expect their ladyships later tonight."

Worry tied her belly in knots. "I shouldn't be here."

He stared down at her. "Where else do ye think ye should be?"

"Anywhere but here. I should never have left—"

"Do not for one moment tell me that ye'd rather be back in yer cousin's tavern fighting off—"

She shot to her feet. When she wobbled, he steadied her, holding her waist firmly in his grip. "No! I was going to say Peppering Eye."

"The village where ye lived?"

"Aye. My stepfather was vicar there."

"Well now, that's all right, then. Do ye have any relatives there?"

"No one but my cousin. I think I told you he is my stepfather's nephew."

"I believe ye may have, lass." He loosened his grip. The heat of his hands mesmerized her. She leaned toward him, and he drew her carefully into his embrace. When she melted into his arms, he pressed his lips to the top of her head. "Ye have no idea what ye do to me, lass."

Melinda reveled in his strength, his warmth, as tingles of awareness shot from the top of her head to the soles of her feet. She wished they could stay this way for hours, but knew he had an important meeting to attend. "You're right. I'm afraid I do not."

"When we have more time, I'd be happy to explain it to ye, lass."

The twinkle in his eyes had her wondering just what he intended to explain to her. Mayhap she should ask Mrs. O'Toole. She'd have to mull that thought over. One thing she was certain of: she wanted to spend more time in James's arms, savoring more of his kisses.

She didn't realize she was staring at his mouth until he said, "If ye don't stop staring at me like that, I'll be kissing the breath out of ye."

Her eyes lifted to his. The intensity of his gaze warmed her even more. Unable to resist, she took another peek at his lips. He'd been so gentle when he kissed her. Unable to stop herself, she said, "I don't mind."

"Ye don't mind," he repeated.

"Would you?"

"Faith, lass, ye're killing me."

"I'm sorry, I don't mean to." When he didn't move, she asked, "Would you?"

He stared into her eyes and rasped, "Would I what, lass?"

She blew out a frustrated breath. He had to know what she meant. When he continued to stare at her, she asked, "Would you kiss me? Please?"

He wrapped an arm around her waist, pulled her close, and kissed her with a passion that stole her breath.

When her brain finally cleared, she was sitting in the chair, and he was standing on the threshold. "Ye're a fast learner, lass. But I've a lot to teach ye, as far as kissing me back."

With a nod, he left, taking the tray—and her heart—with him.

CHAPTER TWENTY-THREE

GARAHAN STEPPED THROUGH the door to the main part of the town house just as Jenkins opened the front door to admit Captain Coventry and Gavin King. Emmett joined him, and they walked over to greet the men.

"Has there been a new development?" King asked.

Garahan was about to answer when a deep voice called out from the top of the stairs, "Chattsworth and I are through waiting on tenterhooks in Sussex."

"Aye," the viscount agreed, joining the earl.

"To be direct, Coventry, you are not to send half-messages concerning the safety of our families in the future."

Coventry's expression remained neutral. "And what of your wives' penchant for following after you?"

Garahan answered, "His Grace and yerself have hired an elite guard. We're accustomed to headstrong women…" He paused to bow his head at the earl and the viscount. "Begging yer pardon for me plain speaking." The pair nodded as they descended the staircase and to join the men. "Since the attack on Wyndmere Hall," Garahan continued, "the lot of us expect yer wives—and the duchess and baroness as well—to end up in the thick of things."

"Ye'll recall," Emmett said, "when necessary, we give their ladyships a quarter-hour head start before following them."

"Why a quarter hour?" Lippincott asked.

Garahan shrugged. "It gives them the illusion that they've succeeded in their plans."

"When we catch up to them," Emmett said, "they've had time to think over yer reaction."

"Aye, and then they're grateful to have our protection," Garahan added, "when ye realize they've ignored yer orders."

"Ignored?" Chattsworth asked. "Don't you mean disobeyed?"

Garahan and his cousins snorted with laughter, while Coventry replied, "Having married a strong-willed, wonderful woman, I can answer for the men—they meant ignored."

King cleared his throat to get everyone's attention. "I have something of import to share with your lordships."

"If ye don't mind, yer lordships," Garahan said before turning to King and Coventry, "I suggest moving the discussion to the duke's library."

"I was about to suggest the same," Earl Lippincott announced, leading the way.

Viscount Chattsworth walked beside him and murmured, "Better be worth the aggravation we'll both have to listen to if it involves our wives haring off to Chalk Farm."

"At dawn to protect us from someone attempting to put paid to our accounts," the earl added.

The viscount was about to reply when Coventry said, "I would think that your wives would choose not to make the tedious journey from Sussex with your infant sons and your maids, considering the paraphernalia required to make the journey."

Emmett added, "A trunkful of nappies and extra clothes the babes will not doubt require."

"Astute observation, O'Malley," the earl said. "One would think you have knowledge of infants."

"'Tis a fact I do," Emmett replied. "Me sisters keep writing asking when I'm coming home for a visit."

The earl and the viscount stopped and stared at Emmett as if they'd never seen him before. "Sisters?" the earl asked.

Garahan shook his head. "Do ye mean to tell me ye never mentioned Grainne, Maeve, and Roisin to their lordships?"

Emmett shrugged. "Why would I? They're back home in Ireland."

"Happily wed," Coventry said.

"With infants of their own," King added.

The earl strode toward the library. The viscount matched his steps, asking, "Why didn't we know the O'Malleys have sisters?"

The earl frowned. "My best guess?"

"For a start," the viscount said.

"Ye did not need to know," Garahan answered as he stepped in front of the men and opened the door for them. "After yer lordships."

The earl asked, "Does Jared know you have sisters?"

Garahan shook his head. "'Tis Patrick, Emmett, and their brothers who have the sisters," he answered.

Coventry cleared his throat to get their attention. As one, the group turned to face him. "If you have any further questions about any of the families," he told the earl and the viscount, "I have all of the information on file, but it is not to be common knowledge in order to protect the families."

The earl frowned, and Garahan wondered why the man had not asked the captain in the first place. The fact that Garahan's position within the duke's guard put his family at risk had always been a concern. More so now, as his brothers, cousins, and himself were becoming better and better known in London—on the docks, in the underbelly of London, and among the cream at the top of Society, the bloody *ton*.

"Now then," Coventry continued, "we have confirmed that Baron Corkendale is the person responsible for starting the rumors about your wives." When the viscount opened his mouth to speak, Coventry held up a hand. "King's men and my own are working to get to the bottom of other disturbing information we have uncovered before we bring him in for questioning."

Garahan and his cousin watched the earl and the viscount for their reaction to news that had the duke's guard on high alert.

"Five years past, the previous Baron Corkendale's wife died in a tragic carriage accident that injured the baron," Coventry said.

"Two months ago, the baron perished when he was thrown from his horse." King paused briefly, then continued. "The circumstances were questioned, as the baron was an excellent horseman—and the weather had been clear for days. The baron died without issue. As his cousin's heir, Corkendale immediately stepped forward to assume the title and everything entailed along with it."

"Anything else we need to know?" Emmett asked.

Coventry frowned and told them, "Apparently there was an indiscretion involving a young lady of impeccable reputation. The matter was quickly handled. Corkendale and the lady in question were married over the anvil in Scotland."

"How quickly after the indiscretion?" the earl asked.

"Days," King replied.

"Did they marry before or after he assumed the title?" the viscount asked.

"Before," King answered.

"Garahan and Emmett are working with my men to find evidence and determine if the current baron can be implicated in any way in his cousin's accident, or the accident that claimed his cousin's wife." Coventry told the group, "If there are no further questions, Garahan and Emmett have duties to attend to."

"How in the bloody hell do Chattsworth and I tie in to this mess?" Lippincott asked.

Coventry met the earl's gaze and answered, "One of our contacts at White's chanced to overhear a heated exchange between Corkendale and another lord. Apparently Corkendale was disparaging the good works the duke and duchess have been doing to aid the widows and children of the men who have served in His Majesty's forces. The duke has taken a firm stand in the House of Lords, lobbying for better conditions for those returning home injured in battle—or not at all. His Grace was quoted: 'The families of our fallen heroes should not have to suffer further waiting for monetary aid from the country their husbands and fathers have given their lives for.'"

"My brother is following in our father's footsteps," the earl said, "championing those injured or who have given their lives for king and country. He has worked tirelessly to clear the tarnish our older brother added to the family name during his short tenure as duke."

"As have you, your lordship," Coventry said quietly. "I would venture to say that any man who tries to discredit His Grace either had ties with the previous duke, or has some unknown reason for this verbal attack on your family."

"Most common reasons are greed and jealousy," King added.

When no one had any further questions, Garahan bowed and took his leave. He was leaving those within the duke's town house well guarded. Emmett would have no difficulty increasing the patrols around the town house with the men Coventry had recently hired at the duke's request.

Garahan paused before the door to the servants' side of the house, hesitating, as the need to speak with the lass filled him. Used to denying need when it did not coincide with his duties, he shook his head and continued along the hallway to the side entrance. He stepped outside and nodded to Findley. "I'll be gone for a few hours. O'Malley will be by shortly to go over the increased patrols now that their lordships have arrived."

The guard nodded. "Garahan?"

Garahan stopped and looked over his shoulder, "Aye, Findley?"

"Is it true?"

He turned around and walked back over to stand beside the man. No point in letting their voices carry. "Is what true?"

"That Viscountess Chattsworth and Countess Lippincott will be arriving tonight?"

Garahan raked a hand through his hair. "Aye. Mayhap in a few hours from now, depending on how many times they had to stop—traveling with babes adds to one's journey."

Findley nodded again. "Are the rumors true?"

Garahan growled low in his throat. "What rumors?"

"That their ladyships have tried to interfere at more than one duel and have—"

"Whatever ye heard, pay it no mind," Garahan interrupted. "'Tisn't yer place to question what their ladyships do—or not do. Yer duty is to protect them with yer life, no matter the cost—whether it be to take a lead ball, knife in the back"—he paused, thinking of his cousin Finn O'Malley's recent injuries in the line of duty—"or a rope around yer neck. Ye vowed to protect the duke and his family with yer life. See to it that ye don't let distractions interfere with that vow—or yer duty."

"Aye, Garahan. You have my word."

"I rely on it, Findley." Garahan strode to the stables. Confronting the lass's cousin would have to wait. He had to run down the baron's footman. Huggleston should have more information for him. The footman would tell Garahan all he knew—or he'd end up under the duke's hammer.

CHAPTER TWENTY-FOUR

M ELINDA HEARD EXCITED voices entering the kitchen and wondered if the rest of the guests had arrived. She hated to be incapacitated, and was beyond uncomfortable being in the duke's town house with James somewhere in London, seeing to his duties.

She knew his position with the duke's guard was an important one. From what she'd surmised, and overheard Mrs. O'Toole and Mrs. Wigglesworth saying, all of the men in the duke's guard were crucial to the protection of the duke, his family, and extended family.

Fretting over the prospect of meeting more servants was exhausting, but all she could do was wait...and wonder. The servants traveling with the viscountess and countess were most likely far above her station in life.

Would Mary Kate or Mignonette be among the servants who traveled from Sussex? She felt more insecure by the moment. It was nearly time for Mrs. O'Toole to arrive with the healing herbal.

Stiff from sitting too long in one position, she rose slowly and walked around the room, stretching her legs. Her shoulder ached but, oddly enough, was easier to handle than the pain in her back had been.

Her troubled thoughts had her wondering if her stepfather had known the type of man his nephew had grown into. Would he have forbidden her to accompany him to London to work for him? She sighed. There was no use questioning something she would never have the answer to.

Needing something to do, she straightened the pile of fresh linens on the worktable along the wall. With her hands busy, her mind drifted back in time to her former life—and the loss of her mother and stepfather. Her grief had nearly debilitated her. Had she missed another option open to her because her thoughts were muddled with grief? Could there have been a position somewhere in the village of Peppering Eye that she'd missed because she was consumed with worry, knowing the new vicar and his family were on the way to move into the vicarage—her home for the last fifteen years?

"Melinda. There you are! I've brought you something to nibble on after you take the herbal draught."

She fumbled with the linens and ended up spreading the pile across the tabletop, instead of in the neat stacks she had been hoping to straighten. "Forgive me, Mrs. O'Toole. I was trying to help—not make more work for you."

"Do not worry about it," the cook assured her. "Should you be up and about, rather than sitting?"

"I was getting stiff sitting in one position for so long. I'm steadier than I was earlier, so I didn't think it would be a problem." At least, Melinda hoped it wasn't going to be.

"How thoughtless of me. Forgive me—things got busy all at once with the arrival of Lady Aurelia and Lady Calliope and their sons."

Melinda watched the smile bloom on the older servant's face. "I'm sorry for taking you away from more important duties. Can I help in any way?"

"Not at all, Miss Waring. James asked Mrs. Wigglesworth and myself to look after you, and we are more than happy to do so. Would you like me to send someone down to sit with you?"

"Do you know when James will return?"

Mrs. O'Toole sighed. "I'm never sure when any of the duke's men are returning—they aren't at liberty to discuss their duties or where they are going." She placed the drink, and the small meal of broth, bread, and calves' foot jelly, on the table next to the chair Melinda had vacated. "Do you need to stretch your legs a bit more, or do you think you'll be able to sit down and eat?"

"I think I got the worst of the kinks out." Melinda sat and reached for the drink first, knowing Mrs. O'Toole felt it her duty to wait until the entire mug was empty before returning to the kitchen.

When she drained the cup, the cook smiled. "You have more color in your cheeks. I know you are probably hungry, but we cannot take any chances on upsetting your stomach, given the extent of your injuries."

"I feel better than the first time James brought me here. Don't worry about me. I'll be fine. Just let me know if I can do anything." She paused for a moment, then continued, "I'm probably not much help, since I'll be using one hand instead of two."

"I'll see what I can find to keep you occupied. Are you sure you don't need help eating?"

"I'm sure. Thank you." Melinda waited until Mrs. O'Toole hurried out of the room before she sighed. Staring at the mug and plate beside her, she wondered aloud, "What does it say about me that I'd rather be working my fingers to the bone than sitting on my bottom all day?"

The deep chuckle had her looking over her shoulder.

"That ye've a fine work ethic," Emmett said from where he stood in the doorway. "Are ye feeling better, lass?"

She frowned at him. "Do you think women having a work ethic is humorous?"

"Nay, lass," he said, stepping into the room. "'Twas something else that ye said."

"I thought I was alone, and frankly don't remember anything that I said being funny."

"Well now, when one is alone and speaking their mind, 'tisn't funny, but when someone walks into the room and happens to overhear the choice of working yer fingers to the bone or sitting on yer—"

Thankfully, he didn't finish the statement. Their eyes met, and she wished she could crawl under the table. The heat swept up from her toes. Why couldn't she have kept her mouth shut?

"Don't give it another thought, lass. I won't be telling himself what I overheard. Garahan would take exception to me hearing and remarking on such. He has a short fuse, though, truth be told, his brothers do too."

"Why would he care that I embarrassed myself in front of you?" She was the one who should care.

"Well now, if ye must know, he'd take it personally that ye mentioned a delicate part of yerself within me hearing."

She covered her mouth with one hand to keep from snorting with laughter. "I'm not delicate—surely you've noticed that by now. I've taken a beating, jumped from a moving carriage, and am still standing—well, not at the moment. A delicate woman would not be able to go through what I have and still have this overwhelming need to do something—anything—so she wouldn't feel as if she were adding to Mrs. O'Toole and Mrs. Wigglesworth's duties."

Emmett crossed his arms over his chest, and she could not help but notice that the Garahans and O'Malleys were extremely fit—though wouldn't they have to be to handle the duties she'd heard bits and pieces of? Just the thought of bare-knuckle fighting, being shot, stabbed, and, if the tale could be believed, nearly hanged—the men would have to be in excellent physical condition...like the warriors of old.

"Lass?"

She shook her head. "I'm sorry, I was woolgathering. Did you ask me a question?"

"Nay. I was telling ye not to give it another thought. Ye've landed in the perfect place to recover from yer injuries, with the likes of Mrs.

O'Toole and Mrs. Wigglesworth to look after ye." He grinned. "And meself, if I do say so."

"I am grateful, Emmett. I just feel so useless right now."

"Ye aren't useless—ye're injured. 'Tis a difference. Now then," he said, handing her broth. "Drink up, lass, then have yer bread. I see Mrs. O'Toole's snuck a bit of butter on it. Last I heard, an invalid's diet did not include butter. 'Tis oft times too rich for an uneasy belly."

She set the broth down and reached for the bread. "I have a strong stomach." She bit into the bread, chewed, and sighed. "Delicious."

"Ah, she has a way with bread and pastries. Be certain to eat the calves' foot jelly. It'll cure whatever ails ye. I've got to check in with the lads on patrol, but if ye have need of me, just send word."

"Thank you, Emmett. I will."

He paused in the doorway. "A word of warning, lass, not that ye'll need it—but Mary Kate arrived with the others. I'm thinking she'll be curious to meet ye. I did not want ye to be surprised."

Melinda could not imagine why the woman would want to meet her, other than curiosity. To be honest, she was curious too.

His concerned look surprised her. "Mayhap ye don't remember, James rescued her, too."

"I remember," Melinda said. Unsure what he expected her to say or do, she sipped the broth, thankful that it soothed the tension in her throat.

She'd heard the tale more than once since she arrived—and how pretty Mary Kate was.

He walked back over to where she sat. "Whatever ye heard, if it was from anyone other than James or meself, I wouldn't worry over it."

Unable to stop herself, she blurted out, "I heard she is very pretty."

"Looks aren't a concern to us, lass. Not one of us can stand idly by when we see someone in need. We'll do whatever we can to help."

She nodded, unsure what he expected her to say.

With an audible sigh, he sat on the edge of the cot so that they were eye to eye. "James has never had his head *and* his heart turned by a lass before. Ye're the first."

Tears welled in her eyes. "I'm no one special," she rasped. "Surely you noticed that I have one leg that's not straight." Lifting her gaze to meet his, she whispered, "You've seen my back—the scars will be with me for the rest of my life." She raised the arm that was in the sling. "Now this," she said before lowering it. "Why would James want someone like me?"

The intensity in Emmett's eyes unnerved her, but she could not look away when he answered, "He's seen what I have, lass—yer giving heart. It calls to those of us who see past what others cannot. Ye've a pure heart. You don't complain—even when ye should be wailing in pain. Ye care about others, even when it landed ye in trouble."

He looked away, then back, and she noticed the intensity was replaced with concern. "Me cousin's a royal pain in the *arse* at times, but as constant as the sun. He's not one for fancy words, lass, but his heart is as true as yers. Trust him."

Emmett's words opened up the hope she'd closed off inside of her because of her limp. She'd been ridiculed, stared at, and laughed at growing up because of it. "I want to trust him—but..." Her throat ached from holding back tears of self-pity and longing.

"Ye haven't seen *his* scars, lass. 'Tis the ones he carries on his heart that would break a weaker man. Not one of us is weak. 'Tisn't how we were raised. Trust him with yer heart."

He rose and handed her the handkerchief from his waistcoat. "Dry yer pretty eyes, lass, or James'll be taking a strip off me hide, thinking 'twas something I said to make ye weep." She wiped her eyes. When she tried to give his handkerchief back, he smiled. "Keep it. Ye'll be needing it for the tears ye've been holding back. Cry it out, lass, so ye're dry-eyed when himself returns."

"Thank you, Emmett." When he had one foot over the threshold, she asked, "You're certain about the scars?"

"Certain sure. Trust me—trust James."

"I'll try."

"Good enough for me, though it won't be for himself. I'll be back to check on ye later."

With that, he was gone, but his words lingered in the small room. They swirled about her, tempting her to see herself through the eyes of someone who could see past what she always struggled to hide— the shame of her twisted leg. She had never said as much to her mum. Her poor mother would have felt even more blame. Mum was not a physician and had no idea that with the way the bone had been set, her leg would not heal straight.

Alone, she let the tears come. After she'd run dry, she mopped her eyes and blew her nose. She probably looked a sight, but no one would notice her in the tiny room off the pantry. Easing back in the chair, she thought over Emmett's words. From the tone of his voice and the set of his jaw, the man believed every word. Mayhap if she let go of her preconceived notions of perfection—and the taunts from her past—she could let herself begin to believe that James saw her differently than she saw herself.

Could he love her despite her flaws? If she took a chance and opened her heart, could she trust that he would not bruise it or hand it back?

She drew in a deep breath and slowly exhaled. There was only one way to find out. It was time to believe in herself and what she had to offer a man like James...

Her love and her heart.

CHAPTER TWENTY-FIVE

GARAHAN RETURNED HOURS later. He stopped to check on Melinda, but the lass was sleeping. Like the lovesick fool that he was, he watched her sleep. Awake she was a sight to behold—asleep, she appeared otherworldly. He couldn't decide if the lass reminded him of an angel or one of the *Fae*. When she mumbled aloud in her sleep, he quietly left the room.

Duty called.

He needed to hear reports from those who stood guard in his absence. He passed through to the main part of the house and was pleased to hear the rumble of deep voices coming from the entryway—more voices than normal. Relief filled him. Their ladyships had arrived with their proper escorts. Knowing their ladyships, it was probably not without a few minor skirmishes—neither one appreciated being told what to do—but in his opinion, that was just one more aspect of their personalities to admire. He didn't actually question whether his cousins and brother would insist on escorting Lady Aurelia and Lady Calliope—it would be a fact. He was sorry to have missed what was bound to have been a lively *discussion* between their ladyships and the duke's guard.

His brother was the first to notice him. "Jamie! 'Tis about time ye showed yer ugly mug."

Garahan cuffed his younger brother on the back of the head with affection. "Some of us are actually working—not enjoying the countryside while escorting their ladyships from Sussex to London."

Aiden Garahan snorted with laughter. "Oh aye, ye know their penchant for"—he looked around the group and lowered his voice—"trouble."

"Don't let their lordships hear ye say such," Garahan warned Aiden before turning to Emmett to say, "Me second meeting with the baron's footman went as planned. Now that the apothecary's bill has been settled, Huggleston's starting to believe I mean to keep me word and include his family with those we protect."

Seamus Flaherty lifted one eyebrow in silent question, which Garahan ignored, noticing Dermott O'Malley nudge his brother, Emmett, in the ribs. Before the O'Malleys started a scuffle, Garahan spoke up again. "Why don't we discuss this in the duke's library?"

Aiden chuckled. "Aren't ye worried that one of us will knock over a vase or land on one of His Grace's favorite chairs and break one of the legs off?"

"Don't be needling yer brother, Aiden," Emmett warned. "He's got a lot on his mind."

Aiden slanted a speculative look at his brother. "I've heard ye've rescued another lass, and she's the opposite of Mary Kate."

Garahan grabbed Aiden by the cravat and lifted him off the ground—surprising not only Aiden but the rest of the group. "Ye'll mind yer words and what ye say about the lass, unless ye want another pounding like the last one I gave ye before we left home."

"They're at it again," Chattsworth grumbled. "Tell me again why His Grace thought hiring the O'Malleys and their kin was a good idea?" he asked Lippincott as they approached the group.

Garahan glared at his brother and released him. To Aiden's credit, he landed on his feet and acted as if nothing out of the ordinary had occurred. Garahan had hoped his brother would stumble, then he could have helped steady him—and sneak in a quick jab to his kidney in the process. He'd not stand for anyone disparaging the lass—or comparing her to another woman. Melinda was not like any other woman he'd ever met.

Despite what life handed her, the lass's kindness and compassion had yet to be tarnished. While he lived and breathed, he planned to see that nothing—and no man—would have the opportunity to besmirch her name or reputation again.

"Problem, Garahan?" the earl asked.

Aiden answered, "Nay, yer lordship."

"A bit of a misunderstanding, yer lordship," Garahan said at the same time.

"There is no time for misunderstandings, if you are referring to what I just saw," Lippincott said.

Aiden stepped in front of James, saying, "It's as Jamie said, yer lordship. A simple misunderstanding between brothers."

The earl raked a hand through his hair and sighed. "Your protection detail has quadrupled with the arrival of our wives and sons. We do not have time for any of your day-to-day infighting."

"Begging yer pardon," Dermott O'Malley said. "'Tisn't fighting of any kind. We're—"

"Honing your skills," Chattsworth interrupted. "As I told the others, practice your bare-knuckle at a set time—and away from the house—so I will know to expect it and not be caught off guard."

"Excellent idea," the earl concurred. "The stables or behind the stables will do while you are in London. No one will be able to hear—or observe your fighting."

"Begging yer pardon, yer lordships," Dermott said again.

Before he could repeat what he just said, Emmett told his brother, "I think they heard ye the first time." With a lift of his chin, Emmett silently urged the group into the library. As the last one in, he closed the door.

"Let's hear your report first, Garahan," Lippincott said.

Garahan nodded and said, "I had a successful *meeting* with Huggleston, Baron Corkendale's footman."

Aiden coughed to cover his snort of laughter at the suggestion it was a meeting.

Garahan ignored the interruption and continued, "He was heard spouting off lies and slander against Lady Aurelia and Lady Calliope." He met the earl's gaze and added, "But not responsible for the ones concerning yer lordship's sister and brother-in-law."

If he had blinked, Garahan would have missed the deadly gleam in the earl's eyes and the lightning-fast movement of his curling his hands into fists before relaxing them. The duke's brother was far better at concealing his anger than Garahan.

"Will he be able to speak, if questioned?" the earl asked.

"I only bruised his jaw," Garahan replied. "Didn't break it."

"Anything else we need to know?" Lippincott asked.

Garahan's gut iced over as he replied, "The baron's offering a reward for finding the scullery maid he recently employed—claiming she ran off without giving notice, causing an uproar in his household. He intends to demand restitution from the lass."

Emmett placed his hand on Garahan's shoulder. The heavy weight of it reminded him of his da. He reined in his anger and put a leash on his temper. He acknowledged the show of solidarity with a slight nod. "Huggleston and I came to an understanding the first time we met. The man is responsible for the care of his younger sister and his ma. 'Twas his sister's terrible fever that had the man accepting extra coin from the baron to spread rumors." The group listened intently as Garahan continued, "Huggleston passed along the information that two scullery maids have been let go in the past few months."

"Is the cook difficult to work for?" Chattsworth asked, while the earl watched Garahan closely.

Lippincott asked, "Is the young woman you rescued the scullery maid Corkendale is offering the reward for?"

"Aye, yer lordship," Garahan said.

The earl inclined his head. "Please continue."

"The cook isn't difficult to work with and 'tisn't why the maids were let go," Garahan replied, his stomach churning at what he'd been told. He hated injustice, bullies, and mistreatment of women and children. The baron would pay!

"Best tell us," the earl urged, as if he sensed what Garahan would say.

"Their mistress fired them," Garahan replied.

"For neglecting their duties?" the viscount asked.

It gutted Garahan to think of the poor lasses working for the bloody bugger to earn a decent wage, only to be violated by the baron. He dug deep to bury his feelings and reply, "The maids both insisted the baron forced himself on them. Even their visible bruises did not sway the woman. She let them go without a reference—or their back pay!"

"Did ye get the lass's names or their direction?" Emmett asked.

"Aye. Fortunately, they have families who took them back—even when it became evident both lasses were impregnated." Garahan's hands ached. He uncurled them, allowing the blood to rush back in. "I've left me name and Coventry's card with Huggleston. The lad showed remorse. I'm thinking he feels the same as the rest of us, regarding the treatment of a serving woman as a vessel for their employer's lust."

"And you believe him, after what he's done—spreading another scandal about our wives?" Chattsworth asked.

"Aye, yer lordship. I slipped him a bit of a convincer." Garahan's knuckles were still sore. "But just for form, mind ye. I believe the man regrets what he felt he had to do."

His cousins and brothers would no doubt know what he was about to share. Garahan had his doubts about the earl and the viscount. Had they ever been reduced to working a job no one else would take to help put food on their families' tables? He thought not.

"He confessed his reasons for trying to bribe our new stable lad—

who is trying to help pay for his ma's bills at the apothecary. Apparently Huggleston's in a similar state, needing extra coin, only it's his youngest sister who nearly succumbed to a virulent fever. Corkendale promised to elevate him from footman to butler if he would spread what the baron told him about their ladyships. Huggleston did not know they were lies when he repeated them at Tattersalls, outside of White's, Weston's, and at that tea shop their ladyships used to frequent."

"Gunter's," the earl supplied.

"Aye."

"How much will it cost us to ensure this footman will not go back on his word to you?" the viscount asked.

"Our promise to send a healer—he is the sole support of his mum and sister, and cannot afford to pay the apothecary on what he makes as footman working for Corkendale."

Garahan was grateful, yet again, for whichever angel sat on his shoulder to guide him through life. He always had to work hard, but his family always had his back. As part of the duke's guard, Coventry and King had his family's back. Who took care of those like Huggleston and Melinda, if not for himself and his kin?

"I have sent word to two friends who have Emmett's gift of healing," Garahan told the group. "Like us, they happen to be in a position to aid those who need saving or are struggling to survive."

"Would sharing their names have an adverse effect on their good works?" the earl asked.

"Aye," Garahan replied. "King would no doubt know them. Coventry is well known to the man. In fact," he continued, "he is considering Coventry's offer of employment."

The earl and viscount were duly impressed. "Joining the ranks of others who have served in His Majesty's forces," Chattsworth said.

"Forced to retire early due to injuries received in the line of duty," Lippincott added.

"Aye," Garahan agreed.

The men discussed and digested Garahan's report. It wasn't unusual for a member of Society to take advantage of those in their employ. Young maids were the ones who suffered more than others, when the master of the house decided to take what wasn't offered—and most often by force.

"We'll keep a close watch on the lass for ye, Jamie," Aiden said. "No one'll hurt her."

Garahan stared at his brother and shook his head.

Aiden misunderstood the action and added, "Even if you don't want our help—"

"'Tisn't that. She's already been grievously injured. I won't go into detail now, but know this—the thought of her suffering even a broken fingernail is unacceptable. I'm counting on ye to see that the baron—and his lackeys—do not get anywhere near the lass. Understood?"

The chorus of *ayes* went a long way to easing the frustration and worry inside of him. "Now then, yer lordship, ye said ye have something to add?"

The earl and the viscount shared a glance before the earl said, "Coventry informed me of a new rumor."

Garahan frowned.

Before he could ask, Lippincott continued, "It rose from the working class and has gained momentum sweeping through the merchant class, rising to the top of Society—and has the *ton* agog with anticipation."

Garahan glanced at Emmett and the others. From the identical blank looks on their faces, it was news to everyone. "We haven't heard of any new rumors about the duke or his family."

The earl smiled. "Coventry has it on good authority that you challenged the baron's footman to a bare-knuckle bout."

Emmett coughed. Dermott cleared his throat, and Aiden elbowed Seamus, who chuckled.

"Would you care to explain the use of my estate in this wager, Garahan?"

The frustration in the viscount's voice had him explaining, "The head groom at Tattersalls started the rumor in defense of me, yer lordship. There's many who know me character—and would never believe the ugly rumor involving Lady Calliope and Lady Aurelia."

Lippincott nodded. "My brother has expressed interest in this bout, Garahan."

"Is His Grace wanting an apology?"

"He sent his thanks, and deep appreciation for donating the coin collected from the wagers to a fund benefiting those injured or have given their lives for king and country."

"I cannot take credit, yer lordships. 'Twas Burton's idea. Not mine. He lost his oldest son in a battle fought on foreign shores. He's been working night and day to support his family and his son's."

"I shall arrange a meeting with Burton—on behalf of the duke," the earl said.

"I have agreed to host the bare-knuckle bout," Chattsworth announced. "And the celebration that will follow."

Garahan's stomach knotted. "Celebration, yer lordship?"

"Your victory will exonerate you in the eyes of those who have judged you based on the rumor mill."

"But what of the truth?" Aiden asked. Garahan shook his head at his brother, who fell silent.

"What me brother meant to ask is, after I win the bout, will the baron apologize publicly and have a retraction printed for all and sundry to read?" Garahan asked.

"We can add that to King's announcement," the earl said, "when he claps the baron in irons."

"Do you think he'll attend the bout?"

"Aye," the viscount replied. "He believes he has defeated the duke and will want to witness your defeat as well."

Garahan squared his shoulders, and the rest of the men followed suit. "If he believes that," Garahan said, "then the baron has *shite* for brains."

CHAPTER TWENTY-SIX

S EAMUS FLAHERTY WALKED down the hallway toward the side door
to the town house—the one the guards used most often. He was
headed to his next position, patrolling the southern perimeter of the
duke's town house. He relished being outside—hated being cooped
up.

Mary Kate Donovan opened the door to the servants' side of the
house and slipped inside.

He shook his head. Women! They just could not leave well
enough alone. He pulled the door open in time to hear Mary Kate's
overly bright greeting.

Bollocks! "I hope she didn't wake the lass." He waved to Mrs.
O'Toole, who was up to her elbows kneading bread, and continued
toward the sound of female voices.

He had yet to meet the lass who'd captured his cousin's interest.
From the way Garahan spoke about her, he was well past smitten. He
cleared his throat, and Mary Kate glanced over her shoulder, clearly
surprised to see him. "Seamus! I didn't hear you."

"I did not intend for ye to. I thought ye were given strict instructions to let the lass rest?"

Mary Kate had the good grace to flush with embarrassment. "I was
only coming to see if there was anything she needed."

He frowned to show his displeasure. "Garahan'll have me head if ye've disturbed her."

Stepping into the room, he introduced himself to the lass. "Me name's Flaherty—Seamus—cousin to Garahan. Is there anything ye be needing, lass?" The poor thing looked exhausted, and no wonder, with an injured shoulder, bruised ribs, and a host of other injuries that had been alluded to, but not discussed. "Are ye in pain? I can ask Mrs. O'Toole for something to ease it."

Her exhaustion faded as a sweet smile brightened her expression and warmed his heart. Garahan would be taken with the lass's smile and her innate need to soothe others—despite the fact that she had to be in considerable pain.

"I'm fine, thank you, just surprised. I wasn't expecting visitors this early."

"Forgive me," Mary Kate said. "I was curious about you. We have something in common. I'm not sure if anyone has mentioned it, but James rescued me right off the sidewalk." She shook her head. "I have no idea what I would have done if he hadn't helped me by bringing me here."

"There's a bit more to the tale than that, Mary Kate," Seamus said. "Don't be stretching the truth." He noted the color that had bloomed on her face had faded. "'Twas me cousin Michael O'Malley who bundled ye into a hack and accompanied ye here to Grosvenor Square."

Mary Kate bit her bottom lip—and Seamus knew the lass had intentionally glossed over the tale of Garahan's rescue.

"You're right, of course, but in my mind—"

"I'm late for me rotation guarding perimeter. I'm certain Lady Calliope has need of ye, Miss Donovan."

"Thank you for introducing yourself," the lass said. "It was a pleasure to meet you, too, Mary Kate."

"And you," Mary Kate replied.

Seamus would deal with Mary Kate Donovan later.

>>><<<

MELINDA KEPT HER face as expressionless as possible waiting for Seamus and Mary Kate to leave. Had she imagined it, or had the young woman hinted there was something between the woman and James before Seamus arrived?

She had to have misheard, because James would not have proposed to her if he still cared for Mary Kate. Her heart knew the emotions she'd seen in the depths of his eyes were true. The timbre of his voice as he expressed his concern and worry when he had not been able to find her was honest.

Her head began to pound, though it was outweighed by compassion for the other woman. She hoped Mary Kate's eyes would open to the truth Melinda knew in her gut and her heart—James Garahan loved her...limp, scars, and all.

Compared to Mary Kate, Melinda knew she was plain as dishwater with her dark brown hair and brown eyes. Mary Kate had a lovely figure, perfectly proportioned, whereas Melinda had an overly large bosom, hips to match, with a smallish waist. With her childhood injury, and the recent ones, she was riddled with imperfections.

Instead of focusing on what *she* perceived as beautiful, she knew others held their own ideals of perfection and beauty. Her trust in James was bone deep. She didn't have to agree with the man's opinion of what was beautiful. He convinced her every time he trailed the tip of his finger along the curve of her cheek, or gazed into her eyes with an intensity that robbed her of every thought. And when his lips met hers...their hearts linked and their souls whispered of a love that would withstand whatever life tossed in their path.

James shouldered his responsibilities easily, would never forsake his vow to the duke to protect the duke and his family. He carried the weight of responsibility for his brothers, their family—and his cousins and theirs.

From the way she'd heard Mrs. O'Toole and Mrs. Wigglesworth speak of James and the men of the duke's guard, each man added those they rescued to the growing number currently under their protection—and still stood strong and ready to answer the call for help.

Her love strong, her mind eased, and she felt the pain behind her eyes lessen. She had just closed her eyes when she heard footsteps heading toward her room. The duke's men often used the rear door to reach the stables. She didn't bother to open her eyes.

"Begging yer pardon, Miss Waring?"

Her eyes shot open to find a tall, broad-shouldered, handsome man with dark hair and dark eyes standing in the doorway. "May I help you?" she asked.

"Nay," the man replied. "'Tis meself offering to help ye. Me brother James has asked us to introduce ourselves before our shift on the interior patrol." When she didn't reply, he added, "I'm meaning members of the duke's guard from Chattsworth Manor and Lippincott Manor."

She smiled, and he relaxed his stance. "Me name's Aiden Garahan. I'm currently on rotation at Lippincott Manor working for the earl and his countess. I am one of the duke's guard who escorted her ladyship from Sussex."

His voice was nearly as deep as James's. "It is nice to meet you, Aiden. Has anyone told you that you resemble your brother?"

He rolled his eyes. "Aye, lass. A time or two. Not that me knot-headed brother would ever admit to the fact. Can I get ye anything before I head upstairs to the rooftop?"

"You're going to patrol on the roof?"

"Aye, lass. Do ye have enough water? Are ye hungry?"

She smiled at his concern. "I'm fine, thank you, Aiden. Don't let me interfere with your duties."

"No interference at all, lass. If ye have need of me, just send word."

"Thank you, I will."

By the time her midday meal arrived, along with her medicinal herbal, she had met the other member of the duke's guard from Lippincott Manor—Dermott O'Malley, who resembled his brother Emmett a great deal.

She was grateful for the quiet, as it gave her time to decide whether to mention the conversation she'd had with Mary Kate. It was clear that Seamus felt the woman had only remembered part of being rescued—James's part.

Melinda could understand what it felt like to lose all hope and, at the last moment, get swept up into the safety and security of James Garahan's arms. But there was a difference—James had asked for her hand. From what Seamus told her, no one had turned James's heart until the night he rescued her.

Needing to stretch her legs, she rose from the seat and wandered around the room. Restless, she straightened the medicinal supplies on their shelves and sorted the linen strips by size. Her balance was much steadier today, and the pins and needles in her arm and hand had all but disappeared now that her shoulder had been repositioned.

She wondered how long it would take for the muscles holding her shoulder in place to heal. She should have asked Michaela or Alasdair. It had only been a day, but she was ready to take off the sling.

Thinking of the pair, she wondered if she could send them a message, thanking them for their help, then thought better of it. No one was supposed to know what they did, where they were...or *who* they were! She would not disclose their whereabouts for the world. She knew there were more women toiling to survive working at difficult jobs and, like her, being preyed upon by men who thought of them as objects...not people.

She had just finished fixing what needed straightening when she heard more footsteps—this time, however, they were definitely lighter and not as loud. She wondered if Mary Kate had returned to continue their conversation. If so, she was prepared to be compassionate and listen to the woman. Mayhap Mary Kate had not gotten over the shock of her dismissal—and how she ended upon the sidewalk on her hands and knees.

In her rush to sit down, Melinda caught her toe on one of the chair legs. She only had enough time to twist so she landed on her bottom and not her shoulder.

"Oh my dear!" a soft voice exclaimed. Without hesitating, that someone had their hand around her waist and another beneath her good arm, helping her to her feet. "Are you lightheaded? Do you feel faint?"

Before Melinda could answer, the woman helping her called out, "Mrs. O'Toole! Come quickly! Miss Waring has fallen!"

Embarrassed to the core, she stiffened. "You didn't have to interrupt her. I'm fine, truly. My toe caught on the chair leg, and I stumbled."

"You could have landed on your injured shoulder!" the woman admonished her. "Here's Mrs. O'Toole and one of the duke's guard now."

"Lady Aurelia, what happened? Did Miss Waring faint?"

Melinda wished there was somewhere to hide from the trio who stared at her. "I'm fine. I just explained to her ladyship—and please pardon me for not recognizing you, your ladyship—that I caught my toe and stumbled. I'm fine."

"You looked flushed. Are you sure you didn't bump your ribs or shoulder on the way down?" a man she vaguely remembered seeing, but not meeting, asked.

"Er...yes. I am certain. I imagine I could have done more damage to myself. The pain would be excruciating if I had."

He nodded. "Having sprained my wrist as a boy, and then falling on it more than once before it healed, I can agree. The second time I landed on it, it broke. Excruciating would be a mild description for the pain."

"You remember Findley," Mrs. O'Toole said. "Don't you? He is one of the men recently hired to assist the duke's guard."

"I thought I recognized you, Findley. Thank you for your help then, and your offer of assistance just now." Melinda smiled at Lady Aurelia. "It is a pleasure to meet you, your ladyship. I'm sorry to have worried you."

"Think nothing of it. I was concerned when I saw you on the floor—especially with your arm in a sling. I remember Her Grace having to deal with the pain of a separated shoulder after…" Lady Aurelia shook her head. "Best not to dwell on the past. Suffice it to say that I'm happy to hear you are not hurt. I cannot imagine how difficult it is to manage with an injured shoulder and bruised ribs—on the same side."

"I manage." Melinda hesitated before adding, "It's sitting still that is actually the most difficult for me. I'm used to working long hours. I have offered my help. Aside from straightening the room—which they insist I do not need to do—I'm at a loss as to what to do with myself."

"James has insisted that you spend the time recovering," Mrs. O'Toole said. "I do not want to sound harsh, given what you've been through, Miss Waring, but he has gone to great lengths rescuing you not once, but twice. I would think you honor his request."

Shame filled Melinda. How could she have ignored all that James had done for her, just because she was tired of sitting still? "Forgive me, Mrs. O'Toole. I promise to do my best to rest and recover—for James's sake and for yours, Emmett's, and Mrs. Wigglesworth. I am grateful to all of you. But I am not used to being idle."

The cook frowned, but before she could speak, Lady Aurelia said, "Why don't you join Calliope and me in the nursery? We've been banished there by our husbands—they think to keep us out of trouble while we are in town. Silly men."

Findley, who was standing guard at the entrance to the room, coughed, but did not quite manage to cover the fact that he'd laughed.

Ignoring the guard, Lady Aurelia continued, "After you spend a little time with our darling sons, Edward and William, you will be longing for a bit of quiet time to rest."

Melinda could not believe her ears. "You want me to join you and Lady Calliope—and meet your infant sons?"

"I believe I just said as much," Aurelia answered.

"Forgive me for asking, but why would you want to spend time with me?"

Aurelia smiled. "Just because Calliope and I happened to marry men with a title—that we both love to distraction—does not mean that we were always living in the lap of luxury." Melinda apologized again, but Aurelia waved it away. "You have no idea how many young women have cast their eyes—and their lures—at James Garahan since he has been working for His Grace. Calliope, Persephone, Phoebe, and I have come to care for the men in my brother-in-law's private guard as if they were family. Only a very special woman would have been able to win the heart of the oldest Garahan brother. Say you'll join us. We'd love to get to know you."

Melinda had met many unusual people in her life—a number of whom lived in the village of Peppering Eye, where she'd spent most of her life. But she'd never met a lady of the *ton* who professed to want to get to know a lowly member of society such as herself. She could not imagine Lady Aurelia working as a scullery maid. Mayhap her ladyship was just being kind.

Unsure of how to answer, she glanced at Mrs. O'Toole, hoping the cook would weigh in and advise her.

The older servant took pity on her. "You'll find that Her Grace, her sisters-in-law Lady Phoebe and Lady Aurelia, and their very good friend Lady Calliope would not be considered conventional by the members of the *ton*. But you'll not find any finer women than the four of them. It has been a pleasure meeting them, getting to know them, and working alongside of them. The experience has been enlightening and enjoyable."

Melinda nodded and turned to answer Lady Aurelia. "If you are certain that I won't cause undue speculation, or rumors, by being in your company, then yes," she said. "I would love to meet Lady Calliope and your darling sons."

Lady Aurelia closed the distance between them, slipped her arm through Melinda's, and led her from the room. "We'll take the servants' staircase," she explained. "It's closest to the nursery."

Melinda was looking forward to meeting Lady Calliope and their infant sons. When she entered the nursery, Mary Kate was speaking to another woman—presumably Lady Calliope.

When she stopped in the doorway, Aurelia peeked around her and mumbled something before saying, "Don't worry about Calliope's maid—Mary Kate has a kind heart, but has yet to accept that James has never returned her feelings. In fact, another member of the duke's guard has his eye on her."

Relieved her faith in James had been confirmed by another person, Melinda nodded.

Mary Kate smiled at Lady Aurelia. "I just changed Edward for you. He's such a good babe." With a glance at Melinda, she said, "I am happy to see you are feeling well enough to be on your feet."

"I am, thank you." Melinda didn't quite know what to expect from the woman but was determined to be open and friendly—mayhap Mary Kate needed a friend.

Lady Aurelia patted Melinda's hand to get her attention. "I'd like you to meet my very good friend Calliope. Calliope, meet Melinda Waring."

"I'm delighted to meet you, Melinda," Calliope said. "I thought you were resting?"

Melinda sighed. "I am supposed to be, but I feel so much better and have difficulty sitting when I'm used to working."

Calliope nodded. "Before I met and married William, I had been working for my cousin and his wife." A look of sympathy filled her eyes. "I was a poor relation, you see, and treated as their personal servant—and…"

Her ladyship's voice trailed off, and Melinda sensed Lady Calliope, too, had been a victim of abuse by her relations.

"But no longer," Lady Aurelia added, her voice bright. "Would you like to meet our darling sons?"

"I would love that above all things. I used to spend time watching the youngest members of my stepfather's congregation." Warmth filled Melinda as Lady Aurelia lifted her son from his cradle. The babe's expression was open and interested. His eyes, a brilliant blue, stared at her. "Oh, he is so beautiful! How I have missed being around little ones." Lady Calliope brought her son over so that Melinda could meet both bright-eyed babes. "They are so beautiful—such dark hair and blue eyes. There is such a strong resemblance—they could be brothers!"

Mary Kate seemed to relax when Lady Calliope said, "Our sons look just like the rest of the Lippincotts. His Grace, his brother the earl—my husband—the viscount—Calliope's husband—and their sister Lady Phoebe's husband Marcus. All are known for their dark chestnut hair and brilliant blue eyes."

"Our babes are cousins—second or third—mayhap once re-moved," Lady Aurelia added. "It will be wonderful for them to grow up together. After all, Calliope and I have been friends since we first met. William and Marcus met Edward after my brother-in-law inherited the dukedom. They are distant cousins on their mothers' side."

In her bid to do something with her time, Melinda had neglected her promise to James to rest. What if he arranged to have someone stop by to see if she needed anything? "It was lovely to meet you, your ladyships, and your beautiful sons, but I should return downstairs. I wouldn't want one of the duke's men to arrive to check up on me—as they told me they promised James they would do—only to find the room empty."

"Oh dear," Aurelia murmured. "I had not thought of that."

"You've only been here a short time," Calliope said. "Are you certain you won't stay longer? We could send word to the men."

"It wouldn't be right to take advantage of James and the others like that. I've caused him enough worry since the other day." With one last look at the babes nestled in their mothers' arms, Melinda made her excuses and left the nursery.

She had just closed the door when it opened, and Mary Kate emerged. "Wait, Melinda! I'll go with you to see that you don't stumble on the stairs."

It was kind of her to offer. "Thank you."

Leading the way, the maid cautioned, "You do have to watch your step. I nearly got tangled in a pile of linens midway down the stairs last week at Chattsworth Manor. Mrs. Wigglesworth mentioned that today is wash day, so we'll need to be extra careful."

Melinda frowned. "I didn't notice any on our way up."

Mary Kate shrugged. "When there are guests at Chattsworth Manor, the housemaids change the linens later in the day. Mayhap they do here as well."

"I'll make it a point to remember that. Thank you for telling me, Mary Kate."

"Of course. I would feel awful if I neglected to, and you stumbled and were injured. I know what it's like to suffer at the hands of another."

Melinda slowed in her descent. "I'm sorry to hear that. You seem to be happy working for Lady Calliope."

Mary Kate smiled. "She is wonderful to work for. You might think she is timid, but she's not—she's learned to be cautious and is soft-spoken. She and Lady Aurelia are great friends and the kindest women I know."

"My mother was much like their ladyships—soft-spoken and kind."

"You must miss her," Mary Kate said as they reached the bottom step. "I'm very fortunate that my parents are still living. I'm sorry for your loss."

The door burst open, and James Garahan stood in the doorway, looking like a thundercloud. "Where in the bloody hell have ye been, lass?" Before Melinda could answer, he glowered at Mary Kate. "And just what do ye think ye're doing dragging the lass up and down the stairs when she should be resting?"

Melinda heard the sharp intake of Mary Kate's breath. "Mary Kate did nothing of the kind," she said. "She was accompanying me down the stairs. Lady Aurelia invited me up to the nursery to meet Lady Calliope and their sons."

James's brows lifted in surprise.

"Mary Kate has been kindness itself, James. I understand you are worried about me, which is why I did not stay overlong in the nursery, but jumping to such a conclusion is wrong."

Mary Kate spoke up. "Miss Waring did not want you, or the other men in the duke's guard, to worry if you happened to stop by to check on her and find the room empty."

James looked from one woman to the other and back. "Well then, I'll apologize to ye, Mary Kate, and will escort ye to yer room, lass."

When Mary Kate turned around to head back upstairs, James said, "I'd like to speak with ye, Mary Kate, before ye return to the nursery."

She turned back and nodded. "I can wait here."

Melinda shook her head. "Please, walk with us." She wanted to ensure that James would not hold on to his anger with Mary Kate.

"Thank you, Melinda."

James muttered something, but Melinda ignored his mumbling, asking Mary Kate about her family. By the time she reached her room, she found she *was* tired.

"Thank you for accompanying me, Mary Kate. Lady Aurelia was

right earlier—I am a bit tired now and believe I'll rest for a while."

"I'll let their ladyships know. I'm sure they'll be anxious to show off their beautiful babes again."

"Mary Kate, would ye mind if I have a quick word with Melinda before I speak to ye?" Garahan asked.

"Not at all. I'll be in the kitchen. I need to speak with Mrs. O'Toole."

When she left, James closed the distance between him and Melinda. "Are ye sure Mary Kate did not say anything to upset ye?"

She decided not to mention the earlier conversation on the chance that she had misunderstood. "Not at all. She is very friendly."

"Aye, she is that." He paused before saying, "But she's had an unreasonable expectation about meself for too long. I may have added to it by avoiding her, rather than taking the time to speak to her."

Melinda had an idea of what he was going to tell her. "Unreasonable?"

"I rescued the lass, whisking her away from an intolerable situation, and helped her find a different position. That doesn't mean that I have feelings for her." His eyes were turbulent, swirling with emotion when they met hers. "Before ye ask, do not assume that I only feel protective toward ye, when I've opened me heart and shared what I feel with ye."

"I believe you, James. I trust you."

The depth and intensity in his dark eyes filled her heart to bursting when she noticed the admiration twined with desire… *Desire for her!* Her breath hitched.

"There's something you need to know," she said.

"Aye?"

"The wounds on my back left scars," she rasped. "I cannot see them, but I've felt them with my fingertips when dressing. They must be repulsive."

James drew her into his embrace and rested his chin on top of her head. "The deed, and the man who took a cane to yer back, is repulsive. Scars are nothing more than the way our bodies heal certain injuries." When she eased back, he pressed his lips to her forehead. "Ye're a strong and beautiful woman. Scars or no scars, I wouldn't have ye any other way, lass."

The love in his eyes warmed her and had her lifting to her toes to press her lips to the strong line of his jaw. Watching his eyes widen, she braced a hand to his forearm and stretched higher to reach his cheek. When he groaned, she gave in to the temptation and pressed her lips to his.

⟫⟩⟨⟪

THE FEEL OF the lass's lips tentatively brushing against his jaw, and his cheek, had relief surging through him. The surety of her lips pressed to his shot through his veins like wildfire—the lass finally believed him!

Mindful of her ribs and her shoulder, he pressed her carefully, but firmly, against him and sipped from her lips. When the leash on his desire for her pulled taut, he plundered her sweet mouth until she sagged against him.

Drawing on every ounce of his control, he ended the kiss and held her to his pounding heart—relieved when hers kept time with his. "Ye tempt me to the limits of me control, lass."

"I don't mean to."

"Ah, that's part of the temptation. I'd best leave ye to yer rest and have a word with Mary Kate."

She stiffened in his arms, and he chuckled. "Worry not, lass. Ye're the one who holds me heart, and no other. I've needed to tell her that I don't have feelings for her, beyond the need to help and protect her, for too long now. 'Tis best I get it said."

When she relaxed against him, he whispered, "I'll be back later—to kiss ye goodnight, lass." He grinned seeing the dazed expression on her face and glazed look in her eyes. "Let me help ye to yer chair."

When he had her settled, he lifted her hand to press a kiss to the back of it. "Remember, ye're the lass I'll be kissing goodnight tonight—and every night thereafter."

Her soft sigh was music to his ears. The lass loved him—oh, she hadn't said it yet, but he knew. Her kiss was proof of that.

He strode down the hallway to the kitchen, going over the apology in his head. He owed Mary Kate an explanation for avoiding her. She deserved to hear him tell her that he did not return her feelings.

He nearly collided with his cousin, Seamus, who was kissing Mary Kate near the kitchen door. He cleared his throat, and the two broke apart. Mary Kate blushed, while Seamus's look was one of challenge, from a man who'd staked his claim with a kiss that left no doubt in Garahan's mind of his cousin's intentions.

"Mary Kate, I'm overdue with me apology. Forgive me for avoiding ye—"

Seamus interrupted, "The lass has known for a while now that ye have no feelings for her beyond protecting her." He brushed the tip of his finger along the curve of her cheek. "Isn't that right, lass?"

She nodded, beaming at Seamus.

"In fact, she's going to allow me to court her, aren't ye, lass?"

"Aye, Seamus." She finally looked at Garahan. "I accept your apology, and thank you for it. Melinda is a fine woman, who, if I am not mistaken, is head over heels in love with you."

Garahan grinned. "Ye're not mistaken. Thank ye for understanding—and may I say, ye'll not find a better man than me cousin Seamus, unless it's one of me brothers."

When Seamus drew Mary Kate close again, Garahan asked, "Don't ye have the rooftop shift? I'm headed to me post on the perimeter."

Garahan waited while Seamus kissed Mary Kate once more, and left her leaning against the wall with a bemused look on her face.

He wondered if the duke was ready for two more of his private guard to fall in love and marry. Shaking his head at the thought, he realized he was faced with the same problem his O'Malley cousins had been—being distracted by the women they loved when there was a volatile situation that needed their full attention.

Distractions were not an option—until after the situation had been handled. Melinda's kiss had been all the confirmation he needed that the lass loved him. She would have to understand the position he was in—and the duty he'd vowed to fulfill, no matter the cost.

As he stepped outside to man his post, he realized he would have to have a conversation with the lass about his position within the duke's guard, and their expectations after they married. He looked forward to asking the lass what she envisioned for their future together.

CHAPTER TWENTY-SEVEN

M RS. O'TOOLE ARRIVED with Melinda's medicinal herbal. "I'm sorry you had to wait for me. We haven't had this many guests at one time in quite a while."

"I'm feeling better than I expected to. Why not let me help? My stepfather used to boast about my cooking. I'd be only too happy to do my part, if it'll ease your burden."

Mrs. O'Toole looked as if she wanted to refuse, but in the end agreed. "If you promise to sit on one of the stools while you help me."

"I promise!"

A short while later, Melinda had convinced the cook to let her remove her sling—as long as none of the duke's men were in the vicinity—and she was happily up to her elbows kneading bread dough. "I have missed spending time in the kitchen, Mrs. O'Toole. Thank you for agreeing to let me help you."

True to her word, Mrs. O'Toole had put Melinda to work, while regaling her of tales the members of the duke's guard that James specifically might wish the cook had kept to herself.

When Melinda asked about Mr. O'Toole, the cook got a faraway look in her eyes before answering, "I've been a widow for some time." She sighed and smiled at Melinda. "I loved that man with every fiber of my being, and was lost without him for the longest time. Thank goodness the duke's father understood my grief—having lost his duchess."

The words washed over Melinda, leaving her with a sense of clarity. Her heart rejoiced upon realizing that she felt the same way about James. The days when she did not see him, she felt at loose ends. The more she got to know him, the more she found herself waiting for the times when he would stop to see how she was faring. Those long hours between when she'd made the decision to leave him and when he came to her rescue—again—were the longest of her life.

She could not wait to see James later that night, because she would finally tell him what was in her heart, and hope that he would ask her to marry him again.

Melinda mixed the ingredients for the scones, while her mind was swept away thinking of James's kisses.

"Do you need help with that?" Mrs. O'Toole asked, coming to stand beside Melinda.

"Oh, forgive me. I was woolgathering." Dreaming of dancing with James, though she knew it could never happen. How could it, when she would more than likely stumble due to her weak leg? "It'll just roll this out—or pat it if you are using the rolling pin."

"I have more than one rolling pin—do not roll them out too thin."

They agreed on the thickness, and Melinda asked, "What do you use to cut out the scones?"

Mrs. O'Toole answered, "I always have a glass on hand. We get more scones per batch that way. The size is perfect with a dollop of fresh jam and clotted cream." Melinda's stomach growled, and Mrs. O'Toole smiled. "I cannot have James upset with us for not feeding you, Melinda. I'll fix us something in a moment."

Melinda's face flamed. "Will I be allowed to eat more than an invalid's diet now that you can see I am on the mend?"

Mrs. O'Toole held a hand to her heart. "I forgot, didn't I?"

Melinda did not want the older servant to fret. "You were not the one to forget. I was supposed to remind you, but I hate to be a bother."

"You could never be a bother," Mrs. O'Toole informed her, as they two finished cutting out the trays of scones.

While they were baking, she urged Melinda to sit at the table. They shared a meal of hearty soup and fresh bread with a pot of tea.

Melinda finished every bite and sighed. "That was delicious. Although I appreciated the care, I have to be honest, broth, bread, and calves' foot jelly are not all that filling."

Mrs. O'Toole smiled. "I saved a bowl of the jelly for you!"

Melinda bit her tongue to keep from refusing the offer. From the delight in the older woman's eyes, Mrs. O'Toole knew exactly how Melinda felt about it. "Thank you."

Together they cleared the table. Mrs. O'Toole was about to start on a batch of berry tarts when Melinda yawned.

"Why don't you take a short rest? You are not used to working, or eating a full meal yet," Mrs. O'Toole said. "It would do you good."

Melinda started to refuse, then remembered her promise to James. "Thank you, I think I will."

"Don't forget your sling," the cook reminded her. "James will pitch a fit if he sees you without it. Here, let me help you put it on." When Mrs. O'Toole had adjusted it to her satisfaction, she smiled. "Off with you. I'll send someone to fetch you in an hour or so."

"Thank you. It was nice being able to pitch in and help."

Back in her room, Melinda decided to lie down. The meal was making her sleepy.

She did not remember falling asleep, but thought she remembered James coming to see her. The heat of his fingertips as he traced the curve of her cheek and line of her jaw soothed her, bringing a sigh to her lips.

"YE'D BEST NOT work yerself into exhaustion again, lass," James said as he brushed a lock of dark brown hair from Melinda's eyes. "What am I to do with ye?"

"Don't wake the poor lass," Emmett said from where he stood in the doorway. "She needs her sleep."

"That she does. Do ye think His Grace will grant me request for a special license?"

Emmett grinned. "Aye, the duke is a romantic at heart."

CHAPTER TWENTY-EIGHT

M ELINDA SLEPT THROUGH until morning, surprised to find a warm quilt covering her. Disappointment speared through her when she realized she'd missed her goodnight kiss. Mumbling to herself, she got up and washed quickly.

A lovely gown of the deepest blue lay across the back of the chair, along with a chemise, and stockings of the finest wool. Grateful to be able to change into a clean gown, she carefully folded her worn clothing and stockings, setting them aside to wash them later.

After she dressed, she lifted her arms above her head, intending to pin up her braid, and gasped as pain shot from her side all the way to her shoulder. She must have overdone it yesterday and would be paying for it today. She closed her eyes, braced a hand to the back of her chair, and waited for the pain to subside.

"Lass! What's wrong?"

Her eyes shot open. The man she'd dreamed about was striding toward her. "James?"

"Is it yer ribs or yer shoulder?"

A tear slipped past her guard, and he brushed it away.

"Both, is it?" he asked when she did not answer him.

She nodded, unsure if her voice would quaver, giving away the fact that she had done what he warned her not to do. She did not want to seem ungrateful, but was afraid her actions would lead him to believe that she was.

"Have a seat, lass." He helped her to sit. When she had, he asked, "Where is it?"

She stared at the strong line of his jaw and the firm set of his mouth. "I'm sorry, James."

He shook his head and repeated the question.

She had no idea what he was talking about. "Where is what?"

He walked over to the pitcher and bowl, picked up the folded triangle of linen, and brought it over. "Do ye need me to help ye put the sling on?"

"I think I can manage."

She had it beneath her arm and was reaching behind her when a callused hand gently nudged hers aside. "After Mrs. O'Toole explained why ye slept through the night, ye'd best be listening to common sense and wearing yer sling for the next few days. Do not take it off unless someone is here to help ye in the mornings and again at night."

She knew she had rushed things and should have listened to reason, but felt so beholden to James and everyone who was trying to help her. "I do not want anyone to think that I am not grateful, or would take advantage of their kindness, allowing me to stay here—"

"For the love of God, lass. Enough! Ye're injured and have yet to heal. Yer ribs alone—it will be at least a fortnight before they won't be needing to be wrapped. Yer shoulder may take longer, lass. It all depends on how badly ye abuse it when I'm not around to remind ye to rest."

Her nose tingled as her eyes welled with tears. She hated to appear weak, and said as much.

"Ah, lass, weak is something ye're not. Besides, tears are not a sign of weakness—'tis the body's way of healing and dealing with grief."

"Why are you being so kind to me when I did not do as you asked? I was bound and determined to help…and now I cannot lift my arm to pin up my hair."

"Did ye put it up yerself yesterday or the day before that?"

"Nay, but—"

"Would ye like me to help ye, or should I ask Mrs. O'Toole when she brings yer breakfast?"

Her eyes rounded at the thought of James's hands in her hair. An image of his undoing her braid as he spread it upon his pillow filled her head.

"Keep looking at me like that, lass, and I'll be closing and locking the door. Then ye'll have no choice but to marry me."

Her cheeks felt as if they were on fire, but she did not look away from him when she rasped, "Are you going to ask me?"

He knelt before her and lifted her chin, lining up their lips. "I'm after me good-morning kiss, since ye wouldn't wake up last night, and missed kissing me goodnight."

His lips were firm, warm, and wonderful as he masterfully set free what she'd been holding back from him—the love she'd been afraid he would not return.

⋙⋘

WHEN SHE ALL but melted against him, he deepened the kiss, drawing a moan from her sweet lips. "Aye, lass, that's it. Kiss me back."

He knew the moment she was lost to the passion building between them. Her hand slipped around the back of his neck, tangling in the hair brushing against the collar of his frockcoat. This time, he moaned as he traced the tip of his tongue along the rim of her mouth, urging her to open so he could taste her fully.

Lost in the intoxicating flavor of her, he did not hear his name being called until someone tapped him on the shoulder. He broke the kiss to say, "Can't ye see I'm busy? Go away!"

"If you do not want to compromise Miss Waring's reputation, I suggest you accompany me to the library. Mrs. O'Toole is here with her breakfast tray."

Garahan shot to his feet. "Yer lordship. Forgive me. I thought it was one of me brothers."

The earl frowned. "And what if it was?"

Garahan raked a hand through his hair and belatedly looked at Melinda. "I'm sorry, lass. I lost me head. It won't happen again."

"Until after you two are wed," the earl finished for Garahan. As they reached the door, the earl paused. "You have asked Miss Waring for her hand, haven't you?"

"Twice, yer lordship."

The earl paused. "I see. Miss Waring, do mind telling me why you have turned Garahan down—twice?"

She looked at James and then the earl before answering, "He deserves someone better than me."

The earl turned around and walked back over to Melinda. "From what I have heard from my brother's staff about the shape you were in when Garahan brought you here, I can only surmise that you were grievously mistreated—and by a member of your family." When she nodded, he continued, "No one has the right to do that to you—to anyone. Do not let them strip you of your self-worth, your pride, or your determination to make a life for yourself. You are a remarkable woman, Miss Waring. Remember that."

As she lifted her gaze to meet the earl's, he said, "I believe James Garahan is *almost* worthy of you. With a compassionate, kind, and loving woman such as yourself by his side—he will be worthy in no time."

"Thank you for having such confidence in me, your lordship," Melinda replied. "I know it is probably not the proper thing to do, but I must disagree with you. James Garahan is far worthier than you grant him credit for. I will do my utmost to see that his reputation is never called into question. He values the work he does for you so very much, and I hope you will come to value him as much as I do."

The earl smiled. "I do value him, as I value every member of the duke's private guard. Forgive me, Miss Waring—and you too, Garahan, for testing your bride-to-be to see if she has the same intrinsic values as you."

When Garahan tried to step around the earl, the man held out his arm to prevent him from doing so. "My study, if you please, Garahan."

"Aye, yer lordship." Garahan looked over his shoulder and promised Melinda, "I shall return later. Try to stay awake this time."

⟫⟫⟩⟨⟪⟪

SHE WAS SMILING as he left with the earl.

Mrs. O'Toole walked in with a teapot, followed by one of the footmen bearing a huge breakfast tray. "Since you missed the evening meal, I thought you might be hungry." She bit her lip, trying not to smile as she added, "And from what I overheard just now, you will need to eat to build your strength up. James is not a patient man—he'll not want to wait to marry you."

"But he hasn't asked me," Melinda protested.

"I heard he asked you already—and you turned him down."

"Only once. I asked him if I could think about it the second time he asked me, after I jumped out of the hackney."

Mrs. O'Toole directed the footman as to where to place the tray and thanked him. When he left, she poured a cup of tea for Melinda. "That was not the best timing to ask, when you were obviously still in such pain, but I understand his reasons why. The man is in love with you, Melinda. Can you not see that?"

"I do not want him to marry me because of a misplaced sense of honor. I doubted the depths of his feelings. When I did not answer right away, he said my not answering was a good as a no—and that he'd only be asking me one last time. He is giving me time to learn to trust him and to believe in his love for me."

"And do you?"

Such a simple question, yet she hesitated a moment before answering. "I do, though I cannot help but feel that a man like James could do far better than a scarred woman with a permanent limp." She lifted her eyes to meet Mrs. O'Toole's and whispered, "He's so handsome, strong, and brave, he deserves—"

"To have his love valued and returned by the woman he loves," Mrs. O'Toole said. "Think about that while you eat every bit of that breakfast. When I return, I'll help you pin up your hair. I'm so glad the gown James left for you fits. You look lovely in that color."

"James?"

"Aye, didn't you know he left the other blue gown for you as well?"

Melinda shook her head. She had thought it was the housekeeper and Mrs. O'Toole who had given her the other gown.

"James is a thoughtful, handsome, strong, and brave man who deserves to have his love returned," Mrs. O'Toole said before leaving.

Melinda held the teacup in her hands, warming them. Setting the cup down, she brushed a hand on the soft fabric of the second gown that James had picked out just for her. She never thought a man like him would pick out and buy such a gift. There were hidden facets to his personality that she wanted to discover.

She was ready to take a chance on love. She could not wait to say yes to James.

CHAPTER TWENTY-NINE

THE EARL CLOSED the door behind Garahan.

"Yer lordship—"

The earl shook his head and held out a folded slip of parchment. "I had it on excellent advice that you would be in need of this."

Garahan unfolded and read the document. "'Tis a special license."

"Aye. My brother requested it a week or so ago. Marry Miss Waring. A woman does not look at a man the way she looks at you unless she is deeply in love with him."

"Are ye certain?"

"I have it good authority... In matters of the heart, Aurelia is rarely wrong."

"I'm indebted to ye—and His Grace."

The earl held out his hand, and Garahan shook it. "I have made arrangements with the vicar for tomorrow afternoon, as the matter involving Corkendale and my family should be settled soon. Do you think that will be acceptable to Miss Waring?"

"Aye. All I have to do is ask her for the third time."

The earl shook his head, mumbling, "Third time."

Garahan grinned. "Aye, 'tis the charm." Thoughts of Melinda and their wedding night had him changing his mind. "Yer lordship?"

"Aye, Garahan?"

"I'm thinking I should give the lass time to heal and to have a say in more than marrying me. Would ye mind?"

The earl smiled. "Not at all. That would give ample time for plans and preparations."

"Aye," Garahan agreed. "And for me bride-to-be to become used to the lot of *eedjits* who will become her family." He curled his hands into fists. "I have one thing I need to do first."

"Oh? And what is that?" the earl asked.

"I need to leave a message with her cousin—one he will not forget."

The earl's gaze met his.

When the earl raised on eyebrow in silent question, Garahan said, "I give ye me word not to maim the man—but for beating me bride-to-be, he deserves—"

"A taste of his own medicine," the earl finished. "Excellent notion. Take Tremayne, O'Malley, and one of King's men with you as witnesses."

Garahan drew in a deep breath, wanting to refuse, but knew better than to contradict the earl, especially after being on the receiving end of the earl's lightning-fast jab to the chin when delivering the news about the rumor about who fathered the earl's son. "Aye, yer lordship."

"Dermott O'Malley," the earl added. "He has not been involved in whatever took place at that tavern."

Garahan disagreed. "'Tis why I'll be taking Emmett O'Malley—he has a stake in this, as does Tremayne."

"I do believe the man deserves a beating, but not from three men," the earl said.

Garahan drew in a breath and counted to thirteen—his ma's lucky number—before exhaling. "What if each one of us has a turn, and takes two swings at the blackguard?"

The earl frowned, considering. "One blow—from the three of you, delivered one at a time! No more, no less."

"Done!" The need to see justice done had Garahan burying the need to see Melinda before he left, but he was afraid if he did, the lass would talk him out of going after her cousin.

He found Emmett at his station guarding the upper floor of the duke's town house. "We've been given an assignment by his lordship."

"Which one? We've two here at the moment."

Garahan smiled. "The earl. I'm to take you, Tremayne, and one of King's men with me."

Emmett's eyes glowed a brilliant green. He didn't bother asking— he knew what the assignment would be. He cracked his knuckles and waved a hand toward the servants' staircase. "Lead the way."

"We'll stop at Captain Coventry's and collect Tremayne, and with any luck, we'll run into one of King's men while we're there."

As luck would have it, Tremayne and Jackson, one of King's men, were stepping out of the door to Coventry's building when Garahan and Emmett arrived. Garahan didn't bother to dismount. "We've been tasked with an assignment that requires the both of you to accompany us."

Tremayne narrowed his eyes, staring at Garahan, before he slowly smiled. "Was it the earl or the viscount?"

"The earl," Garahan answered.

"There are rules," Emmett said, waiting for the two men to mount their horses.

Jackson shrugged. "King lives by the rules—it won't be a problem for me."

"What rules?" Tremayne demanded.

Garahan snickered. "Each one of us is allowed one blow."

"Hardly seems fair, given what the bloody bastard did to Miss Waring," Tremayne grumbled.

"It's the rules," Emmett reminded him.

Garahan turned to Jackson, who rode beside him, "You are the exception, Jackson."

Jackson grinned. "Unlimited blows? Sounds fair to me."

"Nay," Garahan answered. "Ye're to be the witness that each one of us had a turn to land one blow."

"A turn?" Jackson asked. "So this won't be a typical fight."

"'Tisn't a fight," Garahan said.

"'Tis repayment," Emmett said.

"For what the bloody bugger did to Miss Waring," Tremayne added.

"Hardly seems fair to me," Jackson mumbled. "To let the three of you have all the fun."

Garahan nodded. "Then again, it would be up to the man who is to witness the deed to ensure that the man does not try to escape while we...collect payment from him."

Jackson grinned. "I could sneak in a jab or two."

"Maybe more," Emmett said. "You're the witness. When we are not taking our turn landing a blow..."

"We were not tasked with the job of keeping our witness from landing a punch or two," Tremayne finished.

The men rode away from the wealthier section of London and crossed into a less affluent area until they were on the border of what some called the stews—and others referred to as London's underbelly.

"I'll be letting ye have the first go at the man, Tremayne," Garahan said.

Tremayne gave a brief nod and dismounted.

Garahan followed suit, as did Emmett and Jackson. "Ye'll be next, Emmett."

For a moment he thought his cousin would argue, until Emmett agreed. "'Tis yer right as the man who is about to marry Miss Waring to deliver the final blow."

Garahan shoved the door open, satisfied when it hit the inside wall, and the tavern fell silent. He scanned the room and found his target. "Remember me?" he asked the tavern keep.

The man swallowed twice before nodding.

"Then you know why I'm here."

The overweight man shrieked, a high-pitched sound that grated on the ears. Tremayne strode up to the bar and reached across it to grab the man's frockcoat. "Remember *me*?"

The man shook his head, and Tremayne delivered a wicked jab to his cheekbone.

Emmett stepped up alongside Tremayne. "Best not let go of him yet." When the tavern owner's eyes met his, Tremayne passed the man to Emmett, who leaned close as he rasped, "Payment for what ye did to the lass's back." He plowed his fist into the man's face. Blood gushed from the tavern keep's nose.

Garahan bellied up to the bar and glared at the whimpering man. He didn't bother to ask his cousin to hold the man still. He delivered a right cross at the same moment Emmett let go, and watched the man fly backward into the wall behind the bar and slide to the floor. "Jackson?" Garahan called over his shoulder.

"You followed orders. I'm satisfied and will relay the same to his lordship."

The crowd never made a sound as King's man—dressed in the red coat that denoted his position as a Bow Street Runner—approached the bar. "One more thing." He walked behind the bar, squatted, and checked for a pulse. "He'll live."

"More's the pity," Garahan said.

Emmett agreed, "If we club Jackson over the head, he won't be witness to the two of us delivering a few more blows."

Tremayne laughed. "I'd love to join ye, but I gave my word."

Jackson stood and shoved Garahan out of his way. "I never thought one of the duke's men would break their vow."

Garahan shoved Jackson into Tremayne. "I gave my vow to protect the duke, his family and extended family with me life. That I've done."

"What of your word to the earl?"

"He asked me to give the man what he deserved. I'm thinking the earl did not realize how much more of a beating Emmett and I think he needs."

Tremayne chuckled as he grabbed hold of Emmett, who was trying to get around him to the unconscious man behind the bar. "Don't you have someone you promised to say goodnight to, Garahan?"

Garahan smiled as he walked through the door, leaving the dishonesty and stifling air behind him. "That I do, boy-o!" He mounted his horse and took off like a shot.

"Guard his back, Emmett," Tremayne said. "Jackson and I will be right behind you."

A FEW HOURS later, satisfied that he'd accomplished his goal—leaving a message that would be remembered—Garahan stabled his horse and rushed through the side door, calling Melinda's name.

She was right where she'd promised to be. "From the look on your face, your conversation with the earl—"

Her words were silenced by Garahan's lips as he savored the sweetness of the woman who held his heart. When he could bear to break the kiss, he whispered, "Say yes, lass."

"Yes!"

He heard Emmett's whistle, broke the kiss, and stepped in front of Melinda, demanding, "Is everyone inside and safe?"

Emmett nodded. "Are we having a wedding, then?"

Melinda didn't wait for Garahan to answer. "Yes, we are."

"That's fine, then, lass. Kiss himself later—he's due to man his post on the rooftop."

To Garahan's delight, she pressed her lips to his, professing, "I love you, James."

He was smiling when he kissed her one last time before leaving. "I depend upon it, lass."

When they were out of hearing range, Garahan asked, "Are the plans in place for the bare-knuckle bout?"

"Aye," Emmett answered. "The earl and the viscount will be leaving with their families in the morning. Will ye be asking Melinda to make the journey?"

Garahan considered the notion. He did not like the thought of being separated from her for more than a day or so. She was embedded in his heart—and his life. "I will."

"Then ye'd best ask if she can ride with their ladyships."

"I'm not sure there will be enough room."

"They'll be only too happy to make room. Besides," Emmett continued, "their ladyships traveled with barely a bag between them."

Garahan nodded. "With one or two bags stashed atop his lordship's carriage, there will be room—unless their lordships change their minds and ride with their wives."

Emmett chuckled. "And their babes? I'm thinking they'll ride back to Sussex the way they arrived in London—on horseback."

"Fine, then," Garahan agreed. "I'll mention it in the morning—'tis getting late."

CHAPTER THIRTY

MELINDA STARED UP at James. He asked for the second time, "Well, do ye want to accompany their ladyships?"

"To Sussex?" Melinda asked.

"Aye."

"Because the journey to London with their babes was exhausting?" she asked.

"Aye," Garahan said for the second time. He couldn't tell her the true reason he wanted her there. He didn't want her in London without him, since he'd heard of the baron offering a reward to get his hands on Melinda.

"Ye don't have a lot of time to gather yer things," he reminded her.

"Am I to stay on in Sussex?"

He rolled his eyes. The woman was full of questions now that she'd agreed to be his bride. "Are ye trying to add to me duties today?"

"No!" she replied. "I am trying to find out what is expected of me and whether or not I will be returning with you."

"As far as I know, ye'll be at Chattsworth Manor—as will I be—for a fortnight at least."

She listened as she gathered what few possessions she had, then stood beside him. "I'm ready."

He stared down at the small satchel in her hands, a lump of sadness lodging in his gut. He'd see to it that Melinda would never have to suffer as she had—or want for anything from this day forward.

"Faith, me ma was right."

"About what?" she asked as they stopped in the kitchen to bid Mrs. O'Toole and Mrs. Wigglesworth goodbye.

"I'd be finding a wife who was the other half of me heart—but would suit me down to the ground."

She paused in front of the door to the other side of the town house. "Because I do not have much to my name?"

He slipped an arm around her waist and dipped his head to kiss her. "Nay, because ye value people more than things."

She smiled. "Things can be replaced—people cannot."

He pressed a kiss to her forehead, opened the door for her, and joined the others gathered in the hallway.

⇶⫷

A FEW HOURS later, Melinda learned the other reason she was traveling with their ladyships to Chattsworth Manor.

"A bare-knuckle bout?" she asked Lady Aurelia. "Is that what it sounds like?"

Lady Calliope answered, "Aye. Two men pummeling one another."

"For sport?" Melinda asked.

"And for the purse," Lady Aurelia added.

Melinda nodded. "Wagers will be placed, I take it." When their ladyships agreed, she asked, "So who will be taking part in this bout?"

Aurelia and Calliope shared a glance before answering, "James Garahan."

Melinda digested the news. "Whom is he challenging?"

"The man who was paid to slander our names—and that of our husbands," Calliope answered.

"But not my sister-in-law and her husband's," Aurelia added.

"Will it be held inside or outside?" Melinda asked.

"Outside—there will be a celebration to follow," Calliope said.

She could not imagine James fighting anyone for money. "Celebrating the victory?"

Aurelia nodded, then added, "As well as the coin that will be raised from the wagering. It will benefit widows and orphans of the brave men who gave their lives for our king."

"So it is a worthy cause," Melinda said. "Is there anything else I should know?"

Calliope bit her lip to keep from smiling when she answered, "The opponents must follow the rules."

"Of course," Melinda said. "That makes sense."

"There is an unusual one—if you ask me," Aurelia said. "But I confess to never having attended a bare-knuckle bout before."

Melinda could tell from the tone of Lady Aurelia's voice that this was something out of the ordinary—well, at least out of what Melinda would consider ordinary. "And what would that be?"

"They will be shirtless."

Melinda felt her mouth drop open and heard Lady Calliope's giggle before she was able to close it. "Will there be anyone else in attendance besides us?"

"We're expecting fifty to one hundred people."

"Shirtless," Melinda repeated softly.

"Only the opponents in the bout," Aurelia said.

Melinda frowned. "In public."

"I'm told it's quite common," Calliope added.

"Oh my!"

CHAPTER THIRTY-ONE

MELINDA'S HEART WAS in her throat as she stared at the roped-off area where James would face down the man responsible for spreading vile rumors about Viscountess Chattsworth and Countess Lippincott.

What if the other man bested James? Would those in attendance believe the rumors as fact—that James fathered the earl and the viscount's sons? She shook her head. That would not be possible, would it?

"Stand beside me," Mary Kate urged. "We can watch from a spot where James cannot see us. You don't want to distract him when he's defending Lady Aurelia and Lady Calliope's honor."

Melinda wished she'd stayed inside, working with the others hired from the village to prepare and serve the surprising number of people attending the bout. "Are you certain he cannot see us?"

Mary Kate linked arms with her. "Do you see Seamus over there by that tree away from the crowd?"

Melinda spied the auburn-haired giant by the base of an oak tree. "Aye."

"It's a good distance away," Mary Kate said. "The crowd will be between us and James."

Worry for the viscountess and countess began to drive Melinda to distraction as they walked toward Seamus. "Won't it be a risk for their ladyships to attend?"

Mary Kate patted Melinda's hand as they neared the guard. "They are innocent and have the full support of their husbands—and His Grace and his influential friends."

Melinda's stomach ached. "What if James loses the bout?"

"Don't worry," Mary Kate assured her, "James never loses."

"But I've heard his cousins talking about how they caught him off guard—"

"Ah, but that was with family," Seamus said as they paused beside him. "Garahan trusts us. 'Tis the only way we get one over on him."

"Breaking his nose?" Melinda demanded.

Seamus chuckled. "No wonder me cousin lost his head over ye, lass. Ye're angry on his behalf."

"There was no call for Emmett to do that."

"Ye weren't there," Seamus reminded her. "Now then, the bout's about to begin. Ye won't want to miss this."

Mary Kate tugged on her arm until Melinda was sandwiched between Seamus and Mary Kate as the two combatants were introduced. The roar of the crowd had her wondering if an event such as this was commonplace.

"There was never anything like this in Peppering Eye. Though I remember their Beltane fires and May Day celebrations."

"Ye don't know what ye've been missing, lass," Seamus remarked.

Melinda followed the direction of Seamus's gaze and knew the man was silently rooting for his cousin.

>>>>><<<<<

GARAHAN FACED HIS opponent—Royce Huggleston—and felt a moment's pity for the younger man. In a bare-knuckle bout, brawn, skill, and experience always won out over age, overinflated ego, and lack of experience.

He allowed Huggleston to connect a few blows, much to the delight of the crowd. For a heartbeat, he wondered if those gathered were there to cheer him on...or see him defeated. His reflexes deflected the jab aimed for his jaw, reminding him that he'd best concentrate on the here and now. Huggleston—and avenging their ladyships.

"How's the jaw? Does it still pain ye, lad?"

Huggleston's face flamed—exactly the reaction Garahan hoped for as he sidestepped an ill-placed punch.

"Ye'll have to do better than that if ye wish to prove yer employer's lies to be truth." Garahan delivered an uppercut that had his opponent shaking his head. "Ye can step back from me and raise yer hand, giving the signal that ye yield anytime."

Huggleston leaned forward, leading with his right shoulder, alerting Garahan to watch for a right cross.

Garahan shifted, and the punch went wide. "Ye aren't even half trying, lad. Try that move again," he said. "This time, don't give it away—try leading with yer left shoulder."

Huggleston reared back and dropped his hands to his side. Garahan didn't want to hit the lad when his guard was down. "Raise yer guard!"

Huggleston's hands went up, and Garahan leaned toward him with his left shoulder, then landed a staggering blow with a wicked right cross.

Huggleston stared at him for a moment before his eyes rolled back in his head and he crumbled into a heap at Garahan's feet.

Aiden rushed to his side and raised Garahan's arm in the air while the crowd roared their appreciation.

Garahan wasn't sure if it was his sense of fair play—not striking the younger man until he raised his guard—or because they believed in the medieval way of settling disagreements—trial by combat.

"Ye nearly gave the fight over. Why?"

Garahan met his brother's gaze and answered, "The lad has a lot to learn and a younger sister battling illness. I plan to continue to help the lad—and teach him a thing or two about sparring."

Aiden shook his head at him. "Ma's right. Ye heart will get ye into trouble one of these days."

Garahan scanned the crowd for a glimpse of the dark-haired, brown-eyed lass who carried his heart in her hands. When he saw her beneath the oak tree—Seamus on one side of her and Mary Kate on the other—he grinned. "Me heart finally found its home."

Turning to his brother, he added, "One day, yer heart will too. Learn from me mistakes, Aiden—don't fight it."

With a nod at the unconscious man on the ground, Garahan said, "Best toss the bucket of water on the lad."

The crowd fell silent. Garahan looked up in time to watch the viscount and the earl lift the ropes and walk over to stand on either side of him. Following along with the plan, he remained silent, waiting for the viscount to speak first.

"Would those of you at the back of the crowd step aside?" the viscount asked.

When they obliged, the earl said, "I believe Baron Corkendale has an announcement to make."

All eyes turned to watch the well-dressed man strutting forward, his head high, the smirk on his face unmistakable. "As a matter of fact," Corkendale said, staring at Garahan, "I do. Trial by combat is a medieval form of justice—you have yet to prove your innocence, Garahan."

"Jamie!"

Garahan looked at his brother, caught the cloth he'd tossed to him, and wiped the sweat from his eyes.

Chattsworth and Lippincott smiled at the baron. "Did you believe this bout was to prove his innocence?" the earl asked.

"Why else would I agree to let my footman accept the challenge?"

Corkendale grumbled.

The earl smiled. "This is a charitable event, Corkendale. All of the men who serve in my brother's private guard are highly skilled in all forms of defense, and bare-knuckle happens to be a particular favorite of the men. Garahan's in particular."

The baron looked taken aback. "You cannot expect leniency for the man when he has been accused of unspeakable deeds?"

The viscount said, "Not that type of charity, Corkendale. The type that begins in our homes and our hearts, giving to a cause we as Englishmen should all support—those who have fought bravely for His Majesty defending the Crown!"

The earl smiled at Garahan, who was helping his opponent to his feet. "Never underestimate the power of an apology—or forgiveness."

The baron's confusion was there for all to see. "I don't understand."

The viscount sighed. "We were afraid of that. Which is why we asked Gavin King of the Bow Street Runners to attend the bout. Before he reads the charges against you, mayhap you would like to consider apologizing."

"To Garahan? Are you mad after he forced your—"

Garahan had the baron by the throat and a foot off the ground before he could finish his sentence. "Ye'll either apologize to their lordships—and their ladyships—or shut yer gob!"

The baron's wild-eyed look had King's lips twitching. "Set him down, Garahan. I believe he needs to hear the full list of charges before he apologizes." Garahan did as asked.

Rubbing his neck, shifting from foot to foot, the baron glared at Garahan. "You wait until—"

"After yer trial for me apology?" Garahan finished. "I can wait, but their lordships and ladyships cannot."

"Later," the earl warned. "King? I believe the crowd who generously donated to the cause would enjoy being enlightened."

King and his men joined them inside the ropes, forming a ring behind the baron. "Stephen Corkendale, you will accompany my men and I back to my office on Bow Street, where you will answer questions regarding the untimely—and suspicious—deaths of your cousin and his wife, the previous Baron and Baroness of Corkendale."

The baron's eyes bulged, and he took a step backward, only to be stopped by the viscount, who advised him, "There's more."

"We have all the evidence we need to hold you until your trial," King said. "Now, as to the other charges…"

"Other?" the baron squeaked.

"Aye. The willful public defamation, and character assassination, of Earl and Countess Lippincott, Viscount and Viscountess Chattsworth, and Baron and Baroness Summerfield, in the form of vile and vicious slander, rumors, and accusations."

"I never made that entry into White's betting book—"

King stared at the baron. "Did I mention White's?"

The earl glared at the baron. "You did not."

"But I—"

"You posted a reward, and made false and derogatory claims against Miss Melinda Waring, who owes you nothing. You, however, owe her an apology and a day's wages."

"I never—"

"Lastly," King announced in a clear, strong voice. "You are hereby charged with violating two scullery maids in your employ."

Muffled whispers started at the back of the crowd, growing in volume as those gathered judged the baron.

"Thompson, cuff the baron," King said.

"No, wait!" the baron shouted as he was clapped in irons. "I'm innocent."

Earl Lippincott and Viscount Chattsworth moved to flank King.

"We have witnesses who willingly came forward with evidence that has been corroborated," King said. "The courts will decide your fate—while you will remain a guest of the Crown, awaiting your trial."

Garahan nodded to Seamus, who'd been watching for the signal. Waiting for his cousin to escort his bride-to-be through the crowd, he held out his hand to Huggleston. "I hear the viscount and the earl are looking to add to their household staff. If ye're interested, I think I can get you an interview."

Huggleston shook his hand, then asked, "Why didn't you take your shot when I dropped my guard?"

"Would you have?"

Huggleston admitted he would.

"Well then, ye have the makings of a fine protector—but not necessarily a shot at a bare-knuckle title. Those are mostly fair fights."

"Mostly?" Huggleston asked.

Garahan grinned. "On occasion, they aren't."

"How do you know when they aren't fair?"

Garahan laughed. "Well now, I'm thinking it would be when yer opponent tosses dirt in yer eyes. Mayhap when yer opponent grabs ye by the *bollocks* and—"

"I understand."

"I thought ye might. Now then, shall I speak to their lordships on yer behalf?"

"Aye, thank you. I think my sister and mum would do well in the country."

"Aye, lad, 'twill be—" Garahan stopped speaking, distracted by the sight of Flaherty walking toward him with his arm wrapped around Mary Kate on his left and Melinda on his right. "Get yer hands—"

"For the love of God, Garahan! Put a fecking shirt on—there are ladies present!"

"Bugger yerself, Seamus! While ye're at it, watch yer language—there are ladies present!"

Aiden tossed a shirt to his brother and sighed. "Begging yer pardon, ladies—me brother should know better than to stand before ye in such a state."

Garahan caught the shirt and tried to trip his brother—who side-stepped the move. "Anyone with an ounce of sense knows it's customary to strip down to yer trousers—how else will those judging the bout know if yer opponent lands an illegal blow if not for the bruises?"

He smiled at Melinda, who was staring at his chest, leaving him to wonder if it was maidenly embarrassment—or if she was struck dumb by his impressive physique. Shaking his head at her, he donned his shirt, then offered his arm. "Care to join me at the refreshment table?"

Melinda blinked and flushed a lovely rose before she answered. "I would, thank you, James."

Garahan ignored the baron's whimpered protests as King and his men led him to the wagon that would transport him to London, but stopped when the earl called his name.

"Aye, yer lordship?"

"Haven't you forgotten something?" the earl asked.

Garahan couldn't think of any part of their intricate plan that he'd forgotten. "I don't think so."

The viscount walked over to him, a black frockcoat in his hand. "Put your coat on before anyone starts the rumor that the duke's guard walks about my estate half-clothed."

While he did, the earl walked over and handed him a length of black cloth. "And this."

Garahan rolled his eyes. "Can ye not forgo the cravat, as I've earned ye a fair amount of coin for a cause ye support?"

The earl's lips lifted into a half-smile. "No. Put on the bloody cra-vat."

"That's what I call the thing. Ye know I hate anything tight around me neck."

Melinda moved to stand in front of him. "Let me help. I'll fashion a respectable knot—and keep it loose." She tied his cravat, rose on her toes, and pressed a kiss to his cheek. "There," she said. "You are now respectable again."

Garahan pulled his bride-to-be flush against him and kissed the breath out of her. When he could bring himself to break the kiss, he whispered, "Faith, ye know you love it when I'm not."

EPILOGUE

Two weeks later…

"**Y**OU MAY KISS your bride."

A cheer went up from his brothers and cousins as Garahan swept his wife into his arms and kissed her tenderly. "I've got ye now, lass."

She cupped his face in her hand. "Don't let go."

Garahan laughed. "Faith, I haven't since the first night I saw ye. Ye're stuck with me forever, lass!"

"Aren't you going to put me down, James?"

"Nay, lass, and before ye ask, I've already made arrangements for Mrs. Romney to pack up a basket for us."

"A food basket?"

Garahan couldn't resist pressing his lips to his bride's. "Aye. We aren't staying for the wedding breakfast."

Melinda stared into his eyes and asked, "We aren't?"

"Nay, lass." He leaned close to whisper, *"Ye're* breakfast." Turning to those gathered, he said, "Thank ye kindly for the feast, yer lord-ships, but me bride and I will leave ye to celebrate over breakfast. While we do the same."

Without another word, Garahan strode from the room.

Hanging on to her husband, Melinda asked, "Where are we going?"

Garahan headed for the main staircase and took the stairs two at a time. "Second floor, last bedchamber on the right."

"I never realized how strong you are, James."

"I've strength and stamina that I've been saving for ye, lass." He stopped in front of the bedchamber. "Open it, love."

She did as he asked, and held on tightly as he whirled her around, then closed and locked the door. Striding across the room, he set her on her feet and lifted her hands to his lips.

"Yer beauty humbles me. I promise to go slowly—but the wait has been harder than I thought. The need to make love to ye is tearing at me guts, lass."

Melinda sighed. "I never know what you'll say next, James. You constantly surprise me."

His laughter was deep, rich, and just a bit wicked as he removed his frockcoat. "Why don't I show ye what I've had on me mind for the last four weeks?"

Instead of striding across the room to the bed, he bowed to her, holding out his hand. She blinked. "What would you have me do?"

"Take me hand, lass—dance with me."

➤➤➤◄◄◄

HEART IN HER throat, she didn't hesitate. James would not let her stumble or fall. Placing her hand in his, she felt the heat of the one he slid to the middle of her back.

"Look into me eyes, lass, and ye won't get dizzy."

Her gaze locked on his as he expertly led her into a waltz. "I did not know you could dance."

"Ah, lass, I've been saving it as one of me surprises."

Undone by the way he lifted her off her feet when he felt her leg weakening, she slid her hands around his neck. "I love you with all my heart, James."

He slowed his steps, pulled her flush against him, and slid his hand to the small of her back. "I never thought I'd find a woman that would suit me down to the ground. But ye do. I love ye, lass."

She eased out of his arms and turned around. "Would you please unfasten me?"

"Ye're trusting me with yer scars, lass?"

"I am."

She felt his hands tremble as he undid the buttons on her gown, bracing herself to hear his reaction to what she had felt with her fingertips—the raised, ugly marks on her back. All she felt was the swish of silk as he lifted her gown—and her chemise—over her head.

Melinda gasped when warm, firm lips caressed the scars across her shoulder blades. "James!"

"Ye scars mark ye as courageous, lass. Let me honor each and every one with a kiss."

Her knees gave out when his lips reached halfway down her back. He carried her to the bed and gently laid her on her stomach.

With each press of his lips to her scars—and his whispered words of praise—she fell deeper in love.

When he reached the base of her spine, she was mindless to control the desire spiraling inside of her. Need had her desperate to touch him as he touched her, pressing her lips along the length of his spine. Would she be able to drive him to the edge of reason?

His weight shifted, and he rose from the bed. She turned over to stare in wonder at the beauty of the man removing the garb that identified him to the world as one of the duke's guard. The impressive breadth of his chest and shoulders were even more evident without a stitch of clothing to cover his masculine beauty.

The man standing before her was riddled with scars across his chest and upper arms that she hadn't noticed in her shock seeing him after the bare-knuckle bout. She wondered if his back was equally scarred.

Before that thought could take hold, she noticed the scar he had alluded to. How long did he struggle to breathe with the noose around his neck before someone saved him? She couldn't ask—wouldn't. To keep from keening in sorrow, she bit down on her bottom lip.

"Ye're worried about yer scars, lass. Well, now that ye've seen mine, should I cover them up?"

She slipped off the bed, wrapped her arms around her husband, and laid her head over his heart, needing to feel the beat—proof that he had survived.

She lifted her head and looked into his eyes. "Why would you hide yours from me, when I have bared mine to you?"

"Ye've a tender heart lass." He brushed a wisp of hair off her fore-head. "I wouldn't want to frighten ye."

"You are so beautiful, James, that you could never frighten me."

She kissed one shoulder, and heard him hiss and draw in a quick breath. A glow flickered inside of her as she left a trail of featherlight kisses along his collarbone.

He exhaled when she reached the other shoulder, only to tense when she dipped her tongue in the hollow at the base of his throat. Power surged through her. She marveled that a man as strong as her husband could react to her caresses.

Before she could ask him to show her another way to pleasure him, he rasped, "Ye're killing me, lass."

When he tried to ease back from her, she murmured, "Mmm, my turn." Gently, with great care, she kissed her way closer to the faint, silvery scar circling his throat. Praying her kisses would have the same effect on him as his had on her, she nibbled and left open-mouthed kisses, following his scar from one side of his neck to the other.

She sensed the quickening of his breath was not because he was upset, and hoped her husband was enjoying her exploration. Gathering her courage, she looked up and was dazzled by the depth of desire in his warm brown eyes.

Watching him closely, she traced a path with the tip of her finger from one pectoral muscle across to the other. He closed his eyes and groaned, giving her the courage to trace an imaginary line from his chest over his shoulder and onto his back. Slipping behind him, she paid homage. With tiny bites and soothing kisses, she completed the circular scar—bathing it with love. One day, she may ask him to share the story behind it, but right now, she had another goal in mind—driving her husband to the edge of reason.

He was silent for too long. Worried that she'd upset him paying attention to the scar that could have ended his life, she used her hands to smooth the tension from his shoulders. Beginning at the base of his neck, she pressed her hands to his back, drawing them toward his powerful shoulders. Once. Twice. Three times.

She repeated the motion along the length of his spine, awed watching the way his muscled backside tensed and then relaxed when she moved her hands to beneath his shoulder blades, drawing them down to his waist.

The tension left him by degrees with each loving caress, until she found the courage to grip his hips and slide one hand lower to cup his backside.

He spun around, then swept her off her feet and onto the bed. "I'll not be able to satisfy ye this night if I let ye continue yer innocent explorations, lass."

He knelt on the bed and lowered his body onto hers until they were skin to skin...heart to heart. Unimaginable heat seared wherever his body touched hers. He nudged her legs apart and settled between them, pressing her firmly into the mattress. "I'm hoping ye know what to expect, lass. I'm not sure I have the patience to explain before I go mad with wanting ye."

Love for James washed over her. "I do. Do not worry about hurting me, James—I've felt pain inflicted with anger...pain from fear."

She caressed the side of his face, and felt his love for her open the last lock on her heart when he leaned into her hand and closed his eyes.

Love was the answer all along. "You love me, James, and nothing that you ever say or do would be to intentionally cause me pain. I willingly give you all that I am, and all that I have."

Sliding her hands along the heavy muscles of his shoulders, she slipped them around his back and lifted her hips. "Make love to me...please?"

※※※

NOTHING BUT CONCERN for his wife—and the knowledge that she understood what would happen in their marriage bed—could have had him hesitating when need battered at the iron links of his control.

The caress of her hands, the touch of her lips, felt otherworldly— magical—and he reveled in it. Her breathless request smashed the first link.

He kissed her with reverence, hoping to ease what pain would follow.

Her unbridled response to his kiss broke the next link and had him kissing her as if the world were about to end and this was their last moment together.

Her passionate kisses, punctuated with the rise of her hips moving against him, begging him, smashed the rest of his control.

He surrendered and slid into her welcoming warmth until he reached the barrier between maiden and wife. He lifted his head and stared down into her soft brown eyes. "I love ye, lass."

Her dazed expression gave him hope that she would adjust to his lovemaking and not shrink back from him.

Plundering her mouth with warm, wet kisses until she began to writhe beneath him, he kissed her deeply and buried himself to the hilt. He was relieved when she lifted her hips and gripped his backside with both hands.

Pain was forgotten as he increased the rhythm of his strokes, drawing out slowly then burying himself deep, surrounded by her pulsating, warm, wet passage.

Shock arrowed through him as his wife locked her legs around his waist and gave herself to him completely. He'd been holding back his pleasure, waiting for her to reach hers. She tightened around him and moaned in ecstasy, driving them both to the edge of pleasure—and over, into oblivion.

As they drifted off to sleep, James knew that no matter where the duke sent him—no matter what duty was asked of him—his true home would be waiting in Melinda's arms.

WHEN HE WOKE, she was just beginning to stir. He held her to his heart, rolled over onto his back, and pressed his lips to hers. "I'll love ye from this breath to me last, wife."

A tear escaped, and he wondered if he had been too rough with her. He wiped it away—and the second tear when it followed. Worry crept up on him. "Lass, did I—"

"Open your heart and love me as I never imagined?" she interrupted. "Aye, James, and for that I will love you from this breath to my last, husband." Tracing the line of his jaw, feeling him pulse inside of her, she smiled. "Will you love me again?"

He gazed into her eyes and chuckled. "Faith, I'm a lucky man to have married a lusty lass. Will ye be praying for a son or a daughter?"

She gasped as he drew her nipple into his mouth, but managed to answer, "Both."

AND BOTH IT was...nine months later.

About the Author

Historical & Contemporary Romance "Warm...Charming...Fun..."

C.H. was born in Aiken, South Carolina, but her parents moved back to northern New Jersey where she grew up.

She believes in fate, destiny, and love at first sight. C.H. fell in love at first sight when she was seventeen. She was married for 41 wonderful years until her husband lost his battle with cancer. Soul mates, their hearts will be joined forever.

They have three grown children—one son-in-law, two grandsons, two rescue dogs, and two rescue grand-cats.

Her characters rarely follow the synopsis she outlines for them...but C.H. has learned to listen to her characters! Her heroes always have a few of her husband's best qualities: his honesty, his integrity, his compassion for those in need, and his killer broad shoulders. C.H. writes about the things she loves most: Family, her Irish and English Ancestry, Baking and Gardening.

Sláinte!
CH

C.H.'s Social Media Links:
Website: www.chadmirand.com
Amazon: amazon.com/stores/C.-H.-Admirand/author/B001JPBUMC
BookBub: bookbub.com/authors/c-h-admirand
Facebook Author Page: facebook.com/CHAdmirandAuthor
Facebook Private Reader's Page ~ C.H. Reader's Nook:
facebook.com/groups/714796299746980
GoodReads: goodreads.com/author/show/212657.C_H_Admirand
Instagram: c.h.admirand
Twitter: @AdmirandH
Youtube: youtube.com/channel/UCRSXBeqEY52VV3mHdtg5fXw

Made in the USA
Middletown, DE
22 June 2023

33222382R00148